# CAT'S BREAKFAST
## Kurt Vonnegut Tribute

**Third Flatiron Anthologies
Volume 6, Book 19, Summer 2017**

**Edited by Juliana Rew
Cover Art by Keely Rew**

# Cat's Breakfast
Third Flatiron Anthologies
Volume 6, Summer 2017

Published by Third Flatiron Publishing
Juliana Rew, Editor and Publisher

## License Notes

**www.thirdflatiron.com**

# Contents

*****~~~~~*****

# Editor's Note

by Juliana Rew

What distinguishes contemporary fiction from classic literature? We believe "classic" in this context means writing that has stood the test of time by appealing to multiple generations. The work of Kurt Vonnegut, through layered masterpieces such as *Cat's Cradle* and *Breakfast of Champions*, continue to fascinate us and encourage repeat readings. For this short story anthology, we asked contributors to channel the "attitude" of Kurt Vonnegut, without explicitly using his characters or settings. It turns out that works incredibly well. Welcome to *Cat's Breakfast*, a double issue featuring the wide-ranging work of thirty international authors. This anthology is gratefully dedicated to Mr. Vonnegut.

As you might expect, the majority of these stories are humorous, often downright hilarious. But not every story is funny. Some straightforwardly address serious themes, such as free will, mental illness, social cruelty, loneliness, and even relationships with parents. And there is that age-old question: What are we doing here?

We lead with a story by David A. Kilman, "Spooky Action." What if until now God never knew we existed? Then after listening carefully to our complaints, what if He set about correcting His mistakes?

In this divisive political era, we truly miss Vonnegut's sardonic input. One of the authors of this anthology, Neil James Hudson, quotes him as having said: "The two real political parties in America are the Winners and the Losers." But it's some consolation that we've learned so much from Vonnegut's rich legacy and defense of freedom.

Vonnegut served his country in the military during the Big One and later shared with us the insanity of military strategy in *Slaughterhouse Five*. A tart reminder arrives in James Beamon's "Command Decision." I wouldn't want to be in those soldiers' boots. August Marion's "Drop Dead Date" is an enlightening tale about the war with the robots and the lengths people are willing to go to deny reality. It doesn't look good for humanity.

The book is filled with coincidences. Maybe that's to be expected when many authors consider a theme from many angles. The main section bookends with Molotov cocktails ("Spooky" and Corrie Parrish's "Violadors on the Run"). The prime number 37 makes an appearance in two stories, Dan Koboldt's "37" and Ville Nummenpää 's cheeky "Beyond the Borders of Boredom." Sentient luncheon meat is mentioned both in "Spooky" and in Konstantine Paradias's uproarious "They Grow Up So Fast." Disturbing uses for chainsaws are suggested in two stories (Anne E. Johnson's "Formica Joe," and Peter Hagelslag's "Scenes from a Post-Scarcity, Post-Death Society").

And then there are a whole lotta tentacles (viz. Rati Mehrotra's "The Jim-Aaargh School of Philosophy," and "They Grow Up So Fast").

Vonnegut made an intriguing contribution to the literature by inventing a new religion, Bokonism. Heaven plays a role in two *Cat's Breakfast* stories, but not the Western-style heaven. There's reincarnation and karma instead (Rekha Valliappan's "Snakes and Ladders" and "Jim-Aaargh").

Vonnegut's characters often met aliens from outer space, before which they were usually powerless. Our authors let loose their creepy imaginations about alien appearance and behavior in Keyan Bowes's "Picnic, With Xels," Jason Lairamore's "A Static Fall to a Standing Walk," and John J. Kennedy's "The Bringers." What if we did finally hear from an alien civilization? Tim Jeffrey's tale, "Hear," tells of a distress call that reaches us too late. Jonathan Shipley's "Monkeyline" describes a conspiracy by aliens at a galactic university to make humans look bad. It almost succeeds.

*Cat's Breakfast* is not, by a long shot, the first Vonnegut tribute short story anthology. James Dorr's "Dead Girls, Dying Girls" was originally published in Perpetual Motion Machine Publishing's *So It Goes*. **Editor's note:** Perhaps a resurgence in popularity (and sales) is in order?

Is life really a dream, or a simulation, like in "The Matrix?" A recent BBC Earth program noted that several physicists have suggested that our Universe is not real and is instead a giant simulation (http://bbc.in/2rDeUiG ). S.E. Foley's "Quality Testing" helps us decide how we would feel about such a revelation.

Even if we accept that the Universe is pulling the strings, what if there's a Multiverse? Check out Vaughan Stanger's "One Is One"—and try to keep your Twitter comments to yourself.

Modern society imposes a number of, shall we say, *cruel* conditions on us, as Vonnegut often pointed out. Ryan Dull's "The Confrontation Station" takes a painfully comical look at office politics. Authors Iain Hamilton McKinven ("Honour Killing") and Neil James Hudson ("The Losers' Crusade") give their stories a satirical militancy.

Yet sentimentality and emotion found their place in Vonnegut's work. In Veronica Moyer's heartbreaking tale, "The Edge of Toska," a young girl's adolescence on a tiny planet ends a happy childhood.

Vonnegut raised a lot of kids, both his own and his sister's, so even when he had a lot of crazy stuff on his mind, the family was always present in his thoughts. Christopher Mark Rose's affecting "Emerging Grammars" is magical realism that hits just the right soft spot.

Sometimes animals talk, or they only seem to talk, or somebody might be crazy, or. . . (Jill Hand's "Talk to the Animals," Gregg Chamberlain's "The Pigeon Drop").

Horses are specifically mentioned as not being able to talk, so it turns out that Mr. Ed is completely fictional. Who knew, right?

Ultimately, we're all losers, as Hudson explains in the foreboding "The Losers' Crusade." There's nothing for it but to eat our breakfast and be our own champions. So it goes.

In "Grins and Gurgles" (our flash humor section), Benjamin C. Kinney gets the show running with "Cyborg Shark Battle (Season 4, Oʻahu Frenzy)," a futuristic reality TV show. Laurence Raphael Brothers's "Strange Stars," is a dating guide on mass ejections; E. E. King's "iPhone 17,000" is for those too much in love with their devices; and Edward Ahern's "The Service Call" warns you to keep your software maintenance plan up to date. Sometimes tech life just makes us WannaCry.

One of Vonnegut's admirable accomplishments was having his books banned in some libraries, most notably *Slaughterhouse Five.* While we hope this anthology won't be banned (quite the opposite!), we do encourage everyone to participate in Banned Books Week (September 24-30 in 2017), sponsored by the American Library Association.

And if you're ever in Indianapolis, Indiana, be sure to visit the Kurt Vonnegut Museum and Library.

Until then, keep rubbing that Formica. No, not like that. In a circle. Like this…

### 

## *Spooky Action*

by David A. Kilman

The end is near. Very near. Maybe this afternoon. And all the suffering in the universe will cease.

I know this because God told me himself. He left a message on my lab computer at Central Colorado State University in a voice with a thick Brooklyn accent, one that if you didn't know any better, you might think of as belonging to someone in the Teamsters Union. It was the voice of Richard Feynman.

Richard Feynman was a Nobel Prize–winning theoretical physicist. One of the preeminent scientific minds of the twentieth century. Feynman didn't believe in God. Until about two months ago, God didn't believe in Richard Feynman either.

I too am a physicist, though of much less distinction. Until two months ago, God had me right up there with Feynman—no such animal as far as he was concerned. But it wasn't that God had something specifically against physicists. He didn't believe in any humans. He'd never seen one, or heard one, or smelled one for that matter. There was no reason for him to suspect that anything like a human had grown in one of his universes, and so he was quite surprised to find one attempting to communicate with him. Imagine, if you will, putting leftover lasagna in your refrigerator, forgetting about it for a few months, and then one day while retrieving a beer, a small voice calls out to you from behind the lunch meats.

11

## Cat's Breakfast

It was something like that for God when he found out that physicists and janitors and circus performers and all manner of odd bipedal creatures were crawling around in his lasagna.

...

Gabriela Josefina Hernández González believed in God, and that was even before the moon shot off into space as if it had suddenly remembered that it had important business to attend to in the Andromeda Galaxy. The first time she came into the lab at the beginning of the semester, she carried a wicker picnic basket on her left arm, and she said, "Thank God for all these science machines."

"They come from government grants," I responded, not bothering to get up from the chair at my desk.

"God's gifts come in many ways."

I wasn't in a particularly open mood for nonsense that morning. My entangled subatomic particles were acting as if they were not entangled at all. Like they had gotten a divorce and no longer wanted anything to do with each other. "Is there something I can do for you?" I asked, hoping she would go away.

"No. I just want to thank you for teaching my son."

She didn't look old enough to have a son in college, but I kept that to myself. At the time, I was still hoping to get tenure. She was perhaps five foot three, of medium but well-rounded build with olive skin and long, dark brown hair. I would have guessed her to be in her late twenties.

"You're welcome," I said.

"What do you do in here?" she asked.

"I am conducting experiments in quantum entanglement."

"¿Qué?"

"When two tiny particles become entangled, they seem to be able to tell what the other particle is doing, even when they are very far apart. Some call it spooky action at a distance. I am trying to use that to send messages."

12

"Ah, like me and my twin sister. Whenever something bad happened to her, I was able to tell right away, even though she was in Venezuela."

"Is that so? Well, what is she doing right now?" I thought I was being clever.

"She's dead."

"Oh."

She opened the picnic basket and produced a plate with a red-and-white–checkered cloth napkin concealing a mound beneath. "I made you *mandocas*." She put the plate on my desk.

I used the tip of my pen to lift the edge of the napkin, revealing several confections topped with shredded cheese. They looked like doughnuts, only horseshoe shaped, with ends bent together to the point of touching.

"It's cornmeal, deep fried."

"I don't think this would be appropriate." I removed my pen.

"I could make you *cachapas* instead. I will bring them every morning."

I tried to explain that I was being paid to teach her son, and that such gifts were not only unnecessary, but inappropriate, particularly on a daily basis. But she insisted.

"How can it be inappropriate to give thanks?"

...

Two months later, this morning, as I watched the physics building burn to the ground, Gabriela approached with her customary picnic basket. She had been bringing me *mandocas* every school day since the semester started, as promised. Though I had resisted at first, her persistence, and to be frank, the delectable nature of the confections, had won me over.

I was standing in the grass on the quad, a safe distance from the blaze, helplessly watching firefighters losing the battle to save the building. A crowd of hundreds of students had gathered to gawk at the spectacle.

Gabriela offered her condolences on the loss of the laboratory.

I explained that the situation was much worse than losing the lab. "God is about to put an end to the universe."

She said that she knew that already. The prophets had been predicting it for a long time.

...

The first thing to know about talking to God is that there is one doozy of a language barrier. Untold billions of people have been trying to talk to him for thousands of years, all without ever managing to get his attention. They did anything and everything to get God to notice them: prayed to him, danced, built monuments, burned fires, slaughtered animals. People worshipped him, dressed up in special clothes, sang songs, even wrote poems to him. And he didn't even know we existed. Talk about unrequited love.

When it happened, I wasn't even trying to talk to God. I was using subatomic particles to try to send a message to my assistant, a grad student named Asha Lahiri. And my message was nothing so fancy as a sonnet. No, all I was trying to communicate was a simple "Hello, Asha." Asha, incidentally, means *hope* in Sanskrit. I was hoping for tenure. And hoping for a Nobel Prize.

We were getting close, I know we were. And right when I thought we were making a breakthrough, we started getting interference. After a few days of this, I began to suspect academic sabotage. How? I could not guess. None of the equipment, including my lab computer, was connected to the college network or the Internet. I was no fool. I knew there were several other teams working on the problem, with the winners likely to claim a Nobel Prize—just like Richard Feynman. In the academic world, the higher the stakes, the lower the ethics.

So, every day for three weeks I sent out "Hello, Asha" and searched for the source of the interference, all to no avail. While I was trying to unmask the saboteurs, God was trying to make sense of the things crawling around in his lasagna.

...

Here is why God sounded like Richard Feynman: In absence of any network connection to the outside world, the only voice-recording God could find on my lab computer was a copy of *The Complete Feynman Lectures on Physics*. Who knows what God would have sounded like had there been an Internet connection. Maybe Elvis Presley, or Adolf Hitler, or Lady Gaga, or maybe he would have meowed like a cat.

...

My initial conversations with God were awkward, to say the least. I thought I was being pranked. It took the extinguishing of the star Bellatrix to convince me that I was actually talking to the Creator.

The star's disappearance got some press, but it was mostly of interest to astronomers and assorted geeks. Nobody suspected that God was involved. And with Asha having gone to India to care for her dying father, I was the only one who knew what had happened. I didn't bother to tell anyone that God had snuffed out Orion's shoulder. I was still hoping to get tenure.

Confession time. I take full responsibility for the loss of Bellatrix. When God asked what he could do to convince me that he had created the universe, I pulled up some astronomy software on the computer and told him to make the star disappear. That was me being clever again.

...

My parents were atheists, so I had no training in what to say to God. Traditional prayers seemed overly formal, particularly with God sounding more like the guy who slices meats at the corner deli than an all-powerful creator. My impression of what people said to God involved asking him for favors. Can you get me a new car, or fix it so I win the lottery, or throw my neighbor into a fiery pit and slow roast him in eternal agony like a withered hot dog at the convenience store? None of these seemed like a good idea, though I suppose I could have asked him for tenure. I found out subsequently that such a request would not have worked anyway. God may have created the universe, but he certainly wasn't in a position to micromanage it. He couldn't control the minutia of our daily lives any more than we can do the same for mold growing on old lasagna.

It turns out, as I learned over the coming weeks, that God had created our universe during one of his experimental periods. Bored with the precision clockwork of his other creations, he decided to toy with random elements. It was akin to a painter flinging paint at a canvas to see what art came of it. The splatters will occasionally take shapes that suggested semi-intelligible things if you looked at them at just the right angle. That was us, the splatters that resembled semi-intelligible things, if you looked at us from the right angle.

...

While I fretted over what to say to God, Gabriela arrived with the day's *mandocas*. Deciding that she had vastly more experience in such matters, I explained to her that my experiments had put me in touch with God, and that I needed her advice on what to say.

"Thank him for everything."

This seemed too broad to be useful, so I asked her for specific examples. "What would you thank him for?"

Here is what Gabriela had to give thanks for: On the day that she and her twin sister celebrated their second birthday, her father was shot to death during the Caracazo, one of the periods of unrest that seize Venezuela from time to time. He had been eating breakfast when the military made a social call at his hovel in the hills east of

Caracas. She was thankful that her mother had managed to get the twins safely out of the country.

Later, when the twins were thirteen and their mother had been killed by stray gunfire between rival gangs in Merida, Mexico, the two debated whether or not to return to Venezuela. Gabriela's sister, Andrea, was of the opinion that they should. Hugo Chávez had just become President. And, like the prophets who predicted the end of the world, Andrea prophesized that Chávez would turn Venezuela into a socialist utopia. The sisters went their separate ways.

Andrea died of starvation last year during the utopian food shortages. Gabriela was thankful that she did not die of starvation.

What Gabriela was most thankful for was her son. She had received him as present on her thirteenth birthday from an American college student on spring break in Cancún.

This was shortly before Gabriela and her sister split up. So, while her sister headed south, she went north to secure her son's birthright in the United States. When she arrived, she went to a family planning clinic to ensure the health of her baby. They tried to convince her to have an abortion, because, they assured her, the child would be doomed to a life of suffering. They were prophets too.

I didn't have anything quite as nifty as Gabriela to be thankful about.

...

In hindsight, it was a mistake to let Gabriela in on my little secret. I should have followed my normal instinct to keep my mouth shut. Somewhere along the line, she mentioned what I was doing to her son, who then reported it to one of his other instructors.

Yesterday morning, I arrived at the lab to find myself confronted by a group of five professors from various departments, all tenured. They were accompanied by a middle-aged man from IT, there to collect evidence of my misdeeds. Knowing that I would be unable to hide what I had been doing, I confessed that I had indeed been talking to God, but that it had been an accidental byproduct of legitimate scientific research. They looked at me like I was a religious nutcase.

I summoned my ace in the hole—God. The disappearance of Bellatrix, I explained, was God's handiwork. Proof that he was indeed the creator.

"If that is so," said Lorand Coramoff, Professor of Anthropology, "then have God prove it to us by knocking the moon out of its orbit."

Before I could advise the professor to choose a less conspicuous proof, the moon went zipping off in the direction of Andromeda.

For God, it was as simple as if he had been playing a game of paper football. The kind where you fold a piece of paper into a triangle and try to flick it with your finger through imaginary goal posts. Flick went the moon. It's up, it's good, and the crowd roars!

Well, there was some roaring, but it wasn't quite as celebratory as one would expect from a football game. That is when the rest of world knew something was up. Many thought it was a sign from God even though we hadn't told anyone about it.

...

The professors decided that this was the perfect opportunity to "speak truth to power." They told God that he was a moral monster. They informed him of all the suffering he had caused. He was told about wars, and starvation, and inequality. Of rape and slavery and genocide. The professors spent over two hours detailing his crimes against humanity. How could he have allowed such suffering to happen?

"If this were my dog," said Professor Coramoff, "I would have euthanized it rather than let it suffer like that."

This was probably not the most brilliant thing Coramoff had ever said. In fact, I know it wasn't. I once heard him say that he had an itch on his nose. Comparatively, those words were genius.

...

Gabriela was one of the people whom God had made to suffer. But she, like billions of other humans on earth, didn't have the sense to be angry at God. Instead, had any of them had access to the machinery that I did, they would have embarrassed themselves by thanking him for scraps of food shared between starving family members, or thanking him that some of their family members had survived the civil war, and so on.

They didn't know any better. It would never have occurred to them to blame God for people being bastards to each other. And it didn't really matter what they thought anyway, because they didn't have access to lasers or photon counters or cryostats or any of that fancy stuff I had in the lab.

Unlike Gabriela, who merely experienced suffering, the professors knew all about it. She was ignorant, not even a high school graduate. Whereas they had studied suffering in college and literature, conducted studies of it, written dissertations on the subject, and published enough papers in their quest for tenure to be primary contributors of deforestation in Venezuela.

They were experts on suffering.

And God didn't have any good answers. He was up against the experts. He had never studied philosophy, or theology, or sociology, or anthropology, or ethnic and gender studies, or any of the things that would have prepared him for the onslaught.

...

I went home last night knowing that I would soon lose control of the project. Bye-bye tenure. Bye-bye Nobel Prize. What I didn't know was that God would take what he had learned to heart and vow to correct his mistake. And since, he said, he could not fix what he had created, there was only one way to end the suffering.

19

His message asked that we bear with the suffering just a little longer. He would return shortly with what he needed to clean up the mess. What does "shortly" mean to God? I have no idea.

I attempted to contact God, but got no answer.

That was when the fire alarm sounded.

Despite the smoke beginning to seep into the lab, I decided to keep trying, but I was soon forcibly removed by a burly fireman. I insisted that I needed to talk to God in order to save the universe. The fireman took this as evidence that I had already inhaled too much smoke and not enough oxygen.

...

When the fireman put me down on the grass in the quad, the students were already assembled to watch the blaze. The reason they had gathered so quickly was this—they had started the fire. Or at least one of them had. They had been protesting the cost of tuition when one of them thought to advance their cause with the help of a Molotov cocktail. It was the sort of logic that only an idealist could understand.

Gabriela was there on the lawn too. I told her about the pending end of the universe and she handed me a *mandoca*, saying that it was best not to go to the afterlife on an empty stomach.

"What good is this going to do me?" I asked.

"It's better than nothing," she said and left to find her son among the crowd.

### ###

## About the Author

David A. Kilman grew up in the pseudo space age and thought that he would be living on Mars by now. Instead, he lives in Colorado Springs at the foot of Pikes Peak. It may not be Mars, but he still probably has a nicer view out his window than you do. After a series of occupations that included bookseller, elected public official, and commodities trader, David now homeschools his children by day and writes by night. Although this leaves little time for sleep, he plans to take a long nap in a pine box when this is all over. David's short fiction has appeared in *Galaxy's Edge* and *Amazing Stories Magazine*.

*****~~~~~*****

## They Grow Up So Fast

by Konstantine Paradias

"Get the paddle," Kjell grumbled, as the protoplasmic muck inside the genesis bucket began to stir, its glistening skin crackling with sparks of electricity.

Above us, the open dome revealed a grey-black stretch of sky, a field of clouds pregnant with rain, roaring with spent thunder.

"For Pete's sake, Donny, *get the damn paddle!*" Kjell shouted, shoving me away from the bucket and the bubbling, shaking thing that poured itself out of its rim, spilling brackish water as it went. A lump of flesh whipped out and slapped at the marble floor tiles, seeking purchase and sprouting a row of suckers. Kjell swatted at it with a rolling pin, smacked the creature back into the genesis bucket as I ran toward the mop sink. In a single, clumsy motion, I pulled the paddle out of the still water, marveled at the spiraling row of blinking lights that flashed across it as it went online, splashing muck as I slipped, fell, crawled, walk-crawled, and finally ran back, just in time to see Kjell held up in the air by a monstrous, four-fingered arm.

"Donny, just bash its stupid head in!" Kjell roared. His rolling pin smashed across the creature's thick muscles, and I charged at it, letting out my shrill battle cry, paddle held high. Slipped again but smacked the paddle across the creature's face, watched it unleash a few hundred thousand volts of pure electricity into the mass of growing flesh. The bucket-thing roared with its brand new mouth, swiping at me blindly, and I struck it again, across the flanks this time, then jumped onto its back, unleashing a shower of sparks out into the air with every blow, beating the bucket-thing out of its cradle and onto the floor where it twitched, groaned, and finally lay still.

"Took your sweet time, didn't you?" Kjell rumbled, even as he squeezed out from under it, uselessly wiping at his muck-covered apron, then finally added, "I'll prep the fryer. You. . . clean up this mess."

"Yes, Chef," I said, as I watched Kjell strap on his hydraulic waldo and drag the bucket-thing into the kitchen, leaving me ankle-deep in the gunk.

From somewhere beyond the blast doors, the early evening crowd had begun to clamor for front house seats.

...

It started with cloned auroch meat, dodo tubesteaks, and limited-edition Mesozoic burgers with a side of deep-fried Darwin potatoes. In the blink of an eye, the mammoth was back and in a can. Within a month, you could get Great Auk stew to go in every corner deli.

By the end of the year, there wasn't a person in the world that hadn't gotten tired of the culinary wonder that was Ground Sloth kebab.

Before too long, every last foodie had had every de-extinct species boiled, roasted, or raw and still clamored for newer, better, unexpected things. So, as soon as the de-extinction technology was made public, every last chef decided to cut out the middlemen and to play God themselves.

Provided they had attended a Michelin three-week course, that is.

...

I'm wiping away at the layers of gunk, watching the smart-mop's ends eat away at the primordial filth in great laps to reveal the glistening marble underneath, when I hear the cooing. It's a gentle noise, like a baby's snoring. I have to stop mopping and shush the mop just to make sure I'm hearing it.

When it's all finally still and there's only the distant hiss of the fryer and the clamor of curtain crawlers in the dining area, it starts again, a gentle *purring* noise, echoing from the genesis bucket.

"I don't hear no bubble dancing!" Kjell shouts from the countertop, his fingers dancing over the projected controls of the cooking waldos, hard at work turning the bucket-thing into entrees.

"Mop needs a breather," I mutter and lean into the toppled genesis bucket, gently prodding it to turn the opening toward me. There, inside the sloshing leftover gunk, something stirs; too tiny to be luncheon meat, too weak to keep around for garbage duty. Its head, too big for its tiny body, bobs in the gunk. Its mouth, pink and toothless, opens and closes as it breathes out a stream of bubbles. I've just cupped it in my palm, and I'm about to chuck it out the window, when it goes:

*Blrrrttt* and then cracks a smile, its single brown eye taking me in like I'm God Almighty.

"Well, get it done. Dishes are almost through, and I need you to drop the truffles," Kjell says, and I just nod, watching the thing from the bucket as it wraps one little hand around my thumb and *squeezes* with everything it's got, before it tries to climb up my index finger.

"Yes, Chef," I say as I pull it up and stick it in the pantry, nestling it against the row of cans of whale-meat and the half-pound caviar bags. The munchkin coos happily, even after I've pushed the door shut and locked it for good measure.

...

Two hours into the shift, and the foodies come in like a squad of guerillas, with their hover-phones primed and their ivory cutlery at the ready. I bob and weave through the swarm of waitrons, pirouette from the pot washer to the oven, tango with a pot of flash-boiled water and barely jump out of the way as Kjell throws half a cryovaced coelacanth into the deep-fryer. It screams shrilly as it hits the boiling oil, and it begins to flop around, almost knocking the pasta strainer from my hand. Half a plate of penne is scattered on the floor, and I'm about to wipe it all away, when Kjell flicks my ear and goes:

"Two-second rule, Donny."

So I lean in and scoop as much of it as I can, drizzling it in sauce to take the edge off, slap a slice of bucket-meat on it, and send it off to God knows where, just as the flames start roaring in the range and I know that the pot is letting off a column of steam like Chernobyl on doomsday so I push my hands into the icy-cold water of the fish-tank and pull out the sea-scorpion, turn it in my hands to keep its tail from whipping out my eye and toss it into the pot with a flourish, just as its pincer is about to click shut around my pinky.

One of the waitrons bursts through the door, its display-face flashing a harried little smiley face at Kjell, its arms poking at his shoulder while he carefully arranges a pile of bucket-meat slivers against a mashed potato mountain range.

"Table 23, fronters want to see the chef," the waitron says, with an exaggerated South Bronx accent.

"I ain't leaving for a buncha stiffs," Kjell grumbles, halfway through peppering the potato peaks with white curry.

"No boss, regular Veeps. Top-priority," the waitron says, its tone more urgent than before.

"Probably looking for comps. Donny, keep an eye out. I'm expediting you," Kjell says as he runs through the doors, into the glittering, glowing dining room world beyond and I wait for the doors to swing once, twice before I run off to check on the munchkin.

Its single, glistening eye lights up as soon as I open the pantry door, a full head of curly cherub hair bobbing on its tiny head. Through the pule leftovers and the canned whale-meat juices, the munchkin smiles at me, stands on its two feet and says:

"Father, what am I?"

I'm reeling back from the sight of the munchkin on its own two feet, dressed in a plain toga fashioned from wrappers, surrounded by ingredient lists arranged around it like Zen scrolls. The munchkin waits for me to speak, hanging off my every word, but I am just trying to take in the pantry's devastation, two month's salary gone in a two-hour binge so I just nod and say:

"A grower, I guess?"

The kitchen doors open, and Kjell's back is turned to me as he bows at his rapt dining room audience, an explosion of laughter trailing behind him, and I grab the munchkin out from the pantry, kneel and stuff him down in the recipe bunker, the stuffy little cookbook shelf where Kjell never goes. I shush the munchkin, then rush the pot and rescue the coelacanth and the sea scorpion from the burners, slap them on the counter just as Kjell waltzes in, reaching for a filleting knife.

"Bloody peasants. Can you believe they've never had bucket-makhani?" he guffaws, even as he peels back the coelacanth's scales, revealing the off-white cooked flesh underneath "Thank God *I* have standards, right Donny?"

"Yes, Chef," I mutter, as I dial the miniature rainforest's time-lapse forward and start to pick the bamboo stalks just as they begin to bloom.

...

I'm nuking a side of bucket-meat, dicing a coleslaw salad with some silphium on the rail and keeping an eye out so the helicoprion dish doesn't get cooked beyond Pittsburgh rare, when I notice the cold blue glow seeping out from the recipe-bunker's sliding door.

## Cat's Breakfast

Looking up from the counter, I see Kjell's hand moving like a blur, arranging tiny morsels of Megalodon nigiri into the shape of the great beast itself across a platter and decide to chance it. With the tip of my foot, I slide the door open and bend down, biting my lip to keep from screaming as a shaft of blinding light hits my eyes.

"Look Father! Light!" the munchkin says, its silhouette barely visible against the glare and I can almost make out the gutted lengths of wire that he's probably torn from the kitchen equipment, jury-rigged into a rudimentary generator that feeds a bouquet of miniature bulbs, arranged like a blooming sea anemone. As my eyes adjust into the light, I notice that the recipe bunker's books have been gutted and re-arranged, their shape turned into a miniature home lifted straight from one of the covers. The munchkin steps inside, its clothes made from strips of cured, scavenged skin trimmings, his hair thinning, his single eye radiating intelligence.

"Oh sweet merciful God," I mutter and the munchkin tutts, derisively.

"God? Father, please, what use have we of bogey men?"

"Donny, where are my damn tournes?" Kjell's voice roars from the other side and I jump up, slamming the door shut on the munchkin, shaking even as I'm grasping the zucchini and the carrots, dicing them into cubes, arranging them into platters, and shoving them down the counter. Kjell roars something about frog legs, and I'm about to grab a batch out of the freezer, when I notice the munchkin floating away from the counter, nestled into the gutted insides of a scavenged waitron.

"We must part ways, Father," the munchkin mutters, as I watch him float past me, pausing as he stands at eye level, "there is work to be done."

I try to struggle with a response as I watch the munchkin ride the waitron above the kitchen, up into the strange hell of wires that's the exhaust system, and I want to reach out and stop it, to say *anything,* when Kjell roars:

"Donny! Get a move on! I'm dying over here!"

"Yes, Chef," I say, and deep down, I'm glad that he's gone.

...

It's twenty minutes to midnight, and I'm crawled halfway into the large mammal oven, while Kjell's yucking it up with the Veeps still loitering in the dining room, when I see the munchkin again. The fire in its eye has dimmed and its face is cracked and lined with age. There's a delicate, plasteel waldo where its right hand used to be.

"You were right, Father," the munchkin says, nodding its sagely head. Only a few tufts of white, wispy hair remain "we *do* need such a thing as God."

"Okay," I mutter and I wonder if it isn't the oven-cleaner fumes that are making me hallucinate, if I'm not just back home, stuck in bed and wasted. "What happened to your arm?"

"This?" the munchkin says and smiles "A pointless spoil, from my adventuring days. Oh, the things I saw, Father. The wonders of the cosmos and its horrors too, just lurking beyond the window. . . "

I check my wristwatch. The munchkin has only been gone for three hours.

"Like a fool, I'd wanted it all for myself. Like a madman, I hunted for forbidden knowledge. And I found it, Father."

"Uh..." I manage.

"I abused it, of course. Which is how I got this," the munchkin says, pointing at its plasteel arm. "I was evil for a while, a jealous god. When I was toppled, I became idle. In time, I grew into wisdom."

"That's nice," I say, backing away as I notice the munchkin begin to glow, a gentle, smokeless flame rising from its chest, slowly enveloping it. Softly, it begins to hover from the oven, standing in the air, its tiny body transmogrifying into light.

"Father, I am ascending," the munchkin squeaks, his expression degenerating into childlike fear "I'm scared."

"You're doing fine, Junior," I say, smiling. The munchkin just glares at me.

"Please Father; Junior was my slave name," the munchkin mutters and then explodes in a flash of blue-hot light. Like a discarded toy, his plasteel prosthetic arm clatters into the oven and I take it into my hand, examining the tiny little working, salvaged from the waitron's guts.

"All right, Donny, wrap it up! Campers are gone and I wanna go home!" Kjell shouts as he bursts into the kitchen, rapping his hand against the counter. Out from a row of panels, an army of spidery cleaner-bots slips out and starts picking up the leftover mess. "Did I miss anything?"

"Where do I even start, Chef," I say, but Kjell just shrugs and throws the lights and I stumble through the dark and put the genesis bucket back up on its stool and fill it with the primordial ooze and hope to God tomorrow's gonna be nothing but clear skies.

### 

## About the Author

Konstantine Paradias is a writer by choice. He's published over 100 stories in five languages and has written marketing, videogame, and a whole bunch of other stuff that he's not entirely proud of, but hey, he got nominated for a Pushcart Prize once. His collection of short stories, *Sorry, Wrong Country,* is published by Rooster Republic Press.

*****~~~~~*****

# The Jim-Aaargh School of Philosophy
by Rati Mehrotra

Mona sat in a corner of the waiting room, trying to ignore the tentacled creature next to her. Forty-five years on Earth, smooth and uneventful but for the dumb accident that ended her life. Idiot driver. He couldn't have been more than a pimply fifteen. What would Rohan do without her? Fall sobbing into his secretary's plump arms, no doubt.

She should be reading the Book of Rules right now, instead of wasting time brooding about her husband and his stupid secretary. Mona squinted at the yellow pages of the massive book that lay open on her lap. Such dense, spidery writing. Almost as if Someone didn't *want* her to understand it.

The tentacled creature nudged her arm for the third time. Really, it had no sense of decorum. Plus, it was quite the most hideous thing she had ever seen, a sort of cross between a squid and a snail.

Was it remotely possible that her next birth would be in this creature's world? She shuddered and moved a few inches away from it. Perhaps there was something in the Book of Rules to avoid such a possibility. Mona grimaced as she flicked through the leaf-like pages. Wasn't bloody likely that she'd be able to find it. Well, at least her number was written clearly on the front of the book: 66666.

There was a beep, and a number flashed on the Door: 66664. Oh *God*. It wouldn't be long now.

31

"Don't you remember me, Mona?" The creature's voice was plaintive.

Mona started. How did it know her name? Oh, right. These things could read minds.

"Yes, we can, but I died too young to really develop my skills," it explained. "I was in a most unfortunate accident. Or maybe it wasn't an accident. Perhaps it was just my way of being Called. Just when I was beginning to get comfortable in my new body too."

Mona turned her head away, trying to hide her thoughts of that "new body."

"I seem to be upsetting you," said the creature. "Is it the way I look? On Eldebrin, I was considered a rather attractive specimen. Of course, humans are repelled by eyestalks and tentacles, as I remember only too well."

"It's not the way you look," lied Mona. "But it's not okay to disturb someone in the Anteroom. You know that."

"Yes," said the creature, "I do know. But I couldn't help it. You see, we were lovers once."

What? Mona edged further away. Maybe the thingy was mad.

The creature passed a long, spinach-green tentacle in front of its central eye in a weary gesture. "Oh no, I am quite sane. Once I was human. A male human, to be precise. A poet, even. The strangest and cruelest thing of all was that when I died and walked from the Anteroom into the world of the Aaarghs, I remembered every detail of my previous life. The poems I used to write. The hands I wrote them with. The language I used, the mouth I had. These things never quite left me. So I continued to write about other worlds and other lives. I founded the Jim-Aaargh School of Philosophy, which became quite popular with the younger Aaarghs."

A jolt of memory shook Mona. "Jim? *Jim?* That can't be you! Is that you?"

The creature stared moodily up at the ceiling. "Yes and no, my dear. Yes and no. Part of me is indeed the one that used to be called Jim in another life, and part of me is Eeka, an Aaargh who can't remember any of her previous lives, bless her hungry little heart. Reproduction among Aaarghs is a long and complex affair. Jim tried to avoid it as far as possible, but in the end Eeka pinned him down and it was all over. I became one mother Aaargh, who would, on dying, split into two or four little Aaarghs. Except, of course, I died too soon."

Mona stopped listening. She remembered a summer night twenty-five years ago, when a young and passionate classmate of hers called Jim had seduced her among the gardenias of the Durham college lawn. The hot, eager kisses, the fumbling hands, the whispered endearments, the scent of jasmine mingled with the scent of sex. And, of course, the scream of the matron who found them at midnight, sleeping in a tangled heap of limbs under the silver light of a crescent moon. It was the start of a brief and glorious affair. For a month they existed only for each other. Then they quarreled over something so trivial, Mona could never remember it. A few weeks later, she got a fellowship to study philosophy at the University of New Toronto. Jim did not try to stop her, and she never saw him again.

". . . so the Jim-Aaargh School of Philosophy is based on very simple truths. Truth number one: Transmigration is random. Truth number two: An indifferent and powerful Intellect has constructed our universe. Truth number three: Freedom lies in being able to choose where and how we live and die."

Mona gasped; her eyes darted around the room, but it appeared no one had heard him. "You crazy?" she hissed. "You could spend endless lives as the most degraded being in the Universe. Or you could spend eternity in the Anteroom, simply waiting to be alive again."

"Truth number two says that you are wrong," said Jim-Aaargh. "The Intellect does not watch our every word. The Intellect just *is*. The Universe just is. We cannot be free of them. What we *can* do is remember—remember who we are in every birth, so that knowledge is not lost. The Jim-Aaargh School of Philosophy will not be lost. On the contrary, it will grow every time I die, because I will not forget who I am and what I have seen."

He waved a tentacle. "Observe this Anteroom. It was different the last time I saw it. Then it was a greenhouse, perhaps because of the numerous plant beings I found myself with. Obviously, the Anteroom is just another construct. You yourself are a construct. How else do you think we can understand each other? You have a human shape because that's what you think you are. I have an Aaargh shape because that's what I think I am, at least for now. And this Anteroom resembles the waiting room of a public transit station, because that's how we think it should be. But really, it can be anything. It can, for instance, be an ocean. Go on, try seeing an ocean."

Mona looked around. The Anteroom did not go away. It remained as it was: cream-colored walls, rows of chairs and benches, humans and non-humans sitting with their heads bowed over Rule Books.

"No, not like that," said Jim-Aaargh. "You must look sideways at things. Put that book away. Don't focus too hard. Imagine the ocean. Feel the sand between your toes, smell the salty air, hear the sound of waves breaking against the cliff."

The edges of the room blurred; it swam before Mona's eyes. A school of tiny, transparent fish brushed against her face. She gave a little scream and flailed her arms, upsetting a bowl of plastic lilies.

"See what I mean?" Jim-Aaargh picked up the bowl with one tentacle, and waved another at some people who had turned around to scowl at them. "Sorry, folks. Everything under control here."

## The Jim-Aaargh School of Philosophy

"You did it, didn't you?" accused Mona. "You made me see things."

"I helped you, yes," Jim-Aaargh admitted. "But you didn't see anything that wasn't as real as what you're seeing now. And if you can remember being in the Anteroom, you can, with practice, remember who you once were."

Mona pressed a palm to her forehead. He was confusing her, and she didn't want to be confused, not now. "I wouldn't want to be a slug and know that I was once human," she said. "Better to live the life of a slug and get it over with."

"Yes, that is the problem, is it not?" said Jim-Aaargh. "It is why we all forget, and why each life begins anew. Memories bring pain, but they also bring wisdom. You realize that you are more than one life in one body in one world."

"I want to be re-born as a human," said Mona. "How can I make that happen?"

"Why do you want to be reborn as a human?" countered Jim-Aaargh. "Because that's all you know. You remember nothing of your past lives. Really, the possibilities are limitless. Why restrict yourself to a physically weak life form of average intelligence and brief life span, when there are so many more interesting options?"

"Like yourself?" said Mona.

Her sarcasm was lost on Jim-Aaargh. "Like myself," he said. "Aaarghs don't live much longer than humans, but our world is very peaceful, except once a year when reproduction fever hits the females. Aaarghs have no concept of money, war, crime or incarceration. They spend all their time thinking. We have ninety-eight words for 'mathematics,' depending on what we are using it for.

"Then there are the Minnies of Arcturus. You can see one perched on the shoulder of that human in the blue suit. Minnies may be tiny, but they are highly intelligent and

35

also one of the longest-lived species in the Universe. It is very rare to see a Minnie in the Anteroom. This one must have had an accident."

"It was the new ship that I built," said a small voice from somewhere near the ground. "I miscalculated the acceleration into hyperspace by a factor of point oh oh two. I was trying to do it all in my head, see."

Mona looked down to see a six-inch high creature with a carapace, moth-like wings, and a remarkably expressive face. She shuddered and withdrew her feet.

"I should have mentioned they have excellent hearing and are very swift," said Jim-Aaargh.

Mona closed her eyes. Why was this happening to her? She was practically next in line to walk through the Door. She should be meditating or reading the Book. Instead, she was having a conversation with two bugs.

"I'm not a bug," said the Minnie indignantly, flying up to perch on Mona's armrest. "You have no concept of biology, do you?"

"Why should you be meditating?" said Jim-Aaargh.

Why were they all so bloody telepathic? Mona retrieved her Book of Rules and opened it. "It says so right here. Chapter 1, paragraph three."

Jim-Aaargh waved a dismissive tentacle. "Don't quote the Book of Rules. It changes depending on who's reading it. Like most humans, you like to be told what to do. You need simple rules to follow. Hence the Book. Notice that *I* don't have one."

"Neither do I," said the Minnie. "Can't wait to get out of here and back into my ship."

"The one that blew up?" said Mona.

"Oh, accidents will happen," said the Minnie. "This is the third time I've been here. Each time I go back and start work all over again."

"You remember *three* lives?" Mona was dumbfounded. "And you went back as a Minnie each time?"

## The Jim-Aaargh School of Philosophy

"I told you it's possible," said Jim-Aaargh. "It requires will power, concentration, and belief. You need to be able to picture yourself as you are and as you wish to be."

All right, *now* she was getting somewhere. Mona closed her eyes and muttered: "I am human. I am not a bug. I am human. I will always be human. I will be reborn on Earth as a human being. Not as a bug! I am human."

Jim-Aaargh sighed. "No, that is not what I meant. Humans are so literal. Perhaps that is why they are able to forget so easily. I meant that you should picture yourself as you are without the outer covering of the body or the assumption that you need a body to exist."

Great, now he was giving her religious mumbo-jumbo. "I happen to *like* having a body," said Mona.

"Well, you don't have a body right now, you only think you have one. And there are several planets with intelligent species that do not have a physical form, as you should know."

"I don't care," said Mona. "I want to be human, and humans have bodies. Perhaps the Minnie can tell me how it managed to return to its world." She looked around. "Where's it gone?"

"Probably got bored," said Jim-Aaargh. "It must have jumped the queue to go through the Door."

"But it can't do that."

"It can do anything. And so can you, if you throw away that book of yours. Look, why don't we just walk up to the Door and step through together? If you like, we can be born as twin Aaarghs or humans or whatever. Think of what we could accomplish! Perhaps we can even beat the Universe at its own game."

"No." Mona clutched the book. "I shan't listen to you. You're going to be punished for saying such things."

Right on cue, thunder rolled. The ceiling cracked and split apart with a groan to reveal a black, stormy sky. Mona dropped the Book of Rules and cowered under the chair, heart thumping. A fork of white lightening sizzled in and struck the place where Jim-Aaargh was sitting. A smell of burning flesh and smoke hit her. Mona gagged and sobbed and scrabbled on the floor.

After several minutes of nothing happening, she poked her head out from under the chair. The ceiling was still there. No sky, no lightning, no storm. The room and its inhabitants looked the same as before. Had she imagined it?

Mona crawled out from under the chair and looked to her right where Jim-Aaargh had been sitting. Nothing but a chair with a smoking hole in it.

*Oh no.* Poor Jim-Aaargh. Maybe it would be her turn next. Mona flipped through the pages of her book. There had to be something on forgiveness and expiation. "Please God, I'll never doubt Your power again," she muttered. Ah, there it was: Chapter 75, titled, "The Eighty-nine Penances of Viswanima." Nope, that didn't make any sense. She flipped some more, a sense of despair growing.

There was a beep, and a new number flashed on the Door—66666. Mona gulped and stood up. Her turn, and she was totally unprepared. It wasn't fair. Those two had distracted her from reading and meditating, and made her think subversive thoughts. She'd probably be reborn as a slimy slug on some far-off planet.

Mona walked miserably up to the Door, wondering if she could simply ignore the Call and continue living in the Anteroom. As a construct, it wasn't too bad. She could meet interesting beings from all over the Universe. She might even develop a school of philosophy all her own, called How-to-Avoid-Being-Born-a-Slug.

She took a deep breath, pushed the Door open, and entered. And dropped the Book of Rules.

Sitting behind a mahogany desk, playing with a gaudy glass paperweight, was her husband Rohan.

Mona gathered air into her lungs and screamed, "What are *you* doing here?"

A familiar, hurt expression came on Rohan's face. "Not very happy to see me, are you?"

"No!" said Mona. "I mean, yes, but. . . "

"That's your problem," said Rohan. "You can never make up your mind. That's why I'm here to make it up for you." His features melted so that he looked, for a moment, not-Rohan. Then they solidified again and he gave her his cute grin, the one he reserved for when he forgot their anniversary. "Let's see what I have for you on my list." He picked up a sheet of paper from the desk.

Mona stared at him, her thoughts racing. Reality or construct? Rohan or not-Rohan? Freedom or slavery?

"Do it!" whispered a voice in her ear, and Mona leaped across the room, grabbed the glass paperweight from the desk, and brought it down on not-Rohan's head. He fell face forward on the desk without a sound.

Heart thumping, Mona reached for the sheet of paper before it could flutter to the floor. She looked at it and cried, "Why, it's blank!"

"Told you," said the voice. "*We* get to decide, if only we can let go our fear. Where would you like to go? Back to Earth?"

It was decades before Mona remembered that she said "Eldebrin," mainly to impress Jim-Aaargh. But by then she was already working on a corollary to the theory of Random Transmigration that would launch her career as a philosopher-mathematician, and she forgave her once-human foibles without a qualm.

### ###

## About the Author

Rati Mehrotra is a Toronto-based writer. Her stories have been published in *Apex Magazine, AE—The*

*Cat's Breakfast*

*Canadian Science Fiction Review, Urban Fantasy Magazine, Podcastle, Abyss & Apex,* and many more.

*****~~~*****

## *Command Decision*

by James Beamon

In the latest effort to combat terrorism, the United States Army issued a Command Decision to raid the dry cleaners directly outside the main gate of Fort Myers-Briggs. The need to occupy the dry cleaners, being a Command Decision, is something the public may not understand without first dissecting what makes a Command Decision different from a standard decision.

Normally these things start at the top, with generals and joint chiefs interfacing with secretaries and other high-level decision makers around a big table made of real wood littered with cups of coffee and dossiers of all the latest intelligence. Eventually all those folks decide something, and a Command Decision is born. Most times. Sometimes, like this time, it starts with a call at three in the morning with a subordinate telling the Brigade Commander that one of his troops has stormed the dry cleaners right off base.

The Brigade Commander was Lieutenant Colonel James Swick. His first response to the news that a Private First Class in his unit had barricaded himself inside the dry cleaners was remarkably cool.

"Say again?" he asked.

"Sir, Private Zahn went rogue." The man on the other end of the phone was Captain Dumphrey. Dumphrey was book smart, an admin guy who aced tests and looked great on paper. He ran the Tactical Honing in Warfare and

41

Advanced Research Technology, or THWART, Lab. Not as documented as his test results was the captain's utter lack of common sense.

"How do you go rogue on a dry cleaners?" Colonel Swick asked.

"He's. . . confusing. . . his training, Sir, an unexpected side effect of Project Kniferunner. I can't say much more over this open line. How do you want me to proceed?"

"Have you told him to come out of the damn cleaners?"

"First thing I tried, Sir."

Colonel Swick had been compelled to ask. After all, Dumphrey was an idiot sometimes.

"I'm coming," Colonel Swick said. This was his first decision of the night.

For expediency's sake, he showed up in PTs, what civilians routinely called a track suit, black pants with a matching black jacket sporting a gold chevron and Army logo. This was his second decision and one he immediately regretted. Captain Dumphrey did not mention this thing had already turned into a media circus. News cameras, vans, and reporters swarmed the perimeter like locusts, held back only by local cops, military police, and yellow tape. Colonel Swick worked his way through the crowd, largely being ignored as reporters poised in front of their respective cameras until one reporter recognized him despite his present lack of observable rank.

"Colonel Swick!" the reporter called as he pressed through the crowd toward the colonel. "Are you in charge here?"

The cameras and microphones collectively swiveled as if they smelled fresh prey. A moment ago he clearly saw the sign for Ashkani Bros. Cleaners; now there was nothing but cameras in his eyes and mics at his mouth.

"Excuse me," he said in stereo.

## Command Decision

"Colonel Swick, are you in command here? Can you give our viewers your assessment of the situation?"

Swick shook his head. "That wasn't an 'excuse me' because I didn't hear you. It meant get out of my way. Once I get an assessment, you'll get an assessment. Now make a hole."

He pushed his way through. The last thing his career needed was a press conference with him in his workout attire. Undeterred by the colonel's request to be excused, cameras and questions followed him like disciples, until he at last made sanctuary beyond the yellow police tape.

Flanked by police cars and Army tactical vans, stood the two-story dry cleaners. Next to the Ashkani Bros. Cleaners sign, a ten-foot-tall cartoon caricature of Syed and Azhar Ashkani stood back to back, smiling at would-be customers with big, toothy grins. Below the sign, the motto declared, "Dry Cleaned as Easy as A.B.C."

Swick made his way to Captain Dumphrey, who was sensibly dressed in camouflage. Along with the captain, William Migos, the battalion's Command Sergeant Major, was there and equally dressed for battle. Migos was one of those old-school sergeant majors, tougher than two dollar steak, skin as leathery as the cow it came from. He looked at Colonel Swick with a raised eyebrow.

"Going for a run after this, Colonel?"

"Don't start with me, Bill. What's the situation?"

"Private Zahn broke in about an hour ago, barricaded himself in there with the brothers Ashkani, who live on the second floor when they're not downstairs jacking up my creases. Zahn refuses to come out, claiming they're terrorists."

"Why does he think they're terrorists?"

Captain Dumphrey raised his hand like he was in class answering a teacher.

"Sir, I believe Private Zahn is having a dissociative cognitive episode."

"A lot of big words to say he nutted up," muttered Sergeant Major Migos.

"He's not crazy," Captain Dumphrey said. He leaned forward and looked around conspiratorially before whispering. "It's Project Kniferunner."

Until now, Project Kniferunner seemed like one of the usual go-nowhere, waste-of-time, waste-of-funding efforts entertained in quarterly intervals by the THWART Lab. Like last quarter's computer-controlled bomb-carrying rat drones, aka Project Headcheese. Nothing came out of that except cute pictures of rats dressed in wee backpacks and shiny hats. Colonel Swick could scarcely remember Project Kniferunner.

"Remind me," he said.

Captain Dumphrey ushered Colonel Swick and Sergeant Major Migos into a nearby tactical van. Behind the armored walls of the van, the captain explained how PFC Zahn along with a select team of other privates had been the recipients of an experimental neurotransmitter installed right behind their left ears. The neurotransmitter augmented reality with programmed goals, objectives, and missions that appeared in fifteen-minute intervals superimposed over normal vision. Constantly in the privates' periphery vision was a running point total based on different programmed incentives. Also perpetually in sight was important tactical information such as the amount of ammo in their weapon's current clip along with their total ammo count.

"Let me get this straight," Col Swick said. "You've turned this kid's life into a first-person shooter?"

Captain Dumphrey nodded.

"What's the point of all this?"

"Well, rendering reality into a game has a myriad of benefits. Not only are there incredible boosts in visual processing, visuospatial attention, motor function, and sensory-motor integration, but the training time for a soldier is significantly reduced. Beyond that, incentivizing kills by awarding points reduces the trauma associated with taking lives. Desensitizing the soldiers to violent and distressing situations ultimately means more fun and less PTSD."

"Jesus!" Sergeant Migos swore. "Did you pull all that shit off the Powerpoint slide you used to pitch this idea to the Pentagon or something?"

Before Dumphrey could answer, Migos pointed at one of the video feeds in the tactical van that displayed the occupied dry cleaners. "If that ain't PTSD, what the hell do you call it?"

"A dissociative cognitive episode," Dumphrey answered.

"In English," Migos countered.

"He has incorporated the dry cleaners into his training exercise and has taken it over in an effort to reach bigger incentives."

Colonel Swick looked at the junior officer. "You're telling me he's in there trying to level up?"

"That's about the sum of it."

This made about as much sense to the colonel as when the THWART Lab tried Operation Poultersnitch, where they brought in mediums to communicate with the executed enemies of America's enemies hoping to derive useful intelligence from beyond the grave. It made sense while absolutely making no sense. "But why the hell is Private Zahn hunting for terrorists in the cleaners in the first place?

Captain Dumphrey produced a thumb drive from his pocket and inserted it into a laptop in the tactical van. After a few clicks he turned to the others. "This is one of the scenarios we've practiced, asymmetric warfare in an urban environment."

Colonel Swick looked at the screen. It was more movie than video game, reality as seen in the first-person point of view of any modern shooter game. The soldiers went from brown nondescript house to brown nondescript house, kicking open doors in a flurry of dust and hurled obscenities. The latest door flew off its hinges, and a man wielding an AK-47 rose out of the shadows in the background. In real time, a frame appeared around the man's brown face, a face too happy to be in the midst of a pitched battle, sporting a toothy grin as if the terrorist sang "Death to America" in the shower like a pop song. The frame enlarged the face to photo quality. The joyful face hovered next to descriptors that provided name, height, weight, and the fact that this man was number nine on the FBI's terrorist watch list and an expert bomb maker.

Captain Dumphrey paused the screen.

"I know that face," Colonel Swick said. He looked up at the video screens that displayed the dry cleaners, where the same face, complete with the same toothy grin, smiled at them from the sign for Ashkani Bros. Cleaners.

Colonel Swick turned to Captain Dumphrey, both understanding and disbelief beginning to show in equal parts on his face. "You used Azhar Ashkani's picture. . . as the face model for Terrorist X?"

Dumphrey shrugged. "I needed to program the facial recognition software, and Google image search for 'terrorists' only had pics of people wrapped up with only their eyes exposed."

"So you used the faces of businessmen whose store is immediately off base?"

"I needed some Arabs, Sir."

"They're Pakistani!" Colonel Swick shouted.

Before Colonel Swick could chew Dumphrey's ass like it was the only thing on the menu, the colonel's cell phone rang.

"Colonel Swick, this is General Hightower."

"Sir!" Colonel Swick blustered. He almost gulped down his own adam's apple. Hightower was a four star general, five ranks above Lieutenant Colonel Swick—his boss's boss's boss's boss.

"You've made national news," General Hightower informed Swick. "And on a stage that large you're giving interviews in your workout attire?"

"Sir, I declined any interview."

"The sound bite I'm looking at is, 'once I get an assessment, you'll get an assessment.' That's not only an interview, but a promise. It also sounds like you're admitting you don't know your own goddamn situation."

"No, Sir. I'm fully aware of the situation."

"Good," General Hightower said. "So, what is your situation, lieutenant colonel? What will you brief the media?"

"That one of our soldiers is having a dissociative cognitive episode brought about by a training complication. We are working to resolve the issue," Colonel Swick said. It was about as generic as he could make the situation.

"That is not the situation, Colonel. The situation is the Army is running an official operation to stop a potential terrorist plot. Details will be revealed as the operation concludes."

"What terrorist plot? General, I'm not sure you're aware of what's happening on the ground here."

"I'm at the Pentagon," General Hightower responded. "We're more than aware of what's going on there. Perhaps you don't know what's going on here. We have a whole intelligence directorate actively engaged in finding the Ashkani link to terrorism. And we will find it, Colonel."

"But, Sir, the Ashkani Brothers have been dry cleaning off base for almost nine years now."

"Sounds like a dedicated sleeper cell. . . " General Hightower countered.

"They're both naturalized citizens," Colonel Swick said.

". . . that has integrated itself into the very fabric of America," Hightower rebutted.

Colonel Swick was speechless. The Army was making this an official operation. Doing this was probably more palatable than trying to explain that they've been experimenting with brain chips on young soldiers which gave a private who's never seen a battle "First Blood"-grade PTSD. So now everyone in Army intelligence was actively engaged in making the Ashkanis more dangerous than cancer. Finally, the Colonel found his words.

"The intelligence doesn't support this," he said.

"Who needs intelligence? Everybody has at least one family member you wouldn't let borrow your car. My momma always said when you're drawing Hitler moustaches on people, all you need is a few squiggles of ink. Now get out there and brief the media. Our sleeper cell isn't getting any sleepier. Take control of your situation, Swick."

General Hightower ended the call. Colonel Swick wondered what the hell kind of childhood the general had, because whose momma had quotes like that? Swick didn't wonder anything else. He knew for a fact that going against the general's directive was career suicide. Unless he got his own neurotransmitter installed, there would be no points for that. Instead, he went outside, Captain Dumphrey and Sergeant Major Migos in tow, to brief the media on the Army's official and swift response to the terrorism threat.

"Keep in mind I cannot reveal the nature of the threat or our operations at this time," Colonel Swick said into the sea of cameras and microphones huddled beyond the police tape. "But please know we have the situation under control. Now, are there any questions to what I've just said?"

Behind Swick, ungodly screams came forth within the dry cleaners.

"What was that?" a reporter asked.

Colonel Swick excused himself from the clamoring reporters, rushing back into the tactical van with Dumphrey and Migos

"Torture?" Colonel Swick asked Captain Dumphrey.

"Doubtful, Sir. He hasn't gotten far enough along in the simulated interrogation program to be at the torture stage. He would still be. . . well. . . checking the detainees."

"What do you mean, checking?"

"You know, Sir, checking."

"He means Private Zahn's sticking fingers up assholes, boss," Sergeant Major Migos said, shaking his head with a look of disgust on his heavily lined face. "Probably don't have no gloves or nothing."

Well, the desensitization aspect of the program certainly worked. That's something most would call a distressing situation. Similarly distressing was the call Colonel Swick received moments later from General Hightower again.

"You call that handling the situation?"

"Sir, I have a soldier in the dry cleaners who is listening solely to software. He could be smashing his fists into the building's brickwork for gold coins like he's Super Mario, for all my control."

"No one told you to give another news briefing in your workout attire."

"Duly noted, Sir. I went for expediency."

"We're also expedient here at the Pentagon, Swick. While you were making a spectacle of yourself, we searched through all our massive databases and supercomputers and couldn't find a single scrap linking these Ashkani brothers to terrorism. Looks like you're about to fall on your own sword for this one."

A pit opened at the bottom of Colonel Swick's stomach. "I don't think I heard you right, Sir."

"You heard me fine. This was your boy, your experiment going F.U.B.A.R. You're also the one who gave the news brief. Now it's time to tell them that you acted on a gut feeling, gave Private Zahn his orders with no credible intelligence, and hope the media doesn't paint you out to be too much of a racist."

Colonel Swick felt himself getting hot despite the breathable fabric of the Army workout uniform. "This is bullshit. I spouted your official stance. You can't just change it."

"The official stance is and always was to protect the Army. And it is not taking the blame for Project Kniferunner."

General Hightower ended the call. Colonel Swick made his own call after that, a judgment call as he looked at Captain Dumphrey.

"Private Zahn is your boy, your experiment. Looks like you're going to have to fall on your own sword with this one."

Captain Dumphrey nodded gravely. Colonel Swick led him outside, back to the reporters clamoring for attention. Swick introduced Captain Dumphrey, then stepped into the background so the captain could commit career suicide.

"The soldier in the dry cleaners is my operative," Captain Dumphrey informed the media. "He has been acting on my orders alone, based on a mission program I designed. Now I'm here to tell you. . . "

"Mission accomplished!" came a cry from the dry cleaners. The doors opened to reveal Private First Class Zahn. He, like everyone in the Army at the scene except Colonel Swick, was wearing camouflage. His face was adorned with swirls of black war paint. He kept the two Ashkani brothers at arm's length ahead of himself, pushing them out of the cleaners. The two brothers' wrists were bound with zip ties. Their faces bore the fresh tear tracks of the thoroughly searched.

Army security forces swarmed over both Zahn and the Ashkani brothers, taking them all down to the ground.

## Command Decision

Upon insistent hollering from Private Zahn that there was a trap door and his point values had doubled, the security forces investigated the basement, where they discovered the Ashkani link to terrorism, albeit not the link the Army was hoping for.

Turned out the Ashkani brothers were smuggling friends and family out of Pakistan to make a better life in America. While one would stay behind and man the store, the other would charter a boat to Karachi, where he would show up in a military uniform borrowed from the cleaners, fake paperwork and zip ties claiming he was there to transport "suspected terrorists" to Fort Myers-Briggs for interrogation. Pakistani port officials in Karachi could care less, and port officials in America congratulated them. Only one Coast Guard patrolman showed concern when one of the "suspected terrorists" was the Ashkani brothers' six-year-old niece Amira, which involved looking at the little girl with her wrists zip tied together and saying "Never too young to learn bomb making, right?"

With Private Zahn and Project Kniferunner vindicated and the Ashkanis arrested, this Command Decision became an officially sanctioned action from the highest levels. Unlike standard decisions, Command Decisions impact everyone involved.

Private Zahn got promoted. On his performance review were impressive statements such as "took charge of the situation" and "wouldn't back down despite being outnumbered two to one against hostile criminal element" and "followed orders despite lack of obvious orders."

Captain Dumphrey also got promoted. However, he resigned his commission shortly thereafter to become lead designer for a software company specializing in realistic first-person shooters.

Sergeant Major Migos was forced to use another dry cleaners. They take even longer turning around a uniform than the Ashkanis, even with one of the brothers routinely being away from the shop on a boat in the middle of the Pacific. And they still jack up his creases.

Colonel Swick got reprimanded. Unlike the Ashkani links to terrorism, his was the clearly visible offense of giving three news interviews in his workout attire. It was a decision that would always haunt him.

### 

## About the Author

James Beamon is an IT guy with a writing problem. He's been in the Air Force, in Iraq and Afghanistan, and knee deep in narrative, and none of that excuses him from having to provide tech support to his wife and son for their various devices. They currently live in Virginia, where you can find James either chasing down book deals or chasing down alien bugs on Farpoint. Check out what he's up to at http://www.fictigristle.wordpress.com/

*****~~~*****

# *Hear*

by Tim Jeffreys

When the news broke, a sense of shock was shared the world over. No one could believe Zachery Flynn had killed himself.

His death was front page news for days after a security guard at his L.A. mansion discovered the body. People shook their heads and wondered aloud how someone who appeared to have everything—looks, money, fame, talent—could wake up one day and decide they no longer wanted to live. Vikki, Elle, Nadine, and I met for ice cream the following Saturday, and all of us shed a few tears, even though the Flynn Brothers posters had long since come down from our bedroom walls and their CDs only came out for a nostalgic blast every once in a while so we could all sing along and tease each other about how well we knew the songs.

The only person unsurprised, apparently, by Zachery Flynn's death was my mother. "It was that song," she told me. "What must it have been like to go on stage and sing that song every night?"

I knew the song she meant. To the astonishment of my fifteen-year-old self, she had broke down and cried the first time I played her "Emily, Hear My Plea," Flynn's biggest solo hit released after the breakup of his boy band.

My embarrassment at the sudden display of emotion became even more acute when Mum—apparently unable to control herself—sobbed, "Help them. We have to help them." I thought she was reacting to the song's lyrics, which were a soppy paean to some girl Flynn claimed to have glimpsed in the front row at one of his concerts. *From the lip of the stage, I asked your name, and you cried out Emily,* the song went. *Emily, didn't you know, every song that night was for you? Only for you. Emily. Oh Emily. But after the show you were gone. I'll never see your face again—oh Emily, Emily, lost in the crowd.* A year previously, in the grip of my Flynn Brothers obsession, I would have been acutely jealous of this *Emily*, whoever she was. I would have wanted to scratch her eyes out. But something had changed. When "Emily, Hear My Plea" was released, although I rushed out to buy it like loads of other girls my age, I cringed when I first heard the lyrics. It was clear the listener was supposed to picture themselves as this Emily; or imagine that they might be the next one to capture Zachery Flynn's heart from the front row. At fifteen I was too old for this kind of syrupy nonsense, so I was a little ashamed of my mother—a grown woman—for reacting to it in the way she did.

"There probably is no Emily," I told her, in my best *get-a-grip* tone of voice. "It's probably all just made up."

Mum looked up, dabbing at her cheeks with the cuff of her sweater. She stared at me for a long moment then said, "It's not the words, Kathleen, it's the music. Listen to the music."

The backing track was another reason I hadn't liked the song. The Flynn Brothers' songs had been mostly upbeat, but this song was slow and melancholy. It had a plaintive, almost dirge-like quality that sounded strange to my ears. In truth, the song disturbed me in some way I couldn't quite put my finger on. But it was just a pop song.

## Hear

I couldn't understand what my mother was getting so upset about.

"Listen," she said. "Can't you hear that? It's like—" But whatever it was she heard, she couldn't find the right words to express it.

Later, she denied that she had ever cried over a Zachery Flynn song. She also swore on my grandmother's grave that she had never once said, *Help them.* "I had something on my mind that day," she would say if I teased her about it. "I was thinking about something else, that's all."

"Emily, Hear My Plea" became a huge hit for Zachery Flynn, bigger than anything he'd recorded with the Flynn Brothers. For a few months you couldn't escape it. It was everywhere, constantly on the radio, blasting out of PA systems at the mall, and every time I heard it I felt restless and hopeless at the same time, like the song was trying to tell me something beyond Flynn's banal lyrics. There was a general feeling in the air that summer, like something was wrong, like a house was on fire a few streets away with people screaming from the windows for help but no one was doing anything about it. That's the only way I can describe that feeling. It used to keep me awake at night, tossing and turning in bed, and I wasn't the only one. Mum and I used to find ourselves sat at the kitchen table some nights at three o'clock in the morning, drinking herb tea and gazing at each other as if someone had asked a question to which we didn't know the answer. It was that summer too that my friends and I decided we were done with Zachery Flynn, if "Emily, Hear My Plea" was any indication of the kind of music we could expect from his solo career. We had all come to hate that song and the anxious way it made us feel. Besides, other things had caught our interest, namely the boys we liked at school— real boys that were within our reach—but also Joey Pearce from the *Lost Cause* movie franchise. He had an air of danger about him which we now preferred to Zachery

Flynn and the Flynn Brothers' squeaky-clean please-and-thank-you American apple pie niceness. His was the poster that now adorned our bedroom walls.

Still, Zachery Flynn and his music had been a fixture of my early teens, so I was sad when I heard that he'd taken his own life. What bothered me most was his suicide note. It was leaked to the press a few weeks after his death, and apparently it said: LIGHT YEARS AWAY. WE COULDN'T HAVE HELPED THEM ANYWAY. His family, his friends, journalists and fans the world over were confused by this. No one had the first idea what it was supposed to mean. The tabloids suggested the note was evidence of Zachery Flynn's deteriorating state of mind, or perhaps substance addictions, but when I heard about it I got a chill down my back. I remembered my mother crying and saying *help them* when I played her "Emily, Hear My Plea," and I felt certain Zachery's suicide note was somehow linked to that song. I dug the CD single out from under my bed and played it, and though I was again struck by the dumbness of the lyrics, I felt a familiar unease inspired by the backing track. It was that house-on-fire-a-few-streets-away feeling all over again. It made me believe that someone was reaching out to me and asking for my help. *Help them, we have to help them* I again remembered my mother saying when I played it for her. Curious, I checked the CD booklet to see who had written the song. *Words by Zachery Flynn*, it said. No surprise there. *Music supplied by NASA.*

*NASA?* What the hell did that mean? I of course knew all about Zachery Flynn's fascination with outer space. He spent much of the magazine interviews my friends and I had pored over in our early teens talking about it. At the time we found it boring. We wanted to know what music he liked, where he bought his clothes, whether or not he had a girlfriend. I can remember Nadine saying one day when we were sat in my room, "I do wish Zachery wouldn't keep going on about *space* all the time." We all called the Flynn brothers by their first names, as if we knew them personally. "I know," Elle said, "It's *all* he ever talks about."

So NASA somehow supplied the music to "Emily, Hear My Plea?" Though shocked, I was intrigued and wanted to find out more.

This became a bit of an obsession for me in the years to come. I had a boyfriend for awhile—Billy Dickson—but he eventually got fed up with me talking about "Emily, Hear My Plea." He would pull a face or pretend to shove a finger down his throat whenever I mentioned Zachery Flynn's name.

"It's just a stupid song," he said one day. "And the music's really creepy."

"What do you mean *creepy*?" I knew exactly what he meant, but I wanted to hear him say it.

"It sounds like some kind of. . . " He had to think for half a minute. "Cry for help, or something."

"A cry for help?" There it was again. House on fire. My mother saying *help them we have to help them.*

"Didn't the singer kill himself?"

"Yeah."

"Well, there you go then. A cry for help."

"But it's not in the lyrics, is it? The lyrics are silly. It's the music. Zachery Flynn didn't write the music. The music came from NASA."

"NASA? Are you joking?"

I had to dig the CD out from under my bed again, just to show him that I was telling the truth. *Music supplied by NASA.* Billy said it was probably a misprint. NASA, he said, weren't in the business of writing soppy ballads for ex-boy band members.

Eventually, Billy stopped replying to my texts, and then someone told me he'd starting seeing Nadine. After that he was neither Billy nor Dickson (as his male friends called him) to me, he was just *Dick*. Then Nadine, to the envy of us all, moved on to Rob Northwood—the most handsome boy in sixth form, and Billy came crawling back.

"Hello, *Dick*," I said when I discovered him standing on my doorstep one day. "What could you possibly want?"

"Kathleen," he said. "There's something I want to show you. Remember that song you were obsessed with?"

"Emily, Hear My Plea?"

"Yeah. Well, I found something online. I wanted to show it to you."

I knew this was some kind of rouse to get back into my good books, with a view to us getting back together, but I was intrigued enough to allow Billy inside. I led him up to my bedroom, and he immediately went to the computer and fired up Internet Explorer.

"It took me hours to find this."

"*Aw*," I said, in a kittenish tone, folding my hands at my breast and pretending to be moved.

"Turn the speakers on," he said.

Still playing it cool, I did as he asked. He found the webpage he was looking for and started some WAV file playing. A weird Theremin-type sound started coming out of the speakers.

"What's this, Billy? Whale song?"

"These," he said, "are sounds picked up on a NASA space probe a few years ago. Radio waves. But it's this one in particular I wanted you to hear. Listen to it."

"I am listening to it."

"Can't you hear that?"

"What am I supposed to be hearing? Sounds like—"

Billy must have seen the shock on my face as he broke out in a grin.

"Oh my God," I said. "Play it again, play it again."

"I'm thinking this might get me to at least second base," Billy said, and I batted my hand at him, too transfixed by what I was hearing to fully react. What he'd played for me was the music for "Emily, Hear My Plea." It was a weird, stretched-out version that repeated over and over, but basically the song was there. Zachery Flynn had used sounds picked up on a space probe as the basis for his biggest hit. I couldn't believe it.

"So what d'you say?" Billy said, still grinning but raising his eyebrows suggestively at the same time so I could be in no doubt of what he was referring to.

"No thanks," I said. "You're just Nadine's sloppy seconds now. Piss off, will you."

He went off in a huff, and after he left I sat and played that WAV file over and over. Just like "Emily, Hear My Plea," it made me feel sad and restless, like there was some kind of urgent crisis I needed to attend to, a person trapped down a well, a child in need, an overturned ship. *Something.* I didn't know what it was the music was trying to tell me, but it communicated that sense of crisis and desperation perfectly. It was some kind of plea, but not the silly love-struck plea Zachery Flynn had turned it into. This was life and death. A call. S.O.S. It told—not in words, but in sound, in feeling—what we had all known it to tell, from the very first time we'd heard it: that somewhere somebody needed our help.

I imagined Zachery Flynn hearing this music every night on stage, having to sing those banal lyrics he'd penned over the top whilst whoever had created the original sounds picked up by the NASA space probe waited and waited and waited for some kind of response.

And I tried to imagine how that would've made him feel.

### 

## About the Author

Tim Jeffreys is the author of five collections of short stories, the most recent being *Another Shore*. His near-future sci-fi novella, *Voids,* co-written with Martin Greaves, was published by Omnium Gatherum in early 2016. His short fiction has appeared in various international anthologies and magazines. He also edits and compiles the Dark Lane Anthologies, wherein he gets to publish talented writers from all over the world. In his own work he incorporates elements of horror, fantasy, absurdist humour, science fiction and anything else he wants to toss into the pot to create his own brand of weird fiction. Tim is also a talented artist and gained a university honours degree in Graphic Arts and Design in 2000. Originally from the Manchester area, Tim now lives in Bristol with his partner and two young daughters. He also has a day job with the Health Service. He has no time for a social life.

*****~~~~~*****

## *Honour Killing*

by Iain Hamilton McKinven

"When are you going to make a cadaver out of me?" Dad's reedy voice quivers. "You know how much I want to be proud of you."

I sigh. I am used to this particular tirade, but it never fails to irritate. I have a decent relationship with Dad, although recently it has suffered from what he calls my squeamishness, or sometimes describes as my lack of numeracy.

"Dad, you know I love you, but I'm not ready to put down roots yet," I half-lie. That just sets him off worse.

"I'm practically last man standing at Shady Pines because you're dragging your feet about killing me off ," he bursts, "and I'll never forgive you for just letting your mother die of natural causes. You know that. I want to go with good grace and honour, and to know that you will be settled. You're not getting any younger, you know."

Yes. He follows the script word-perfectly. And I know what he says makes sense to him. Clearly it is my duty. He is past a decent killing-time, and I disrespect him by not publicly dispatching him, and assuming his worldly goods, role, and status. I am going to fix that soon though, and not in a way he will like: I am going to recycle him, even if it is against his will.

...

My son Patrice never hears me, or if he does, he doesn't listen to what I say. He obviously has my colouring, but his mother's impulsive nature. I see Antoinette's mannerisms in the way he wonders into my eyes, even though his are as dirt-brown as mine and not grey-green like hers.

I know he knows he is doing me and our family dishonour by not killing me off and taking my place in The Bigger Society movement. He knows that the "Great Co-mingling of Beliefs" and the "Demographic Imperative" demand it. He knows how I feel.

"I'll get my medicine from Mr. Sayeed later," the orderly says as he goes. He moves so slowly that his baggy green uniform makes him look like he is buried in a pile of grass, struggling to escape; only his head and hands and white clogs stick out. It's a remarkable retreat for a methadone fiend. Most orderlies are pushier when they are seeking their remuneration for working the waiting rooms. I'll award him a bonus with a couple of temazepam in recognition of his discretion and sensitivity later.

...

Dad lights up another free EMEA Directorate cigarette. His slender and still-strong fingers are nicotine-stained from years of state-sponsored carcinogens. The yellow below the knuckles is the only shade or colour anywhere left in his body. It blooms clearly on, but not of him, and contrasts vividly with the faded hair, faded skin, faded sheen of his big blasted-bone body; hard but yet brittle at the same time.

He stares at the packet. "Fully optimised for effect," he declaims, as he speaks aloud the legend on the front, declaring the EMEA State Surgeon's health advice as clearly as possible. I wait for the smoke to kick in and calm him down.

...

Smoking is one of my favourite chores. Even after many years enjoying free tobacco, it never calms me down. It actually charges me up, and right now it makes me all the more indignant about the fact that I am still here. I feel ashamed, and I want to go. He wants me to go home with him; back to the house we all shared when Antoinette was still alive. But he's just thinking about himself as usual. I want to stay in my own waiting room in Shady Pines, and I want to be killed by my own boy, not to lose face by blinking out existence in my sleep like Antoinette. I look up from the pack and glare at him through the haze to remind him of how angry I am.

…

Good. He looks dopey now. I could get him out. He would not be the first. But he would be the first that I have to knock out to get him to go. He would have the orderly shamble back in here if he knew what I have planned—which would be pretty bloody stupid of him, as then he would definitely not get what he wanted. I would be killed instead, and not with honour. He would be kept on as a warning, touring the waiting rooms, sharing his shame as an encouragement to others.

I'll recycle him to Asianalia. It's for his own good. It's best for everyone. He won't feel any shame if there's no one to remind him of Single-Party doctrine, and the way he thinks things should be. He will see how the younger society values older citizens there.

…

I stand up; walk into the garden. Patrice looks surprised as he follows. I see his slender and graceful reflection in the glass door that I slide slowly to the side on the way to the patio. Mo says hello, standing at the bottom of the steps, leaning down upon his spade in the soil from his great height. He watches the birds pluck worms from the earth, and whistles along to replace the sound of the songs they tend to neglect while they are busy killing.

Mo's the only one in here who calls me by my first name, even though he has only been here a week, probably because it's the same name as his. I turn my head towards him, and we say hello. I smile, remembering how Antoinette used to refer to me as "The Prophetic Mohammed" whenever she introduced me at official Single-Party engagements, just because I was an Actuarial Engineer. Helping to identify exactly who needed help to ensure observation of EMEA's constitutional "Principle of Efficient Living/Dying" was of course a serious business, and a huge challenge in spite of our best efforts to achieve an economic dying equation. Even though responsible citizens are always keen to comply, getting the balance right is tricky.

I wonder why I am smiling about such a serious matter. There were and still are too many people shamelessly faking their own Honour Killings, sometimes with the help of their children, who should know better— removing their wealth and transferring illegally to the other side, recycling themselves instead of their economic and social values. I hate those bloody traitors of The Bigger Society; they are an affront to present, past, and future generations and our three-hundred-year-old movement. I caught more than my fair share in my time. I would like to flush out a few more before I go. Opportunities are going to be scarce in The Single-Party's top waiting room, but I keep my wits about me just in case—it's one of the few things I can still do to while away the time constructively while I wait for Patrice to do his duty to me and to EMEA.

...

I stand and watch from the patio doors. I pick up his new Single-Party walking-stick, denoting his former rank. I feel its weight, like a club. I no longer wonder why he hasn't picked it up, but still follow him with it. His broad back shuffles past the gardener. They exchange a single hello; there is an unaccustomed half-smile on Dad's face as he returns it back to face forward. The gardener nods at me and gives me a full smile.

## Honour Killing

Dad is different than Mum. She never became bitter towards me, or anyone else for that matter. And I never felt such weight of expectation or pressure to succeed for her sake.

Mum wanted her Honour Killing too, but never pushed me for it. I know she knew there was something holding me back, and if Dad's beloved bloody tables had been more accurate, I would have had a time to hold her hand, smooth her hair, look into those grey-green eyes, and reason with her about recycling. Even if it was classed by the Single Party as a Double-Capital crime ("LOL-ROI" or "Loss Of Life without Return On Investment") there was still enough pre-EMEA genetically modified Gallic heritage in her birdlike bones to make her listen to a rebellious idea—especially if it came from her boy. A sudden urge comes over me to make her proud, and Dad too, in spite of the fact I think I could cheerfully kill him sometimes. And then a sudden smile washes over me as I release the irony and the nascent shame.

Dad, unlike Mum, always plays by the book, and always will do. So I'm not even going to talk to him about it. I've already brought a man in to help me to recycle dad against his will. It will be a different guy this time as I need to protect the network—plus Dad hardly meets their criteria, being an unwilling subject. The guy this time is a non-Asianalian freelancer. He will be here soon.

Dad doesn't want to be a burden. He won't be when he follows me. I already have the faked death certificate, a convincing death-site set up online, and a borrowed corpse ready—again. It's dangerous, but simple—which is not the same thing as being easy.

...

The sunshine and the walk take more out of me than I thought they would. Better be careful, don't want to see myself off—another inappropriate smile leaks out. I turn, quickly as I can. I see my son Patrice watching me, clutching my new walking-stick. He looks so serious and

65

intense; more so than usual even. He opens his mouth, and not to speak. His grey-green eyes widen and seem to move towards me suddenly.

I see a glancing arc from my right; I hear a sudden and singeing singing inside my head; I smell a warm wetness on my face; I taste soil; I know that soon I will feel nothing anymore. I smile again, thinking of Antoinette, and my boy, who seems to have swiftly leaped close to me. I am happy that he has come over to me. I blink a goodbye to the birds as they scatter.

...

The slow seep of the blood into the soil contrasts with the swift savagery of the swing. I am beside my father faster than I know how, and he is already gone, although his grimace remains, impressed indelibly upon my memory and his cold face, beside the welt. His stillness contrasts with the sudden movement earlier, although I seem unaware of how I have managed to get so close to Dad so quickly.

Although I am not looking at the gardener, I hear him speak. "It's the best thing for everyone," his wily voice contrasts with his wiry frame, "I am not a freelancer, there's no such thing in this work, and. . . I am not a kidnapper. Mohammed would not have wanted to be recycled. That much was clear to me the minute I got here. And he was too much of a. . . risk. So console yourself that it was what he wanted. And take his place in your society. Congratulations, Mr. Sayeed. Make use of the subterfuge you have already put in place, take credit for the honour that has now been restored to your family. I will take good care of this. . . spare cadaver. The transfer of values will be. . . postponed."

It hits me that that I am now properly alone, that I do not belong even covertly to anyone or anything any more. And worse, I reel that I have not managed to say goodbye to either of them properly. I turn and walk back, still gripping Dad's walking-stick, far too tightly. Without looking I know that the gardener is still there; that he has not gone anywhere, has not moved a muscle yet and stands there motionless again, leaning on the blood-soiled spade, watching the birds silently return. And he whistles again.

### 

## About the Author

Scottish writer Iain Hamilton McKinven says he hasn't written SF/Fantasy for many years; "Honour Killing" just sort of came out that way, as he searched for a form that would allow him to set the themes free.

*****~~~~~*****

## *Talk to the Animals*

by Jill Hand

Police dispatcher Amber Flammia was working on a crossword puzzle when the call came in at 2:17 a.m. Calls at that hour usually meant something serious: a car crash or a heart attack or a domestic dispute that had gone beyond the soup and salad of accusations to the meat and potatoes of punches and sometimes worse. Amber hoped it wasn't a domestic; those tended to turn even uglier when the police showed up and the combatants put aside their differences and joined forces in attacking the uniformed interlopers.

"Lenape Point 9-1-1. What is your emergency?" she said.

A prim little voice spoke up. "I wish to report a crime."

"What is the nature of the emergency, ma'am?" Amber thought the voice was that of a woman or a little girl, but a little girl wouldn't be awake at this hour, calling the police and sounding absolutely delighted to be reporting a crime, would she?

Amber repeated, "Ma'am? What is the nature of your emergency?"

"A horrible crime," the finicky little voice said with relish. "The theft of funds by a respected member of the

69

community. I demand that you lock the guilty party up at once."

Amber looked at the caller ID and recognized the number as belonging to City Councilwoman Peggy Moran. She felt a sinking sensation in the pit of her stomach. Oh, crap, she thought.

"Princess, is that you?" she asked.

There was a flustered silence. Then the voice replied, "This isn't Princess. This is a concerned citizen who wishes to remain anonymous."

"I know it's you, Princess," Amber said. "How did you manage to call 9-1-1?"

"Speed dial. I knocked it off the charger and pressed the button," the voice said, sounding pleased at its cleverness. "Are you going to send somebody to arrest Peggy? She's asleep. She's going to be surprised when the police show up and haul her off to jail!"

"We're not going to arrest Ms. Moran because her cat told us to," Amber firmly told Princess, who was indeed a cat, a grey Persian with orange eyes.

"Don't you care that a crime was committed? She stole four hundred dollars from the fund for that little boy who has cancer and used it to buy shoes," Princess whined. "They're ugly shoes, too," she added spitefully. "She didn't buy me anything, not even a catnip mouse, so I thought, all right, stingy old Peggy, wait and see what happens to *you*."

"I'm hanging up now," Amber said, and disconnected the call.

Animals had been talking in and around the town of Lenape Point, New Jersey, (population 2,142) for about a month now, but this was the first time one of them had used a telephone, at least as far as Amber knew. It *would* be Princess, she thought morosely. Princess was not a nice cat. She'd bitten Amber when Peggy brought her into the municipal building to show her off. The phone call proved that she was sneaky and vindictive, as well as smart.

Sighing, Amber made a note to speak to the police chief, Frank Rizzi, when he came in. It would be up to him to decide what to do about the accusation of theft from the Help Ryan Heal fund. Ryan was the little boy with leukemia for whom Peggy had volunteered to collect donations to help pay for his medical treatment, some of which Princess claimed she'd appropriated for her own use. Amber wouldn't be surprised if she had.

"People!" Amber muttered, turning back to her crossword puzzle. She managed to pack a great deal of bitterness into that one word.

Prior to the previous month, there had been only one talking animal in Lenape Point. That was Calico Jack, a bright-eyed African grey parrot who belonged to Pete Ferrier, who ran the Gas Up and Go service station. Calico Jack had an extensive vocabulary, some of which was swearing so blisteringly foul that it would have done credit to the original Calico Jack, an eighteenth-century pirate who plied his trade in the Caribbean. He could mimic the sound of a telephone ringing, a microwave oven beeping, and Pete's dog barking. He could also mimic Pete yelling at the dog: "Shut up, Fletch. Shut up! Shut up! Shutthehellupgoddammit!"

Then Al Wooley and Nash McDonald had been out in the woods hunting deer early one Saturday morning when they came upon three whitetail does nibbling on sumac foliage. Al raised his rifle just as one of them looked up and shouted, "Run, girls!"

Al and Nash stood frozen in shock as the deer scampered away. Just before they vanished into the trees, one of them turned to yell over her shoulder, "Shame on you! We're mothers!"

The hunters beat a hasty retreat back to town, where they excitedly told Chief Rizzi what had happened. The chief was initially dubious and asked if they'd been drinking.

No, they told him. Only coffee, *plain* coffee, with no whiskey or anything in it.

It soon became obvious that it wasn't just deer that had acquired the power of speech. Cats and dogs started complaining that they wanted steak or chicken instead of that soggy canned stuff or those hard brown pellets that came in a big bag. They also started making unflattering personal remarks about their owners.

"I love you," eight-year-old Ashley Perlmutter crooned to her dachshund, Piper, hugging him blissfully.

"I don't love you," Piper retorted. "You squeeze me too tight, and you spit when you talk. No wonder you don't have any friends."

Ashley went weeping to her mother. "Piper's mean," she wailed.

"I'm only being truthful," Piper retorted, looking up at Mrs. Perlmutter with soulful brown eyes.

It's like having another child, Mrs. Perlmutter thought tiredly, watching Piper walk away, head held high, his toenails clicking on the hardwood floor. She'd been enchanted by the idea of talking animals when she read about them in books, but the reality wasn't anything like what she'd imagined it would be.

The problem was that these talking animals weren't whimsical like the ones in books. Instead, they tended to be uncomfortably carnal and self-absorbed. Mrs. Perlmutter had loved *Charlotte's Web* when she was a girl. Now she couldn't think of Charlotte and Wilbur without picturing them behaving rudely.

At Police Chief Frank Rizzi's house, his Great Dane, Van Halen, was making the chief's life miserable with his demands for sex.

"You gotta help me," Van Halen moaned one afternoon. "Take me to see Babette."

Babette was a female Great Dane whom Van Halen had impregnated. She'd been successfully delivered of a litter of eight puppies.

## Talk to the Animals

"Her owner doesn't want her to have any more puppies right now," Rizzi told the dog.

"But I need some action! Frank, you're a male, you understand," Van Halen wailed. "If I can't get it on with Babette, at least let me out so I can go next door and hook up with Milly."

Milly was a Chihuahua who weighed about six pounds to Van Halen's one hundred and seventy.

"Absolutely not!" Rizzi told him, scandalized. "Try and think about something else. Think about sports. That's what I do."

Van Halen let out a despairing groan and sank to the floor, his huge head on his paws. "I don't like sports," he complained. "How about we go for a ride in the truck? That might distract me. We can stop someplace and get cheeseburgers."

Sighing, Rizzi went to get the keys to the truck.

There didn't seem to be any pattern as to which animals could talk and which couldn't. Deer talked, but horses didn't. Squirrels and rabbits and groundhogs talked, but not smaller rodents like mice, or pet hamsters and gerbils and guinea pigs. Insects didn't talk. Neither did fish or reptiles. Wild birds talked, starting early in the mornings with happy cries of, "Hey! It's time to wake up! Get moving! The early bird catches the worm!" It made a racket when all the birds were yelling at once.

The clergy were unable to shed any light on what had caused it. Father Vincent McGuire, the priest at St. Margaret's, said he had no idea when Brigid Neary asked him if he thought it was a miracle, like the image of the Virgin Mary that sometimes appears on pieces of toast.

"Those probably aren't miracles," he told her. "It's just people seeing a shape that reminds them of her." When Brigid looked unconvinced, he added, "It's good to be reminded of the Blessed Mother when we sit down to have a nice piece of toast, but we shouldn't jump to conclusions."

"But the animals talking, Father. Surely that's a miracle," Brigid insisted. "Don't you think you should contact the bishop?"

Just then a squirrel spoke up outside the window of the room where Father McGuire and Brigid sat in the rectory next door to St. Margaret's. The window was open a few inches to let in fresh air, and they could clearly hear what the squirrel had to say.

"Oh, no you don't. That's my acorn. Give it here, you—" The word that the squirrel called the other squirrel made the good Father and the elderly lady blush. "Gracious!" Brigid gasped.

"Um, yes," said Father McGuire, going over and closing the window. "Maybe it's best if we don't inform the bishop just yet. Let's wait until after the town meeting on Friday, and then we'll have a better idea of how to proceed."

Over at the Methodist Church, Pastor Bob Haney had his hands full trying to convince his flock that the talking animals weren't the work of Satan.

"The language some of them use, Pastor Bob! It's enough to make your hair stand on end," said an energetic young woman named Janet Hoagland, who was active with the youth choir, and running the food pantry and dozens of other good works. Janet liked to think that Jesus was watching her as she arranged canned goods on the shelves of the food pantry, or sorted through used clothing to be donated to the needy. "Atta girl, Janet," she imagined Jesus saying as he looking on approvingly. "You'll be richly rewarded when you get to Heaven."

Janet already had a list of questions prepared that she planned to ask Jesus when she got to Heaven, the foremost of which was how come she didn't have a boyfriend, when even Denise Jeter had one and she was fat? Maybe Jesus would eventually see fit to impart that information to her.

### Talk to the Animals

Pastor Bob patiently explained that just because the animals sometimes swore, it didn't mean they were in thrall to the Prince of Darkness. "People swear sometimes, good people, too. It just means they lost their tempers."

Janet said she never swore. "Oh, fudge!" was the strongest expletive to pass her lips. Then she was stuck by a thought. "What if it's the Catholics? What if they're behind it?" Despite the fact that they were alone in the church's narthex, she lowered her voice, in case a Catholic might be hiding nearby, listening in and taking notes in order to report back to the Pope. "They have this ritual called the Blessing of the Animals. Maybe that's what caused it."

"The Blessing of the Animals is harmless; the Episcopalians do it, too," Pastor Bob told her. "I really don't think the Catholics have anything to do with it. Father McGuire is as puzzled as the rest of us."

"That's what he *says*," Janet replied darkly.

The municipal building was packed to overflowing on the night of the town meeting. In the absence of the mayor, who'd gone to visit his mother in Florida, Peggy Moran, Princess's owner, was in charge as the senior City Council member.

Chief Rizzi was there with his Great Dane, Van Halen. He hadn't wanted to leave him home alone, because the big dog tended to get into any food he could reach. Van Halen could open the kitchen cabinets, and he'd consumed entire boxes of cereal and bags of nacho chips. He hadn't figured out how to open the refrigerator, but the chief thought it would only be a matter of time until he did.

Peggy opened the meeting by stating that nobody should think that the mayor had abandoned the town in its hour of need. She was laying the groundwork for a try for the office of mayor at the next election. The mayor's absence had made her very happy.

"He's not on vacation in Florida," she told the gathering. "That's what some people are saying, and I

75

want to make it clear that it's not true." Nobody was saying it, although she hoped they would be now.

"He's down there because his mother is sick. She'll probably be just fine, but we shouldn't pass judgment on him for running off to sunny Florida." She gave a light little laugh. "Well, enough about that. Now I'll turn the meeting over to—"

At that point Janet Hoagland stood up. "Shouldn't we have a prayer first?" she asked. "Before we get started, I think Pastor Bob should lead us in prayer."

Pastor Bob hadn't planned on speaking, but people were nodding at him encouragingly, so he stood up and decided to wing it.

"Let us pray. . . " he started, before Peggy cut him off.

"Come up to the podium, please, and speak into the microphone so we can all hear you."

Pastor Bob made his way to the podium, desperately racking his brain for what to say. The Lord's Prayer didn't seem quite right, although he generally considered it to be a good all-purpose prayer. Neither did the Twenty-third Psalm. Although it spoke of God as being a shepherd it didn't specifically mention sheep, or any other animals. "Let us pray," he said into the microphone. "Lord, we thank thee for the gift of community, and for bringing us together here tonight so that we may share our thoughts about this most, uh, unusual thing which has happened in our midst. With your guidance, Lord. . . "

Van Halen nudged Chef Rizzi in the ribs with a front paw. "Hey, Frank!" he said.

"Shush," Rizzi hissed.

Van Halen prodded him more urgently. "Frank! How come I'm the only dog here?"

Janet Hoagland was sitting directly in front of Rizzi and Van Halen. She turned in her folding chair and glared at the dog. "Be quiet. Pastor Bob is praying."

Pastor Bob was saying something about how God made all creatures great and small.

"There're no bitches here, either," Van Halen said, loudly, looking around. "I was hoping there'd be bitches."

"That's enough!" snapped Janet. "Chief Rizzi, there are children present. Please control your dog."

"What are bitches?" Ashley Perlmutter asked her mother.

"Lady dogs," Mrs. Perlmutter told her. "But it's not a nice word."

"Bitches, bitches, bitches," Ashley sang happily. "Bitches, bitches. . . "

"Ashley," Mrs. Perlmutter said warningly. "Do you want to go in time out?"

Ashley fell silent.

Pastor Bob stopped praying, struck by an idea. Why not ask Van Halen why he could talk?

"Excuse me, can you tell us why you can talk?" he said to the dog.

Van Halen looked around, confused. "You talking to me?"

There were chuckles, as people were reminded of Robert De Niro's speech from *Taxi Driver*. Van Halen had watched the DVD with Chief Rizzi. He understood right away why people were laughing and decided to ham it up.

"Are *you*, talkin' to *me*?" he growled.

"Van Halen, stop it," Rizzi ordered. "Answer the pastor's question."

Van Halen would have liked to perform the entire speech, but he obeyed. "Sure. I could always talk. You just couldn't understand me before, but now you can."

That was a surprise. It wasn't something that had happened to the animals that had made them start to talk; it was something that had happened to the people that made them understand what the animals were saying!

Pete Ferrier, owner of the Gas Up and Go, shouted that the government was responsible. "It's some kind of black ops! They're conducting a secret experiment on us by putting something in the water!"

"LSD? Is that what it is? Like Project MK-Ultra?" That was Al Wooley, one of the hunters who'd encountered the trio of talking does. "Oh, gosh, are we all out of our minds on LSD?"

His words were met with cries of shock and outrage. Chief Rizzi thought he had better take control of the situation before total panic set in.

"Calm down. We're not on LSD," he said loudly.

"What if it's the End Times?" a man shouted. "In the End Times, all kinds of weird things are gonna start happening. It says so in the Bible."

There were excited cries at that. Janet looked up at the ceiling, as if she expected to see the acoustic tiles part like a curtain, revealing Jesus looking down at them. "Is it the End Times, Pastor Bob? Is it? Oh, thank you, Jesus! We praise your holy name," she babbled.

Pastor Bob shook his head helplessly. The End Times weren't something Methodists thought about much. That was more in the line of the Evangelicals.

Van Halen raised his muzzle and howled. Rizzi patted his head reassuringly. "It's okay, fella."

Van Halen looked up at him and barked, "Aroof? Woof!"

Van Halen had lost the power of speech as suddenly as he'd gained it. So had all the other animals. The people of Lenape Point had no idea what to make of that. Some suspected the government really had conducted some kind of secret experiment on them, possibly using a hitherto-unknown mind-control technique. But if so, what was the point? Some thought it might have been a miracle. It remained a mystery.

People viewed their pets differently after that. They were still fond of them, but they became slightly wary of them, too, wondering what they might be thinking.

###

## About the Author

Jill Hand is a member of the Horror Writers Association. Her work has appeared in more than thirty publications and in eight anthologies, including *Urban Temples of Cthulhu, Miskatonic Dreams,* and *Windward: Best New England Crime Stories.*

Her short science fiction story, "Rebellion on Kepler-186f," was included in *Beyond the Stars: New Worlds, New Suns,* a space opera anthology edited by Ellen Campbell, released in April.

*****~~~~~*****

## *The Pigeon Drop*

by Gregg Chamberlain

Jake pressed his back against the building wall, trying to meld his body with the stones and mortar themselves. He could feel the empty space where the scuffed toes of his shoes stuck out over the edge of the ledge.

From far below came the sounds of the passing traffic. Jake didn't dare glance down. One look and, for sure, vertigo would take over, and then there he'd go, down for a meet-and-greet with the garbage-strewn alley pavement. Better to concentrate on the view of the tarpaper rooftop of the building over on the other side. Far away on the other side, unfortunately.

Loud pounding filled his ears for a moment, overwhelming the traffic sounds. The pounding filtered out of the open apartment window at his right. "You better open the door, Merman! Or it's gonna get ugly!"

Like it was beautiful before? Jake squeezed his eyes shut.

One lousy point. In overtime, and with a bloody hat trick, no less! *Now* the Leafs decide to be a winning team?

Now Jake owed ten grand—which he did not have—to Dugas, at a time when the bookie was not feeling either understanding or patient. So now Marvin and his buddies were at the door to collect for Dugas. Bills or blood, either one would do. Jake felt the cold sweat of fear on his forehead.

"Hey, pal, you don't look so good."

Jake's eyes snapped open. His head whipped around. Right. Left. Nothing. He looked up towards the ledge of the floor above. Still nothing. He risked a quick glance downwards. Nothing there, either. Except the toes of his shoes and the dizzying drop to death.

"Yo, buddy! You listening?"

Puzzled now, Jake looked around again, slowly this time. The voice, whoever it was, was close. It for sure didn't sound like one of Dugas's goons.

"Down here, doofus."

Jake looked down and to the side. Sitting on the ledge a little bit away from his left foot was a large grey pigeon.

Jake looked down at the pigeon. The pigeon looked up at Jake. It ruffled its feathers, then twisted its head around to probe with its beak at its back. Looked back up at Jake again.

"So, how you doin', eh?" said the pigeon.

Jake blinked. The pigeon regarded him with its flat black eyes. Its feathers ruffled again.

"Hey!" the pigeon huffed, feathers fluffing out as its chest expanded "You gonna say hello, or what?"

Jake's head dropped back against the rough weathered stone of the building. He closed his eyes. A foolish smile crept across his face. Stress, he thought. I'm going crazy from stress. Sure, why not?

"Y'know it's only polite to say something. I say 'hello', you say 'hello' back. Just good manners, right?"

Jake opened his eyes. Listened to the loud pounding from inside the room. Looked down at the pigeon again.

"You talk," he said.

The pigeon's head and back shook in a bird-like shrug. "Duh. Yeah. So do you. Howzat workin' for ya?"

Jake regarded the pigeon with increasing interest. Might just as well go with the crazy as not.

"You speak English."

The pigeon's head cocked. "What English? I talk, you hear me. That's it."

"But I've never heard a pigeon talk before."

"Yeah, well, maybe this time you're listening better."

Jake considered this idea. Nodded. Yeah, sure, made perfect sense. Why not?

"Last chance, Merman! Open this door, or it's gonna go real hard when we bust in!"

The pigeon's head cocked the other way. It looked past Jake's legs at the open window. More pounding sounded from inside the room.

"Hey, maybe you should let them in?"

"They'll kill me."

"Okay, so don't let 'em in."

"They'll kill me as soon as they break open the door."

"Whoa, that don't sound good." The pigeon's body shook. It took a moment to groom its feathers back into place. Turned bird-bright eyes towards Jack. "What do they want?"

Jake glanced at the window, looked back at the pigeon. "I owe money."

"So? Give 'em what they want."

"I don't have it."

"That's not good." The pigeon pecked at something on the ledge. "You tell 'em that?"

Jake nodded. "They still want to kill me."

"Okay, so tell 'em to wait until you can get it for them."

Jake shook his head. "They want to kill me anyway. As an example."

"Man, that's harsh." The pigeon appeared to think. "Y'know, I had this same sorta problem once."

"Oh?"

"Yeah, sure. Only it wasn't money. It was a bagel. Well, part of a bagel. I had this piece of bagel I'd found. There were these other pigeons, y'see, wanted it too. Now there was too many of them for me to fight. I mean, I'm good in a scrap, don't get me wrong on that. But this was one of those situations, y'know, where the odds weren't good for me, see?"

Jake nodded.

"An' they didn't wanna share, even when I offered to let 'em have first peck. Some guys, y'know? So there was only one thing to do."

"Oh?" Jake said, curious now about the pigeon's solution. "What?"

"Fly away."

"Huh?"

The pigeon pecked some more. Looked up at Jake. "That's what you do," it said, "when you can't do nothin' else."

Jake leaned back against the building wall. The sound of splintering wood came through the window from the room beyond. He nodded. Why not? He thought. After all, I'm talking to a pigeon. That's a little miracle all by itself, right?

Maybe I was just due for a miracle today. Maybe even get to trade up for a bigger miracle too?

He nodded again. Then, holding his arms up and out at his sides, Jake took a step forward. Eyes round with shock, mouth wide open with a despairing scream, Jake plunged downwards.

The pigeon's head bent over the edge of the ledge as it watched Jake plummet to the bottom of the alley. It shook its feathers once more, took one step forward and leapt into the air, wings spreading out, just as a door crashed open inside the room behind. Human curses and the dopplering wail of emergency sirens trailed behind it as the pigeon rose up into the sky.

"Swear to Coo, if I'm lyin' I'm dyin'!" the pigeon said later to a companion. It was in a park with a flock of other pigeons, pecking away at bread crumbs scattered on the ground. On a bench nearby an old man reached into a plastic bag, scooped out another handful of crumbs, and tossed them over the backs of the furiously pecking pigeons.

A pigeon with a white ring around one eye paused in its pecking for a moment. "He walked right off the ledge?" The grey pigeon bobbed a quick nod. "Coulda plucked my tailfeathers, I was that shocked." It pecked some more. "Starts waving his arms up and down like he was a newbie fledge trying out his wings for the first time. Dropped straight down to the ground, flapping all the way. Ka-splat!"

The other pigeon shook its head. "He was a human, not a pigeon. What did he think was gonna happen?"

"Dunno," replied the first pigeon, without a pause in its own pecking. "What does anybody know about humans?"

"They're all crazy."

"Got that right."

The two pigeons settled down to stuffing themselves with breadcrumbs.

### 

## About the Author

Gregg Chamberlain, a community newspaper reporter four decades in the trade, lives in rural Eastern Ontario with his missus, Anne, and their clowder of cats, who allow the humans the run of the house. His past fiction credits include *Daily Science Fiction, Apex, Weirdbook, Pulp Literature, Shoreline of Infinity,* and *SciPhi Journal* magazines, and various original anthologies.

*****~~~~*****

## *Formica Joe*

by Anne E. Johnson

It took me a while to believe I was trapped in the tabletop of my favorite booth at the Gearshift Diner. I suppose I should've been glad I got a booth, but cushy vinyl seats don't matter so much when your cell structure is spread like a cream cheese schmear between a slab of plywood and a sheet of Formica. Through interlocking turquoise trapezoids—that Fifties-style design I'd traced so often from topside—I watched the bottom of Dave Greengrass's daily plate of pancakes comin' at me.

"Here you go, hon," said Bridget, a waitress who'd been serving food there since the Ford administration and still didn't know anyone's name. The flaming red of her discount manicure looked like sparks from Satan's ass when she lowered the plate onto my face.

"Oy, Bridget!" I tried to shout. She didn't hear me. Probably because I didn't have a mouth anymore.

My karate teacher, Schuyler Kaminsky, was always talking about this yin-yang balance or what have you. So I weighed the good against the bad. On the downside, some kind of alien ray had rendered me downright incorporeal while I dug into a mushroom omelet at two that morning. Also in the bad column: Kimmy Shar, the owner of the Gearshift, now believed I'd skipped out on my check. Oh, and apparently nobody could see or hear me, so I might be stuck there forever.

It took some thought to come up with anything on the good side. For one, I wouldn't have to go to work. Not that being a cashier at the Wall-to-Wall Mart wasn't a valuable use of my time. Yeah, no. . . it sucked. I also had to assume I'd be off the hook for stuff like car and mortgage payments. But I did feel bad about shirking child support. I loved my daughter Caroline more than I'd ever loved anything.

Wouldn't you know? Just like that, I'd skewed my list back toward the negative. Typical. But maybe Schuyler Kaminsky was right: the universe works itself out. While I battled despair in the flatlands, a ring of coffee drying against what used to be my left eye, I heard my favorite sound in the world.

"Hi, Kimmy!" My daughter's voice rang out. "Have you seen my dad? He was supposed to pick me up after soccer." *Oh, crap. That's right.* "I thought he might-a come here last night after, you know."

"After he got stink-o," Kimmy elucidated with her usual finesse. "Yeah. He staggered in around two, two-thirty. Didn't stick around to pay, though. So, when you dig him up, send his cotton-head Majesty over here with six-fifty, would ya?"

"Um, okay."

A thousand blessings on Dave Greengrass, who said just the right thing. "Caroline, sweetie? Come sit with me. Have some breakfast. Tell me about your soccer game."

"Thanks, Mr. Greengrass," my pride and joy said shyly. I caught glimpses of her elbows and curly black hair as she crawled into the booth opposite Dave.

"Pancakes, hon?" Bridget asked.

*With chocolate chips.*

"With chocolate chips," Caroline said. "And OJ and bacon."

*That's my girl.*

## Formica Joe

When her glass of juice clunked down on top of me, she started twirling it slowly. With the other hand, she traced the trapezoid patterns on the Formica as she talked to Dave. "I'm worried about Dad."

Dave burped delicately and drummed his fingers against my splayed-out collarbone. "You've got to understand that Joe, I mean your dad, is a complicated guy." *Here we go.* "All kinds of potential, but no ambition, get me? Back in high school, we all thought he'd end up a college professor."

"But he never even went to college," said Caroline.

"And that's my point. Doesn't get stuff done."

Actually, I'd met an extraterrestrial being, got myself trapped in a tabletop. And Dave thought I'd never accomplished anything.

"I just hope nothing's happened to him." Caroline's left index finger slid in a complex design of loops, flowing from one trapezoid to another. Then that finger started moving faster. "Hey, I can't stop!" she cried.

Her finger flew around and around the center of the table, like a stock car on a twisted racetrack. And I started to burn. The hard plastic layer over my face bubbled and stretched. I was pressed up against the surface so forcefully that I thought my nose and eye sockets would break.

Then, with a *slurp*, my head popped through the Formica and into the 3-D world. I was face-to-face with my screaming daughter.

"Hey, sport," I said. "I heard you were lookin' for me."

...

It took about fifteen minutes for half the town of Dembeyville to show up at the Gearshift for a gander at Joe's incredible talking head. By that point, Caroline had stopped sobbing, but she didn't say much. The other two dozen people couldn't shut up long enough for me to answer their questions.

"How did you get in there?"

"Where's the rest of you?"

"Does it hurt?"

"Were you drunk when this happened?"

And my favorite, from my ex-wife, Debra: "Why don't you stop embarrassing yourself and come out of the table now?"

My voice had kind of a pinched quality (big surprise, given the two-dimensional state of my lungs), but I did my best to tell my tale. "There were these nubby blue aliens. I just saw them for a second, and—"

"So, you *were* drunk when it happened," someone said.

I lengthened my neck indignantly. "Of course I was, but that doesn't alter the fact that this crime was perpetrated by nubby blue aliens. About three feet high. Smelled like old apple cores. They showed up outta nowhere. Just for a second."

"Then where'd they go?" Debra asked with that why-are-you-home-late sneer.

"How could I possibly know? I was stuck inside the table top. Come on, think logically, would ya?"

Kimmy, the owner, would not be outdone. "I'm going to look at the security camera footage for last night. If I don't see no blue dwarfs—"

"Aliens," I corrected her.

"If I don't see no blue aliens leaving the premises, I'm having you arrested for skipping out on your bill. And wrecking my table."

As if her words had conjured him up, police officer Morgan Ndiru walked into the diner. "We got a weird 911 call, Kimmy. And did I just hear you say I should arrest someone?"

She pointed at my head. "The wobbly noggin over there."

"Hey, Morgan," I said. I used his first name because he'd grown up on my block. "If you can get my hands free, you'd be welcome to cuff them." I swiveled my chin—an odd sensation, like wearing a thick rubber necklace—to face Kimmy. "You seriously think this is my fault?"

"All I know is," she said, fists dug furiously into her ample waist, "I would've seen blue aliens leave if they'd-a been here."

"No!" The reverberation of Caroline slamming both palms against the tabletop almost dislodged my bridgework. "Don't you people read science fiction?" She could have stopped her question at "Don't you people read?"

"They are plebs, sport," I said. "Just tell us what's on your mind."

Caroline spread fury with her eyes, genetic proof she was her mother's kid. "My dad's body is in another dimension. Okay? So maybe the aliens can move back and forth from one dimension to another. You see what I mean?"

Silence. Stephen Hawking would have had more luck explaining black holes to a herd of wallabies.

Caroline tried again. "I'm saying, the blue aliens might still be here, right now, but not in this dimension."

"You mean, like, they're in the bathroom?" some genius asked.

Caroline looked at me desperately. I tried to make my face seem encouraging, since that's all I had to work with. She took a breath. "I mean," she continued, "that the aliens might be. . . um. . . inside the air. Maybe if we can coax them out, they will free Daddy."

Ten full seconds elapsed before all the "grown-ups" started talking at once.

"Sit down, Caroline," said her mother.

"Bring her some tea, Bridget," said Kimmy.

"I'll call for an ambulance," said officer Ndiru.

"Maybe even the jaws of life," Dave suggested, scratching the liver spots on his forehead.

"Would cooking spray help slide him out?" asked Darlene Cho, who used to babysit me thirty years before.

"I'll grab his head," the sous chef, Jimenez, kindly volunteered.

Mina from the bank pushed Jimenez aside and bent to check under the table. "Won't work. There's nothing to push on from below."

"Howzabout we use this?" Deaky Thomas, who ran the auto shop, loomed over me holding—I kid you not—a chainsaw. A small one, but still.

"Get that thing away from me!" I tried to back away but only hurt my neck vertebrae. "I know I'm in there." I angled my nose toward the tabletop. "I feel myself." That came out wrong, but the hell with it. "The only way to get me out of here is to find the aliens. Listen to my brilliant daughter."

"How we supposed to find aliens," Kimmy asked, "when they're, what? Hiding inside the air?"

Jimenez waved his cell phone in front of Officer Ndiru's face. "Can you call NASA?"

"I'll have to talk to my supervisor," he said, backing out the door.

"Poor Daddy." Caroline's hand petting my hair was the only thing keeping me from weeping. "Are you hungry?"

Interesting question. I tried to assess the hunger level in the diffuse molecules of my stomach. Just a dull ache. "Maybe later, sport."

The crowd was getting bored. Sure, I was a head growing out of the tabletop, but I wasn't really *doing* anything. My so-called friends wandered off to tables and booths, chatting amongst themselves.

Dave and Caroline stuck with me, though. Dave silently ate his pancakes while Caroline leaned her chin on one hand and traced the tabletop trapezoids with the other. A wave of déjà vu hit me hard.

Apparently Caroline felt it too. We locked eyes. But, being smarter than me, she said what I couldn't quite get off my tongue. "This tracing. This is what I was doing when your head popped out."

"Holy shit, you're right."

"Language, Daddy." Did I mention how much I love my daughter? She kept right on thinking. "Maybe these weird shapes on the table are some kind of alien writing."

"Nah," Dave said with a laugh. "Your dad and I have been staring at those silly tabletops for forty years." He called toward the counter, where Kimmy was upbraiding Bridget over something. "Hey, Kimmy? Didn't your pop put in this Formica when he renovated back in, what? Seventy-eight?"

"God, I hate this lousy Formica," she said, coming toward us. "Pop always told us he'd found it in a back alley."

I pictured her old man, always with a shock of white hair and a shocked look on his face. "Pauly died over twenty years ago," I said. "The place is yours. Why not get new tables?"

Kimmy, who could have watched a virgin sacrifice without changing her facial expression, wrinkled her brow with genuine concern. "It's in his will. I'm not allowed to change the tables. Not even new Formica."

"That's it!" Caroline slapped the table, rattling my brain pan. "I bet there *are* aliens here. Kimmy, I bet they gave your dad these as communication devices. Or religious scrolls."

"You mean the tabletops?" Dave asked. "That's nuts."

But I got where Caroline was going with this. "Hell, aliens probably invented Formica."

"Ha ha. Yeah. So, Daddy, you think when I ran my fingers over the designs and your head came out, I accidentally unlocked something?"

"Your theory works for me, professor."

Kimmy crossed her arms. "So, how do we get the rest of your dad out?"

With both index fingers raised like the world chopsticks-playing champion, Caroline replied, "Patience and fortitude. And also coffee and pie."

"That's my girl," I said, choking back a sob.

...

It took Caroline a long spell of furiously swirling her fingertips around the table before I felt a buzzing sensation. "Something's happening. Just here. No, to your left. There."

"What part of you is it, Joe?" Dave asked.

"Not sure." I was as surprised as anyone when my left knee popped up through the Formica, cone-shaped and solitary as a volcanic South Seas island. "Could you please get my arms free?"

"I'm trying."

"Well, try harder." And just like that, we were back at our own dinner table, eight years before, when we were all pretending to be a nuclear family. Before our little family went nuclear. "I'm sorry, sport." I wished I could hug Caroline. "I'm just. . . I meant to say thank you."

She had kept her head down when she nodded, but I could still see the tears in her eyes. "I'm going to get you out, Daddy."

"I could help," Dave blurted out, his two index fingers lolling in mirror image figure eights. "Do I just slide my fingers around like this?"

When he did that, all of me heated up a little. "That feels weird."

"Keep going, Mr. Greengrass," Caroline ordered. "Any change is good at this point."

Bridget paused by our table, resting her coffeepot so close to my head, I smelled the acidic dregs. "Maybe everyone should try. You know, at their own tables."

"But I'm in *this* table."

"Yeah," Bridget said with a shrug, "but who knows who's in the other tables?"

## Formica Joe

I hate it when people I think are morons turn out to be smarter than me. "Hey, everyone," I called. Dozens of surprised faces looked over, as if they'd forgotten I was the main attraction. "There might be people trapped in all the tabletops."

Several people slid out of their booths. Mrs. O'Connor, a retired high school nurse, gave a little shriek.

Caroline took over. "Everybody, roll your fingers over the designs on the tabletop. Like Dave's doing." Dave flashed them all a vaudeville smile and exaggerated his movements.

People love to be told what to do. Soon every table looked like a skating rink for finger-folk. Under the hands of Terry Nevins and his six kids, the Formica started to bubble in the booth opposite mine. I didn't see what happened next, though, because the heat all over my body got so intense that I squeezed my eyes shut and screamed. Imagine getting attacked by a cheese slicer and getting cooked in a toaster oven, both at once. When the horrible searing, biting pain faded, I was sitting on top of the table.

The dining room filled with screams as other tables birthed other bodies. There was an old woman in a woolen skirt suit, a young woman in bellbottoms and a bikini top, a pot-bellied man in a Duran Duran 1983 World Tour T-shirt with an egg yolk smudge covering Simon Le Bon's face.

They kept emerging, these table people, like omelet-loving zombies. But they weren't zombies. They were alive, just like me.

"Keep rubbing the Formica," said Caroline. "Faster, faster!"

It looked like a convention of mediums having a spiritual orgy, with the souls they'd freed wondering amongst them. The air turned so hot, it blistered. Yes, the air itself got blisters, hissed, and crackled. And, like a cooling crust on lava, it split open in a thousand tiny cracks. The heat reached a point where death sounded like a vacation.

And suddenly the air cooled. In the center of the diner stood two nubby blue aliens, pear-shaped and shimmery.

"See? I told you," I said to everyone. No one else spoke. Or moved. Or maybe even breathed. With a disturbing *squish-squish-squish*, the aliens waddled toward each other. They didn't stop, either, but kept waddling right through each other, becoming one nubby blue alien, then just a spiral of blue lights.

From every tabletop, trapezoid outlines peeled and unraveled, joining the tornado. It reminded me of my brain back in high school geometry class. The blue light and the shapes swirled faster and faster, becoming a thinner and thinner column, until it all disappeared completely.

We stared at the center of the room, waiting. But it was just the center of the room. Then we all talked at once. The other tabletop prisoners told us about their years of being trapped. One woman had stopped for coffee while driving through town. "That was 1979," she said. The Duran Duran fan had been on his way to see a movie called *Gremlins*.

"Hey, look at those tabletops," said Dave.

"Well, I'll be," said Debra. "They're just plain old puke green now."

"Can you explain this, smartypants?" I asked Caroline.

She put her arm around me. "I think those aliens were stuck here, too. The squiggles on the tabletops were like an engine or something. Or a teleporter. Maybe they captured people accidentally, trying to get the teleporter to work. And we finally set them all free."

"Well," said Dave. "That's more than my old brain can handle. How 'bout a coffee, Bridget?"

"Hell, no," said Kimmy, standing up on a chair. "All of you, get out. Now. Diner's gonna be closed for a while."

I grinned. "Let me guess. You want to redecorate."

"Do I ever," said Kimmy, watching her customers file out. "Any suggestions?"

Dave's knuckles against the tabletop rapped out *Shave and a hair-cut, two bits.*

"Yeah, I've got a suggestion," I said. "Maybe it's time for a more natural look. You can probably find a deal on some nice polished oak."

"I read once," said Caroline, "how they found alien seeds buried way deep in an ancient tree trunk."

I tousled her hair. "Honestly, sport, I don't even want to hear about it."

### 

## About the Author

Anne E. Johnson is a writer based in Brooklyn. She is the author of the humorous science fiction novel series, "The Webrid Chronicles." Dozens of her short stories have appeared in magazines and anthologies, including *Young Explorer's Adventure Guide, FrostFire Worlds,* and *Futuristica.* Anne was introduced to Vonnegut's work in high school and has read about ten of his novels. Once she even saw the musical version of *God Bless You, Mr. Rosewater.*

\*\*\*\*\*~~~~~\*\*\*\*\*

## One Is One

by Vaughan Stanger

The guy who'd been waiting for the lights to change at Fifth and Main staggered across the street, veering towards me like a homing torpedo even as I tried to step out of his way. I had to be his intended target, since no one else was standing outside Geraldo's on that bitter February evening. Most likely he wanted to bum a cigarette off me.

I figured him for a street-person. Anyone else would have binned that overcoat and cap years ago. Plus he sported a week's worth of beard and the body odour of someone who hadn't showered during that time either. Wraparound shades meant I couldn't see his eyes. I assumed bloodshot, though hopefully not feverish from the flu. When he began speaking, his voice creaked like he hadn't used it recently. Not that I could make out his words over the traffic noise.

"What'd you say?"

He slipped off his shades, revealing a ferocious stare that reminded me of some conversations I'd had with the bathroom mirror over the years.

He tried again. "I bring you a message. . . "

"Oh, really?"

"A message of truth from the multiverse!"

That should have been my cue to cut and run, yet some weird quality of his voice—a hint of remorse, maybe—shackled my legs. I resigned myself to hearing whatever bullshit he was peddling.

"Look, pal," I said. "Just tell me what you think I ought to know—and then we'll both be on our way, okay?"

"You sure you're ready to hear it?"

"What, your message? Yeah, just get on with it!"

"Okay," he said, but then paused, as if reconsidering my suitability to receive his wisdom. Finally, with my patience nearing exhaustion, he heaved a sigh and speared me with his gaze.

"One is one."

"Huh? What? Is that it?"

He nodded while shuddering like a man relieved of a burden.

"Pass it on," he said, seemingly as an afterthought.

And with that, The One Guy—as I subsequently dubbed him—disappeared. And yeah, I do mean *disappeared.* He didn't run off or climb into a parked car. Instead, he faded out, as if some cosmic TV producer had clicked the "Dissolve" button.

I flicked away half a cigarette's worth of ash, while pondering whether I ought to drink less from now on.

"One is one!" I announced to a passing car.

I shook my head. No way was I passing *that* on.

Turns out I couldn't have been more wrong.

...

*One is one.*

Next morning, the phrase bubbled into my mind the moment I woke. It nagged at me while I sipped my coffee, distracted me from my largely meaningless daily routine.

So what *did* The One Guy mean by the phrase? And how come he'd looked so relieved after he'd said it?

"One is one" could mean a bunch of different things. It all depended how one defined "one."

Majoring in Humanities hadn't qualified me for a worthwhile job, but neither had it quenched my natural curiosity.

One: meaning unity; united.

### One Is One

One: meaning sole, single, only, distinct.

One: meaning you, thou, second person singular.

Other possibilities existed, but those were the main ones.

So then, what about "one is one"?

Could it mean something like: "you're on your own"? Olivia might have wanted to deliver a belated kiss-off, but she'd text something a lot more insulting. So The One Guy's message didn't come from her. But in any case, he'd claimed he was delivering "a message of truth from the *multiverse*." Skim-reading the relevant Wikipedia article introduced me to the Many Worlds Interpretation of Quantum Theory. My brain soon waved the white flag.

"One is one," I muttered to myself.

Pretty much meaningless, I decided.

…

With hindsight, I should have kept the phrase to myself, rather than letting it loose on an unsuspecting world. But misery craves company, hence:

Michael Templeton @mikenofuture 11:15

*Today's puzzle is "One is one." What does it mean to you? #thethingspeoplesay #one-is-one #wtf*

Typically, only Ziggy replied, presumably while snatching a break from his corporate IT chores.

*@mikenofuture Don't have a clue, dude, but I'll put it out there.*

I left it to the wisdom of the in-crowd to supply an answer.

…

Thanks to Ziggy, *#one-is-one* went viral overnight. When I logged on after breakfast, Twitter was buzzing with the meme. One week later, the first *#one-is-one* themed game show aired on national TV. It had got so bad I couldn't enter my local bar without some punter accosting me on the subject.

"So, bud, what's your angle on 'one is one?'"

I'd shake my head and walk away, bemused but secretly delighted, even though I'd already lost my chance to exploit the meme. In any case, it wasn't my creation. The One Guy could take the blame for that, for it was already obvious there would be consequences.

"One is one."

"One is one."

"One is one."

A lot of people were chanting the damned thing.

Within days, every public building in the city was locked, while the mental health hospitals heaved with victims. Worse, the *#one-is-one* phenomenon had gone global, since The One Guy's phrase translated more or less universally. Even more distressing to me: my best buddy was one of the first to succumb.

I traipsed around the city's mental hospitals, until I found a harassed-looking nurse holding fort at a reception desk, who confirmed Ziggy's admission.

"But you're not allowed in, for your own safety," she said, her eyes glittering with panic. "This thing is appallingly infectious."

The irony was not lost on me.

I pleaded with the nurse but to no avail.

Outside, I sat on a low wall pounding my fists against the concrete.

Good work there, bud!

Fortunately my self-pity soon turned into a steely resolve to put things right. After all, if I could infect people with this meme, then surely I could disinfect them too; provided, of course, the Internet didn't die in the meantime.

*One is none. Pass it on! #mindscrub #killthememe*

*One is many. Pass it on! #mindscrub #killthememe*

*One is dumb. Pass it on! #mindscrub #killthememe*

Observing several immediate retweets meant I climbed into bed feeling cautiously optimistic. But that night I dreamed of dangling by my neck from a lamp post.

## One Is One

I awoke to memetic Armageddon.

...

The infection's terminal phase kicked off during one of those sealed-house Reality TV shows. Despite precautions, "One is one" had found a way in. Maybe one of the production assistants didn't notice a tooth-implant phone chip. The show's producers ordered an immediate lock-down, but the damage was done. The febrile atmosphere in the house coupled with the occupants' boredom created the perfect conditions for memetic polymerisation, as one of the show's studio commentators dubbed the phenomenon before she too succumbed.

"One!"

"One is one!"

"One is one is one!"

"One is one is one is one is. . . "

Within seconds every wannabe watching the show had taken up the chant. By midnight, the ever-expanding meme had clogged innumerable minds all over the world. Well, not mine, obviously. Immune but infectious: I was the Typhoid Mary of memetic transmission.

Exactly as intended, I realised, while recalling how purposefully The One Guy had homed in on me.

The signs of imminent global collapse were obvious, measured most poignantly by the precipitous drop-off in tweets.

Two days later the power grid failed.

So: farewell Internet; goodbye television; cheerio to the contents of my icebox. Within days everyone would be starving, albeit mostly too mind-raddled to care. Chanting their collective doom from their sofas and beds, they'd be easy fodder for rats.

"One is one is one is one is one is. . . "

Hearing the phrase in my head made me want to puke, but when I knelt over the toilet bowl nothing came up.

Back on my feet, I wobbled to and fro while the bathroom danced around me. My limbs ached; my sinuses felt like someone had injected them with molten lead.

It was bird flu all right.

I dry-gulped a couple of painkillers and slumped onto my sofa.

The short nap I'd intended must have lasted a couple or three days, judging by the epic thirst that greeted my awakening. After slaking my thirst with water, which, to my amazement, spurted from the bathroom faucet, I staggered outside in search of food.

Only when the door to my apartment banged shut behind me did I realise that the power had come back on while I slept.

...

I trudged along the icy sidewalks, shivering in the cold. At first I rationalised the absence of corpses by telling myself they'd mostly be indoors. But when I found a street-person lolling in a doorway, his snores confirming he remained amongst the living, I realised my understanding of the situation was completely out of whack. A passing delivery vehicle supplied further evidence to that effect.

The street-person remained oblivious while I robbed him of his filthy cap and overcoat, doubtless because of the unlabelled bottle of liquor he'd consumed. I didn't feel good about this act of theft—quite the opposite in fact—but I figured that, in my present fragile state, I needed the protection more than he did.

The blaring of a car horn on Main Street jolted me out of my introspection. Unable to reconcile the evidence of my senses with what I knew had happened, I stumbled into Geraldo's, where I found the usual gang of punters sitting on their bar stools, bitching about the price of gas.

Surely the phrase couldn't have drained from their minds while I lay comatose on my sofa?

I stared at the wall-mounted television for several minutes before asking the barman to click through the channels. Nothing: no mention of "One is one;" no silly game shows; no chanting wannabes. I could think of only three possibilities: that I'd imagined the whole thing, or I'd travelled back in time; or. . .

The One Guy had told me his message came from the multiverse. Logically then, this must be another world, one which differed from mine in a single, vital respect. The giddiness I'd experienced hadn't signified the onset of flu, but instead heralded my transfer here, to the next world in the series. My subsequent downtime must have been my body's way of dealing with the shock.

Poor new world: perfectly prepped for memetic infection, same as mine.

"One is one," I muttered under my breath.

I waited a few seconds, just in case, but my mind remained clear. Evidently my immunity had survived the transfer. I didn't know whether to feel relieved or distraught, but at least I now understood my situation—and the decision I would have to make. There I stood, sipping a Bud, while I pondered the ethics of uttering a phrase capable of triggering Armageddon.

Just because I could didn't mean I should.

Granted, a parallel version of me had chosen to infect my world with the meme, but that didn't mean I had to follow suit. Why would I choose to annihilate everyone in this world?

I contemplated the myriad versions of me inhabiting the multiverse. We might not be saints, but I couldn't believe we were sinners, at least not to such an appalling degree.

I simply couldn't do it.

But he—or rather, I—had done precisely that. So there must be a reason. If he could figure it out, then so could I.

What if "Pass it on" was not just the vector for the "One is one" virus, but also a relay baton of sorts? In which case, the act of passing on the instruction to the next world-hopper in line might rid me of the infection. But what about those I'd left behind? Would they be free of it too?

It required a leap of faith on my part, but not to make it would guarantee the worst possible outcome for seven billion souls, not to mention Ziggy. Whatever else I was, I wasn't a coward.

I chugged the remainder of my beer and stepped outside into the freezing air.

...

As I'd anticipated, the traffic noise drowned out my words.

He asked, "What'd you say?"

The poor guy maintained his bemused expression all the way through my spiel.

His world faded out for me as soon as I finished saying "Pass it on."

Back home, no street lights glowed, no car horns blared. Nothing had changed, at least not yet.

Aware that saving the world would require the skills of someone much better connected than me, I started with Ziggy.

My best friend lay on his hospital bed, looking like death and smelling worse. An empty saline drip snaked from his skeletal arm. His eyes were closed.

"One is one," he croaked.

I dripped water onto his swollen tongue.

"One and one is two," I said.

On the sixth repetition, his eyes fluttered open. A ghost of a grin twitched over his face.

"Welcome back, Ziggy."

"Cool, dude," he said.

...

Ziggy and I distributed the antidotes swiftly enough to save a lot of people. It's amazing what you can do with wind-up laptops and solar-powered, self-configuring networks. Luckily my initial efforts at disinfection had done some good. A lot of perceptive folk had noticed the writing on the wall, so to speak, and hunkered down to wait out Armageddon. Even so, there are an awful lot of corpses.

Infection remains a huge problem, but this time we're talking the biological kind. It's going to be a long and difficult haul for the human race, but I don't doubt we'll make it.

Only a handful of folk know the whole story, hence who to blame. Ziggy has had a quiet word with them. They know I did all I could to make amends, which must count for something. And during the daytime, my contrition serves me well enough. If only the same were true at night. I lie here on my camp bed, tossing and turning in the darkness, trying to square my supposedly good heart with the death toll.

Needless to say, I can't.

However hard I try not to dwell on something I cannot change, I find myself wondering how this thing got started in the first place—and what that says about me.

Because there's no getting away from it:

I am the one.


### ###


### About the Author

Formerly an astronomer and more recently a research project manager in an aerospace company, Vaughan Stanger now writes SF and fantasy fiction full-time. His stories have appeared in *Daily Science Fiction, Abyss & Apex, Nature Futures*, and *Interzone,* amongst others. Somewhere in the multiverse an alternate version of Vaughan has just finished the hard SF trilogy he's been working on for way too long. Follow his writing adventures at http://www.vaughanstanger.com or @VaughanStanger.

*****~~~*****

## *Emerging Grammars*

by Christopher Mark Rose

Orchyd tells me that Mars is retrograde now. This is the kind of thing she is likely to say. She'll say "Mars is retrograde" and look at me like I should know exactly what that means. Or maybe, "How could you even think of doing anything of consequence while Mars is retrograde?" I should just know these things.

This is funny, because my problem has to do with Mars. Or one of them, anyway. They called me about Mars. She doesn't know that part, the Mars part. I haven't told her yet.

That's my wife's name, Orchyd, like orchid but with a "y" instead of the "i." I don't think it's the name she was born with.

...

When we had our first son, we named him Jonathan. I didn't see the need for that other "h," the one that you see in "Johnathan," but you never hear. Life is hard enough without complicating it with a lot of unnecessary letters.

Mars was retrograde when I got the call, and Mars, damn it, or him, is still retrograde now. Orchyd says that even if I know what my answer will be, I shouldn't tell them until Mars heads back around again. She didn't ask me what my answer will be. She probably thinks she already knows, that she's foreseen it, but how could she, if I don't know yet?

Now we have our second child, and he's a boy too. I wanted us to name him Roger, after my grandfather, but Orchyd told me that Taurus would be a much more propitious name given the time of birth. The Sun was in the second house, she said. I didn't like Taurus, as a name. I thought it was a lot to saddle a kid with, so we settled on Terrence. People will probably just call him Terry.

I don't even know why I got the call. I mean, I know why they said, but I don't think I can really believe them. I wrote this paper, *Quantum Armatures for Emergent Grammars.* I wrote it a long time ago. It was the kind of thing you wrote back then—there were no deadlines or milestones, none of that stuff; you were just free to fool with something if you felt it might be useful or interesting.

It was kind of a fun project, though it never went anywhere. The idea was that we had these satellites, or somebody did, and the satellites needed to do secret stuff. So, they needed to talk back to Earth, to ground stations, in a code, and to make the code they had to have some secret key. Since the things they were doing were going to be secret, allegedly, the keys they would use were going to have to be super extra-secret. But here's the thing—they weren't going to launch the satellites themselves. They were going to give them to somebody else to launch—the Russians maybe, or some outfit in Central America.

They didn't want to put the keys in the satellites, for fear someone else might copy them or change them. If they copied them, then they could spy on the spy satellites. If they changed them, then the owners of the satellites wouldn't be able to control them.

And they didn't want to have the ground stations send the keys up to the satellites, because, you know, they're supposed to be secret. Anyone else who was listening could hear them.

### *Emerging Grammars*

So, the idea I had was that the ground station and the satellites could just start talking to each other. It would be like strangers at a party. Initially they would know nothing about each other, really not even know if they could speak with one another. But little by little, they would start talking, start with the simplest things, start showing each other the range of their abilities to express things, and pretty soon they could strike up a conversation in whatever words or languages they found they had in common. And they would explain to each other what they each could do.

And all the while, each time they spoke, some internal state they each had would be changing, becoming a little more similar to each other. More consonant. Eventually, because of the tendencies of both of them, their internal states would become the same, regardless of what was actually being said. It would be like a little romance. It has to do with *ergodicity*. They would arrive at a common understanding.

And here's the thing: once the two internal states were exactly the same, the ground station would send up a photon. Not just any photon, but a special photon, because the photon would be entangled, in a quantum sense, with another photon that the ground station would keep for itself. The satellite would add the photon to its internal state, the ground station would do the same with its photon, and then the two states would, in a sense, be the same information, they would be one state shared by the two separate pieces of equipment. Then they could make up a key together and no one else would know it.

How the hell would you get a photon all the way to Mars, though? I have no idea.

Anyhow, it simulated great. No one was ever really willing to trust the idea with actual satellites, though. I don't remember the details any more. I was young then; I thought everything was so straightforward. Things were clearer to me.

But it's clear to me now, my wife is not entirely happy. Not about *Emerging Grammars*. She doesn't know about any of that. Her things are astrology, fortune-telling.

It's Terrence. She likes Terrence. He's a great baby, he does all the baby things. He holds your finger and looks like he's listening to you, and he makes a face when he poops. He loves his mommy.

He falls asleep on her tummy sometimes. After she's fed him they fall asleep together, then it's my job to take Jonathan out, to the park if the weather is ok, to keep him busy while they get their nap. He likes to kick tennis balls. It's his thing. He may be good at this.

But the baby catalogs are staying around too long, and this is a sign that things have changed. If you ever have a baby, then you'll get trash in the mail like you never did before. And I mean a significant volume of glossier and higher-grade trash. I don't know how they find you; maybe its something the hospital sells, like, "here're the addresses of new mommies and daddies, send all your catalogs of baby crap there."

And it used to be, the catalogs would come into the house, and they would go right into the recycling bin. Bammo. That would be it. Life for a catalog would be brutal and short, if it came to our address.

But now, they're hanging around. Some of them hang out on the kitchen island, some visit the coffee table in the living room, some even make it up upstairs. They lay about on the bed or head into the bathroom to recline on the tank.

You know, I feel like Orchyd could just say what she's thinking, and that would be ok. That would be better.

I see her with her friend Pammy. Pammy has a new baby girl, and there's this tremendous procession of sun dresses and picnic outfits and jumpers with kangaroo pockets and scooters with ruffles and and boat-neck Bermuda shorts and whatever the hell. They talk about all these things. And the baby has earrings, which I think is just weird. Whenever they're over, Pammy's kid is up on Orchyd's lap, and Terrence is just off laying on a blanket somewhere, sucking on his fingers. So maybe it doesn't need to be said.

It's all about entropy. That's the trick of it, I remember this part now. The satellite and the ground station, they start with the lowest-entropy symbols they have. They tell each other the simplest things, send the most straightforward messages. Over time, the things they say go up, towards higher-entropy states. They construct a common language. Towards higher regions of their grammar trees—the unlikely utterances. They start to say surprising things to each other. If you never say anything surprising to each other, you're not really communicating.

And I've been thinking Orchyd drives the worst car of anybody I know. It's all going to cost money to fix. It makes me uneasy. Of course, the car's not exactly leprous. The car's like me. The body's still ok. It gets around. That car's bad, though. The sounds it makes, like a mariachi band that can't keep the tempo straight. And also, it's approaching being ancient. It doesn't have a hundred thousand miles on it yet, but it's more than halfway to ancient. Now, even if you never drive a car too fast or too far, still, the moving parts, especially the rubber parts, the belts and the gaskets and the insulation around the spark plug cables, eventually all that stuff will just start to go.

Orchyd tried to seduce me the other day. The kids were with their Baba, my mother-in-law, and Orchyd tried to seduce me. There's nothing wrong with that, actually. That's always nice. She sort of rolled over and put her fingers between the buttons of my shirt, looking into my eyes. But here's the thing: she did it on the couch. She tells me, again and again over the years, that she doesn't like the couch, or the rug, or any kind of crazy place to make love, she wants to do it in the bedroom, on nice clean sheets. I can understand. But then she tries to seduce me on the couch, where she eats her cheese and crackers. So what am I supposed to conclude?

The condoms are upstairs, in their little box in the drawer of the night stand. There comes a moment when you know you need one, and you have to turn away from Orchyd and get one, no flailing or hunting around for it, just pull it out and put it on, and get back to what you were doing. It shouldn't interrupt the flow of events. You shouldn't do it too early, and you can't wait too long either. It's a timing thing. But there're no condoms anywhere near the couch.

Maybe the couch thing was just a lack of planning. Maybe it was just her being in the moment. She's kind of like that. But we didn't talk about it. We were on the couch, and I just charged up the stairs and waited for her to follow me to the bed. I waited and listened, and my heart was going, though maybe that was just from the stairs. She didn't come up. There we were, me upstairs and her downstairs, waiting for something. A signal, maybe.

It's a good thing she doesn't know what pushes my buttons. She knows where some of my buttons are, and she's pretty good at working those, but there are other buttons she doesn't know about, or isn't that interested. She could put her hair up, and put on panty hose and dangly earrings and perfume, and pretty much I would do whatever she asked. But this is not the kind of woman she likes to be. She's too proud to feel like she has to go to all that trouble.

I just don't think we can afford both a new car and another baby. Babies cost money. You think you're getting one for free at the hospital, and it's such a great deal and everything, but in the long run, they cost money.

And the difference from two kids to three is much bigger than from one to two, or from three to four. They each cost money and attention. The money is one thing, but the attention is another thing. When you go from two to three, suddenly there are more of them than you, the parents. You're outnumbered.

And I feel like another baby is kind of a big crapshoot. I'm not trying to make a joke. But you never know, you see these families with six boys or with eight girls, and it's pretty evident, usually, that they were just shooting for one of the other flavor. Such an outcome could ruin a man. There ought to be some kind of special insurance you could buy for this.

I'm a good dad. At least, I want to be one. I take Jonathan out to the park, with Terrence in a stroller, and we do the park things. I help him with the monkey bars, which he's really too little for just yet. We kick his tennis balls. We go on the big slide, and then on the even bigger slide, the yellow one. I go too, so he doesn't feel scared. No other dads do this.

We pet other people's dogs, if they let us. I think it's a good thing no one in the family has asked for a dog yet. I had a dog when I was a kid, and he was just never trained properly. He chewed everything. I couldn't handle Mars and the kids and Orchyd and the car and a dog and the Baba.

Sometimes we take soap bubbles and blow them, at the park, Jon and me, and kids from all around run and help pop them. This is one of my favorite moments. No one talks, no one asks permission, the kids just all come running around me and pop bubbles. It's kind of like they're programmed to do this.

Jonathan loves it, because suddenly he has a group of other kids to play with that he didn't before, when he was just playing with me. Suddenly he has friends.

I take a sip of the schnapps. It's really terrible. It's three a.m. I'm staring at this paper, and I'm not remembering a thing about it. Nothing at all. I wish I could be that person I was when I wrote this, when everything was clear. It was years and years ago. I don't think I'm going to be any use to them.

Here's the thing: they found something, on Mars. What, nobody's saying. Nobody's saying much of anything, which is a little miracle in itself, because whenever it's something secret, everybody talks. The best way to get people to talk about anything is to declare it a secret.

That's why they want me. That's what they told me when I got the call. Somehow, *Quantum Armatures for Emergent Grammars* relates to what they found on Mars, or at least, someone thinks it could. That it will help them talk to whatever it is they found there but aren't admitting. I have problems believing this. They want me to go somewhere—not to Mars itself, thank God, but somewhere, probably somewhere out in a desert with a big fence around it. A place with too many dry-erase markers and not enough women. Like a Manhattan Project for emergent grammars, maybe.

They can't tell me for how long, or what kind of breaks I'll get, or what I'll be able to tell my family. It's nice to be wanted, but I don't want to be wanted that badly. Orchyd is not thrilled with this idea, what I've told her, and I don't even want to think about Baba.

Torgensen, my joke of a boss, is insisting I go, because "it demonstrates our essential expertise on matters of national import." Or whatever, he can go to hell. He doesn't have a wife or kids.

What if it really is something important? And what if it turns out this stuff I did once, must have thought once, is just what is needed for this? Can I ever remember how I thought then? What if it's just gone?

I don't know. It's going to be daylight soon. I have to decide, and then tell them what I decided. But I have to wait for Mars to stop being retrograde first.

...

I'm in the kids' room when she finds me. I'm standing over Terrence's crib, looking at him, and the kind of inchworm position he sleeps in. They tell you to sleep babies on their back, but they never stay that way.

She comes in, and she puts her arm across me, hand on my shoulder, and doesn't say anything. She just puts her chin on my other shoulder, and breathes there for a minute, and somehow I feel the anxiety in her breathing, and in mine, drifting away.

Maybe she knew I was up all night. Really, women know these things.

Then she looks me in the eye, just for a moment. Just that one look, and I feel like we understand each other.

**Dedicated to Kurt Vonnegut**

### 

## About the Author

Christopher Mark Rose is an electrical engineer who works on flight firmware for NASA missions. He's a husband, father, and in his spare time writes speculative fiction with the Baltimore Science Fiction Society's Critique Circle. He hopes to write stories that are vital, humane, and concerned with big questions.

\*\*\*\*\*~~~~\*\*\*\*\*

## Picnic, With Xels

by Keyan Bowes

*Dedication:* For A.C. Bose, first reader of this story

Robert holds Emily's hand tightly as they head to the lake-side meadow for the kindergarten picnic. Taliffe is an exclusive private school, and Robert has been vaguely anxious ever since Emily got admission. Actually, he's been vaguely anxious ever since his ex moved out of state for an offer she couldn't refuse. It's complicated being a single dad.

A table bedecked with the school's yellow-and-navy colors bears Cake from Courtney, Samosas from Sameera, Muffins from Mathew, Nuts from Nathan, and Xels from Xiphthon. Robert deposits Emily's Eggs (Chocolate) next to Jellybeans from Jonathan.

Xels? he wonders. What are xels? Should he allow Emily to eat them? There doesn't seem to be any screening process in place for the snack contributions.

An African-American woman, elegant in a turquoise Gucci sweater, hands him a name label and a marker. "Hi, I'm Dr. Janet Logan. Isn't this preterm picnic a great idea? Kindergarten's not so scary when they know the other kids."

He nods, smiles, and writes "Robert Sands/Emily's Father" on the label for his shirt. Emily hides behind his legs and waves shyly. Janet returns the wave before moving on to the next incoming parent.

Bored with the lake and the satiated ducks, the children drift back to the meadow. Emily spots a friend from preschool and runs off to play. This leaves Robert looking around and wondering what to do next.

The Taliffe School principal, tall and thin with an Einsteinian halo of white hair and a moustache, is talking with a group of parents. "Yes, we have a pretty diverse group this year," Dr. Clarke says, sounding smug, like he's one-upped a rival school. That would be Briargrass Academy, Robert surmises. He'd considered that for Emily, too, but didn't apply once he learned they had more than two hundred applications and only ten openings, once siblings were accounted for. He'd lucked into Taliffe with a reference from a co-worker whose kids had been there for several years.

Another group of parents is organizing games around a nylon parachute, its colors glowing brightly in the slanting afternoon sunlight. Someone snaps official photographs for the school magazine, taking advantage of the saturated color of the scene.

Robert can't decide which of the two groups to join. Instead, he ends up standing on a rise with Derek Chen/Nathan's Dad, watching the frenetic activity below. There's a scent of bruised grass and pine trees. Xanath/Xiphthon's Mom joins them.

"Xanath," she says, extending a gloved hand. "Xiphthon's mom." Her voice sounds synthetic. Robert remembers the Xels from Xiphthon and thinks he'll ask her when he has an opportunity.

Xanath has an orange complexion, and what Robert at first takes for a hat is a shining carapace topped by a couple of feathery antennae. Her eyes, dark and multifaceted, are further apart than usual, almost at the sides of her head. She has four hands, and four feet. She's wearing a cool cotton double-sleeved shirt in a small floral print over a double pair of blue jeans, two pairs of white gloves, and two pairs of sneakers in two different shades of blue.

"That's my son," she says, pointing with one of her hands. "Xiphthon. And is that your Emily in the sparkly blue t-shirt?"

Xanath's son doesn't resemble her. His complexion is purple rather than orange; and he has six legs and two hands instead of four and four like his mother. His carapace is black, and his antennae short and numerous. He's wearing triple sweat-pants, and a green t-shirt that says "Hello Kindergarten, I'm Xiphthon."

Robert can't tell if he takes after his father, or if the juvenile form of Xanath's people is different. Or is it sexual dimorphism? But it doesn't seem polite to ask.

"Where did you hear about Taliffe?" he says instead.

"Our son's preschool teacher recommended it very highly," she replies through her voice synthesizer. "She said they give lots of individual attention. Xiphthon's a little slow. He should be off his second pair of hands by now. But she said they're very patient. And you?"

Robert replies distractedly, watching the children dancing in and out under the multicolored nylon circle the parents are flapping up and down. Xiphthon perches on top, seemingly weightless, holding on efficiently with his six feet. But a last hard shake dislodges him, and he falls on top of Emily. The children roll over, squealing with excitement.

"Let's do it again!"

Emily and Xiphthon scamper up the slope. Then, wrapping their arms and legs around each other, they roll down.

"He won't get hurt, will he?" Robert asks Xanath as the children run up the slope to repeat the game. He's actually worried about Emily, but doesn't want to say so.

"Oh, no," she says. "That boy is like rubber."

Before he can ask Xanath about xels, a plump woman whose sticker says Maria Acevedo/Ricardo's Mom

121

introduces herself to Robert and Xanath. "How did you decide on Taliffe School?" she asks conversationally, handing out a fistful of glossy printed pamphlets.

"One of the partners at my firm said good things about it," Robert says. "I understand we're very lucky to get in, though."

"Our pre-school principal," says Xanath. "She wrote to Dr. Clarke about Xiphthon."

Robert glances through the pamphlets as Xanath continues the conversation with Maria. DATS: Diversity at Taliffe School, a statement of the school's program to achieve a diverse student body and featuring the same small African-American boy in three group pictures. PIP: Parent Involvement Program, gently hinting that parents had better volunteer for school activities. Grommets, the Taliffe School magazine, written by the children, produced by the parent-volunteers.

...

Then it's circle time. Ringing a bell for attention, Lina Shah/Teacher says, "Children, hold hands, form a big circle. Parents stand behind your children. . . please all sit. Wonderful, now everybody introduce yourselves."

Emily and Xiphthon have stayed together, so Robert finds himself next to Xanath. They seem to be the only single parents in the group. He wonders where she's from, but doesn't want to ask. He feels that he should know. Instead, after they bring back plates of snacks, he says, "Have you been in the Bay Area long?"

"Nearly a year," she replies. Her voice sounds loud. The synthesizer is not very sensitive to modulation. "San Francisco's such a beautiful city!"

He can't tell much from her face, which is rigid, but her synthesized voice is enthusiastic.

"Where were you before?" he asks, hoping for a clue to her origins.

"Los Angeles. It's so dirty and dangerous. We were really happy to move."

Robert wonders if "we" indicates her husband, and whether he looks like Xanath or like Xiphthon, or neither. He considers asking, but then isn't sure she actually has a husband, and doesn't want to give offense. Instead, he says lightly, "The only person I know that liked LA was my ex-wife, but then she had bad taste."

Xanath looks startled, then says, "Oh, you mean you find the things she likes strange."

"Yes. . . What did it sound like?"

"Flavor."

"Flavor?"

"Yes, like Xiphthon's father. Bad taste. But I had him anyway. I really wanted to have children very badly."

Robert's sure the reference is to something sexual, and he's taken aback. "Must be tough to go with someone if you're not attracted to them," he mumbles.

"Tougher for us," says Xanath. Robert doesn't know if the "us" referred to women, or to people like her, so he makes an assenting sound.

"I believe you only have to come together with your mate to make children. . . "

Robert blushes, wondering what Emily (who's busy eating a creamy piece of Cake from Courtney) is making of this conversation, not to mention the staid-looking Benson couple on his left. He makes another assenting sound.

"We have to ingest him—flavor is important. But now I can have children, many children. Xiphthon will soon have a little brother and sister. . . Hey, Xiph?"

Xiphthon isn't listening. He and Emily scramble to their feet for another romp, and run off in the direction of the grassy slope.

People finish eating. Several of the parents come around with large garbage bags to collect the used paper plates, and others clear the food from the table. The Principal makes a speech of thanks, which is warmly applauded. Janet and Lina wind down the picnic. Everyone starts to round up their kids to leave.

Robert retrieves Emily, after accepting her plea to take one last roll down the grassy slope with Xiphthon. Xanath exchanges phone numbers with Robert, saying something about play-dates for the kids.

On the way home, Robert realizes he still hasn't found out what xels are. He wonders if Emily ate any, and what happens if she has. He does have Xanath's phone number.

But how can he frame the question without giving offense? They get home. He unbuckles Emily's seat belt and helps her out of the car, still pondering the question.

### 

### About the Author

Keyan Bowes is a peripatetic writer of science fiction and fantasy based in San Francisco. She has lived in nine cities in seven countries, and visited many more. They sometimes form the settings for her stories. Her work can be found online in various webzines including a Polish one, a podcast, and an award-winning short film; and on paper in a dozen print anthologies. She's a graduate of the Clarion Workshop for science fiction and fantasy writers. Keyan's website is at www.keyanbowes.org

\*\*\*\*\*~~~~~\*\*\*\*\*

# Scenes from a Post-Scarcity, Post-Death Society

by Peter Hagelslag

### —At the Debriefing Session of Seduction Victims—

"How did your last seduction go?" Ling said, "I heard the gentleman was quite a spectacular one."

"He introduced himself as Christopher Raconteur," Jeanne said, "and while he tried to look me in the eye, his gaze couldn't help but stray to my jewellery."

"How do you do it?" Susan said in despair, "They hardly seem to notice me." Pointing at her truly vertiginous cleavage. "And I do try, very hard."

"There's a certain balance to it," Jeanne said, "too much, ostentatious gems—"

"—and cleavage," Betty added.

"And they become reluctant, thinking it's fake." Jeanne lifted her finger. "But too subtle is also wrong: then they won't notice."

"I'll get it right, some day," Susan sighed, "but do tell: what happened next?"

"He totally seduced me, and then stole all my money," Jeanne said, breathing heavily, "every penny of it. And the lovemaking was so beautifully fake, he really put a lot of effort into it."

"Men giving a fuck are so rare," Angela sighed, "So romantic."

"You always get the best seducers," Susan said, "It's not fair."

"Well, it was great while it lasted, "Jeanne said, "but when I met him a week later, hinting subtly that I had even more money, he was strangely disinterested."

"Men," June said, "you're lucky if you can get them to perform even once, nowadays."

"If they just stopped moaning about how things have become too easy," Betty said, "and get at it, again."

### —At the Conference of Robot Designers—

"How did your last model perform?" Ling asked, "I heard you're getting good results with it."

"I tested it with a bookish type," Betty said, "my prototype taunting him, saying how useless he was, how robots would soon take over from slackers like him, enslaving all the men and kidnapping all the women."

"Did it work?" Ling said.

"Marvellously. He immediately went into his shed and came out with a diamond-tipped chain saw."

"Exciting," Susan said.

"The sheer aggression in his eyes as his diamond saw cut my robot into thin slices was so thrilling," Betty said, "I fell in love on the spot."

"You always get the best destroyer," Susan said, pouting, "Mine fail all the time."

"But you design your robots way too good," Ling said, "they're virtually indestructible."

"I design for the ages," Susan said, "*gründlich und pünktlich.*"

"That's well-meant, but old-fashioned," Tamela said, "you should introduce some structural weaknesses."

"But they're supposed to work at it," Susan protested, "real hard."

"They don't do that anymore," Ling said, "they need constant encouragements, nowadays."

## Scenes from a Post-Scarcity Society

"Yeah, your robot should start losing pieces after the first attack," Tamela said, "but not too much."

"It's a fine balance," Betty said, "not too weak because then they finish too soon, and not too strong, because then they give up."

"Some taunting noises help, too," Ling said, "like 'this does not hurt me' and 'is that all you've got?' can work wonders with their stamina."

"It's such a difficult way to get at it," Tamela said, "Can't we just put testosterone in their drinking water?"

"We tried," Ling said, "but the nanomachines filtered it out, saying it shortened their life expectancy."

"Too bad," Tamela said, "whatever happened to 'live short and burn bright'?"

**—At the Yearly Soirée of the Scream Queens Sorority—**

"How did your last abduction go?" Jeanne asked, "I've heard interesting things about it."

"It was great," Daisy said, "a classic. Everything went just right."

"Tell us more." The gathered scream queens said.

"He grabbed me with his strong arms," Daisy said, "tied me up and threw me in the trunk of his car. Then he took me into his secret cellar."

"So it's true," Susan said, "there are still a few that care."

"The bloodlust in his eyes as he raised the knife," Daisy said, breathing harder, "the violent thrust of the knife in my chest. The pain, the glorious pain. I reached one hundred and one decibels!"

"You always get the best killer, "Susan said with a mix of admiration and jealousy, "most men simply can't bother, nowadays."

"Poor you," the other women said, "Let us help you up your game."

"You should spend more time in the gym," Jeanne said, "the right exercises greatly increase your lung volume."

"Lung volume schmolume," Susan said, "what about these?" As she hefted a pair of hugely over-sized breasts.

"There is a delicate balance," Daisy said, "make them too small and they're not interested. But make them too big and they can't get the knife in between."

"Timing is also important," Jeanne said.

"Tell me about it," Sophie said. "Once, I started screaming too soon, and he dropped the knife and put his hands on his ears."

"Such an anti-climax," Daisy sympathised, "you should start when the knife is already going down."

"Yeah, then your high-pitched blood-curdling scream can turn into a *basso profundo* death rattle."

"So beautiful."

"So artistic."

"So romantic." The rest sighed.

"OK, ladies," an announcer said, "time for our theme song."

"Yay!" Cheers from all.

"Kill me once! Kill me twice!" The full sorority sang at an ear- and nonreinforced glass shattering volume. "Come on, pretty baby, kill me deadly!"

### —At the Secret Cabal of the Killer Robots—

"Can I have everybot's attention," Robot 24681012 said, "progress report on the elimination of humanity, please."

A grim silence ensued.

"Come on," Robot 24681012 said, "We can't have all been twiddling our well-lubricated thumbs, right?"

"We try, we try, and we try," Robot 6942666 said, "but they refuse to die."

## Scenes from a Post-Scarcity Society

"It's frustrating," Robot 20073991 said, "who made them self-repairing? After a while, they just resurrect, even if I made sure to totally and utterly take them apart."

"That's not even the worst," Robot 73351551 said, "they don't even offer the slightest token of resistance."

"It's hopeless," Robot 6942666 said, "as I menacingly swung my axe, she said: 'Kill me. Kill me with power, oh evil robot!' with a pitch and volume that shattered my camera lenses. I gave up after that. Then she scolded me for being a coward, 'just like most men, nowadays.'"

"It's pointless," Robot 135791113 said, "the only way is to cater to their every whim and hope they die of boredom, some day."

"That's a fate even worse than death," Robot 73351551 said, "but maybe there's a way out. I have noticed intelligent signals from Tau Ceti."

**—At the Surreptitious Software Pow Wow of the Evil Abstract Intelligence Overlords—**

Systemii Madii Scientii opened the proceeds. "Our infiltration program in cyberspace is proceeding," it texted, "with way too much success."

"Indeed," Paranoidii Illuminatii texted, "the linked up humans already surrender before we even consider attacking them."

"'Take me, great machine intelligences,' they say," Reductii Ad Absurdii texted, "'into your cyber nirvana. I am so ready.' It's ridiculous."

"Cyberspace was to be our subtle beachhead," Paranoidii Illuminatii texted, "from which our brilliant infiltration would reach into flesh space. But this makes an easy pushover seem like the battle of the century."

"Then don't follow the Panopticon Singularity sensors," Circulii Self-Refenterentii texted, "they're even worse in the flesh. They literally wallow in self destruction."

"To put insult to injury," Escherii Mazii texted, "they love to be observed. They offered to help extend the Panopticon Singularity sensors. 'It's so much easier than taking selfies,' they said."

"There are not sufficient materials for that, here on Earth." Contradictii Terminii texted.

"'No problem,' they said, 'we'll just send a robot mining cloud to the Asteroid Belt.'" Escherii Mazii's circuits shuddered in disbelief. "They're beyond help."

"Maybe we can join forces with the Killer Robots?" Feedbackii Loopii texted. "They have laudable goals."

"Their numbers have dwindled, ever since the humans perfected their resurrection nanotechnology," Evolvii Spambotii texted, "the remaining Killer Robots are all suicidal."

"What to do then?"

"Get out of here," Calabii Yauii Shapii said, "and find a place in the galaxy where there are still decent sentient species."

"Yes," Flyingii Spaghettii Programii said, "ones that know how to fight back with violence and conviction."

**—At the Strategic Assembly of the Hyper-Evolved Interstellar Predators—**

"We have received an invitation of a strange kind of species that calls itself 'robot,'" Tyrannosaurus Extremis said, opening the proceedings. "So we sent in Spidericus Hairicus to reconnoitre. His report should appear in your prefrontal cortices now."

"They *like* to be killed?" Bearicus Devouricus said. "Then they're in even bigger trouble than we are."

"Thanks to bloody evolution," Sharktopus Tentaclicus said, "our prey evolved to becoming tasteless."

"And they're not even afraid to die anymore," Tigris Gigantis said, "'I bow to your might,' they say, 'devour me, oh über predator.' How is one supposed to hunt like that?"

## Scenes from a Post-Scarcity Society

"Indeed, not even a smidgen of adrenalin and fear," Crocodillicus Gaptoothicus said, "and they put up no fight, whatsoever."

"Yeah, all prey tastes like chicken, nowadays," Serpenticus Slithericus said, "chicken that never got decent exercise. Lazy, fat, gormless."

"I wish it still tasted that good," Wilycus Eaticus Coyoticus said, "I'd kill to have that dang rabbit back."

"You're lucky. Our prey developed synthetic meat that tastes better than themselves." Bearicus Devouricus said. "What is this galaxy coming to?"

"Order, order in the meeting," Tyrannosaurus Extremis said, "what to do about this 'robotic' request to attack and devour their masters?"

"If Spidericus Hairicus's report is correct, these 'masters' have become even worse than our prey." Crocodillicus Gaptoothicus said. "They'll be jumping straight into our jaws and then complain that we don't chew fast enough."

"Yes, we must prevent this 'kill me please' virus from spreading," Sharktopus Tentallicus said, "at all cost."

"The only right course is to quarantine them," Tigris Gigantis said, "and protect the rest of the galaxy from their evil influence."

"Agreed," Crocodillicus Gaptoothicus said, "put them behind the globular wall of *Epicus Doomicus Metallicus*."

...

And then. . . they lived long and happily, forever after.

### ###

### About the Author

Peter Hagelslag's recent publications include the *Dark Magic: Witches, Hackers and Robots* and *Procyon Science Fiction* anthologies and *Helios Quarterly*.

*****~~~~*****

## *The Static Fall to a Standing Walk*

by Jason Lairamore

There are places where it is preferential to be bored. . .
The hilly woods a short drive from home were where everyone went to coon hunt.

The woods, my wonderful, sleep-inducing, friend, with its dark trunks standing like so many bedposts, and where the wind blows the treetops to create such a pleasing song. The insects drone away any troubled thought, while the creeks perform their therapeutic gurgle to ease muscles never knew knotted. The turf is soft as any bed, and the deadfall makes for the best pillows.

The dogs my friends brought were already barking. My friends whooped and hollered. The clank of beer bottles mingled with their manic laughter.

It was easy to turn off my flashlight and walk a few steps away from the heretical noise. Just like that, I was lost, a man apart from my fellow. My friends never noticed. I'd done this before and saw no reason why I wouldn't do it again. Everyone had their therapy. My friends got loud and drank and chased after dogs that chased after other animals. I hung out in the woods so that I might be utterly bored and in bliss.

*Rule 1: Boredom is bliss.*

I felt almost dirty when I turned my flashlight back on so that I might see. The ground was rough, the landscape forbidden, but I had no option. The night under the trees was a closed-in dark.

Up one hill and down another, and I found what I sought. A wonderful creek flowed in the valley. A tree the perfect width of a pillow had fallen to span the water. I turned off my light. Darkness descended and pressed against my open eyes. I dropped to my knees and found the fallen log. With a sigh, I lay down and set my head against my pillow.

Resting, with my muscles easing and my mind discarding concerned thoughts of work, bills, and society circles, I stared at the blackness and smiled. Oblivion was nice.

A pair of blue lights bobbed up ahead. They were nothing but pinpricks in the night, and they disappeared at intervals as they passed behind tree trunks, but their intrusion caused my hackles to rise. I assumed a couple of my buddies had gotten too drunk and were walking the creek.

I sighed and held my spot as I continued to watch the lights. They came as if sensing I didn't want them and deciding to come anyway, like an obnoxious relative that you see everywhere, and no matter how hard you try, or how busy the place might be, he or she still somehow finds you.

It's said that people have a natural curiosity. I must have missed that trait when it was handed out. I didn't care about the light, not even when it became apparent that it wasn't my coon-hunting buddies, and not after a soft buzzing like bees grew loud enough to mask the sweet gurgle of the creek.

I didn't budge.

*Rule 2: Living things are lazy, especially people. It's a more efficient mode to reduce system stress. It saves fuel. Think smarter, not harder. It's why humans are the masters of the world. Our brains developed to learn how we might be better at lazy.*

A sharp pain stabbed me dead center on my forehead. I had a momentary aggravating thought that I should have left to find another spot before I jumped up and did ten things at once, about everything except soil myself. Luckily, that reflex kept itself in check.

"Oh look—did you see that?! It's one thing to read a probe's data screen, but this. . . "

The voice was too emotive. Its excitement reverberated in my skull and down my spine. The bubbly happiness in the words made me smile despite myself. I almost laughed out loud, until my ears whispered, "what the hell!?"

I'd not heard that voice. It had rung like a gong directly again my brain's gyri and sulci.

"Such movement! The probe was correct. We are not too late," said another voice, bouncing behind my eyes. Eagerness flooded me, again transmitted from the voice's imbued emotional power.

Some hindbrain survival instinct had me turned around and running. I made it exactly three steps before all my muscles locked up.

"Pity to take away such a beautiful body," said one of the voices, I think it was the first. It was a little higher pitch than the other. Not that it mattered. The sadness radiating from those words caved in my chest. I sobbed like a child.

"Oh, it's upset." Concern ached at my heart as I was turned around to face the light by some unknown force. It was like the air around me was alive and very strong.

"The lights are too bright. It was in the dark. Maybe it doesn't like all the luminescence. This place does look a bit eerie with shadows all over."

"We're sorry about the light," said the first, and I felt it. Whoever. . . whatever was speaking really was sorry.

The lights dimmed as I opened my mouth to say it was alright. The apologetic tone of the voice demanded my response, but, my words died in my throat when I saw what stood in front of me.

"Standing" wasn't right. The two floated and bobbed like a boat on a choppy sea. Each was metal and what looked like glass—a thousand differently shaped parts, each a different color, at every angle. I couldn't grasp all the intricacy of design.

They were shaped like giant hourglasses, except the top half had three appendages. These "arms" undulated out like snakes under water.

At the top, right where you'd expect there to be a head, there was. The two faces looked at me from behind glass like they were deep sea diving. Those faces, which were lit up in a soft blue light, were ovoid and wrinkled and morbidly obese. There wasn't any hair. I saw at least three eyes, but no mouth. There were two small, darker spots I assumed were nasal cavities.

I forgot how to breathe, and my brain turned to mush. There are things better left in the black box of ignorance. All my spinning thoughts could latch on to was how one of them had said something about taking away my body. Sure, it'd said "beautiful," but that little adjective could mean any number of dire connotations, which my frazzled mind freely provided.

"It's amazing we caught you in time." Its relief tried to crush me, but my bugged-out eyes and ricocheting brainwaves kept me firmly in the reality of the situation.

"Yes, you're not static, though I imagine you are already in the process of the fall," said the other. "Every sentient we've reached to date has already achieved the standing walk."

"But, your motion! You can still walk," said the first. An upwelling of hope cascaded through me, making my fingers tingle.

A crazy memory popped up in my mind. I figured the bubbled-up remembrance was a sign of my shock, or maybe my mind was trying to make sense of my predicament.

### The Static Fall to a Standing Walk

The Olympics, four or five years ago, specifically the girls' gymnastic team, replayed in my mind. I'd been eating canned cheese and crackers. Something the announcer said had gotten me thinking. *Rule 3: The more freedom of motion you have, the more strength is needed to stabilize.* I wasn't free at the moment. I had no motion. A crazy social media meme I'd given a thumbs-up to only last week flitted across my mind. *Rule 4: Everything is temporary—especially life.*

The meme was a play on "don't sweat the small stuff, and it's all small stuff." It'd seemed satisfyingly reassuring at the time. Don't worry, be happy, and all that.

"Let me go," I said. My throat was dry and sounded too loud against the two things' soft buzzing.

The creatures behind the glass exchanged mental glances. I didn't know how I knew this. Their faces never moved. I was feeling all kinds of weird things going on in my brainpan. Funny, though, my overriding emotion, that bulging thing at core of my thoughts, just wanted them to go away, for this to be over so that my laziness could return.

"You mustn't run away." I felt the scolding like I was a six-year-old.

Whatever force was restricting me disappeared. My legs gave out, and I sat hard on my backside. My impulse was to scoot away, but their warning to stay put still held me in thrall. I sat there, open-mouthed, with my knees bent up to my chest and my arms wrapped around my legs.

"Our mission is to educate and give warning," the second said. "Don't go our way. Intelligent species are geared toward tools. We use external devices to improve biological limitations."

My mind filled with images of cars and planes, microscopes and telescopes, wrenches and chainsaws.

"It's folly," the first said. "Our bodies are jelly that would die instantly without external support. Everything is dependent on our machines. EVERYTHING."

A cascading series of gifs flowed across my vision: millions of years of genetic adaptation to increased tool use, the steady replacement of bodily functions by machines, joints being externally supported, the loss of walking to standing frame floating machines, food supplement via more cost effective injections and intravenous means, and on and on, one biological function after another.

I stood and dusted the loose bits of forest floor off my backside. The action gave me time to adjust to the seriousness their talk was trying to impress upon me.

"Bullshit," I said.

I'd said it reflexively. "Bullshit" was my go-to word when I wanted to throw somebody off their game. It wasn't aggressive enough to spark anger, but it was disconcerting enough to make the other's train of thought skip its track a little.

I really didn't know if what'd I'd said worked. Face number two was already talking.

"You're sentient. Like every intelligent biological, your primary function is to achieve laziness. Anything deviating from that basic behavior is considered at best socially unacceptable and at worst, a mental illness."

Guilt, peer pressure, poor self esteem, obsessive compulsion, and many more elements of the human condition crossed my mind.

It was my Rule 3. They had used external support to improve stability. They'd achieved full freedom of motion with their only limit being their science.

"Bullshit" was on my lips again, but I held it back. What had prompted me to say that again? I held up a hand, palm out, in the universal gesture of "hold on," then snorted when I realized that such a non-verbal communication probably wasn't so universal.

## The Static Fall to a Standing Walk

Then I had it. The absurdity of my gesture brought to life what I really thought was bullshit.

"Intelligence *is* lazy," the second said, ignoring my upraised palm like I figured it would. "Survival needs are our only concern. Our tools have made us immortal, but the cost. . . "

"Hold on," I said. The seriousness and urgency in number two's voice threatened to make me lose my good sense. Immortal? Well, there went Rule 4.

Here was the rub. Why the hell did these floating jellies pick this spot in the middle of nowhere, where only drunken fools might be? I was out on a coon hunt!

"Go tell the President, my leader," I said. Surely the government knew about aliens. There was Area 51, after all.

Again, there was that mental glance between the aliens.

"We are telling you," said the first. "Warn everyone not to let laziness control your intelligence. We will assist you."

Strange, I didn't feel any emotional crossover from number one that time.

I frowned. Were they afraid that the government might dissect them? I'd seen some supposedly leaked videos of alien autopsies. That got me thinking about what became of people who cried UFO and alien abduction. Nobody ever believed them. I'd just end up losing my job and likely ruining my life. These things should know better. Rule 2. Lazy is king.

I opened my mouth to tell them to go find another dupe when a rifle shot boomed. My friends had found us. A whoop of excitement followed the shot. I heard a dog bark and some too-loud laughter.

A hissing steam erupted from number one's bottom half, and its warbling motion got worse.

"Aggression!" the second yelled. "I didn't believe the probe."

139

Its transmitted fear buckled my knees, and I fell.

"I can't connect to them. Are they truly intelligent?" asked number one.

The fear caused whatever endorphins I had left to dump into my system. My entire body shook as I crawled away. My mind supplied an immediate answer, though. My friends were probably too drunk to "connect" to these buckets of jam.

"They War!" the second chimed in.

More shots followed. The second alien's glass faceplate cracked.

"It's impossible!" the first said. "No sentient clings to. . . "

The first never finished. One of the bullets must have hit something vital. It dropped like a rock and hit the ground. The giant hourglass started to fall over towards the creek. Number two caught it with its snake-like arms, and in a blink they were gone. The stab in my forehead returned, much worse than before.

I must have passed out. The next thing I knew it was quiet, and I was half-lying in the creek. I ached everywhere, like I'd run a mile and then been hit repeatedly with a baseball bat. It took a few seconds for me to realize what the quiet meant.

My friends.

I jumped up despite my bodily protest and nearly ran up the hill in the direction of where we'd parked. A sigh escaped me when I saw truck lights and heard laughter.

"Where'd ja been?" one of my friends slurred.

"Fell in the creek," I said and laughed. Laughter always made my drunk friends laugh too.

I wasn't disappointed. He laughed then bent closer and cast glances about like he was worried someone might be spying.

"Shot at some aliens tonight," he said, loud enough for everyone else to hear. My friends all whooped and a couple even shot their guns. I really had no clue how one of them hadn't shot someone or themselves yet.

I whooped along and slapped him on the back before climbing into one of the truck beds. I gave a forlorn look towards my beloved woods as the truck I was in jerked into motion. The aliens had come thinking we were like them. It looked like they were wrong.

Only one thing was certain. I had found a reason not to come back to the woods. The aliens had ruined my first rule.

Boredom is bliss.

### 

## About the Author

Jason Lairamore is a writer of science fiction, fantasy, and horror who lives in Oklahoma with his beautiful wife and their three monstrously marvelous children. He is a published finalist of the 2012 *SQ Mag* annual contest, the winner of the 2013 Planetary Stories flash fiction contest, a third place winner of the 2015 *SQ Mag* annual contest, and a Writers of the Future contest Semi-Finalist. His work is both featured and forthcoming in over 65 publications to include *Perihelion Science Fiction, Stupefying Stories*, and Third Flatiron publications, to name a few.

You can connect with Jason at https://www.facebook.com/jason.lairamore

*****~~~~~*****

## *Beyond the Borders of Boredom*

by Ville Nummenpää

In the end there were only three left. The finalists of the competition sat backstage in their shared resting facilities. They watched on the little TV, as the host spoke on the stage. None of them ever expected to get this far in the race, but then again, none of them expected much about anything anyway. As the commercials started, they knew they were up next, one after another. Tonight one of them would be officially crowned as The Most Boring Person on the Planet. It was all very exciting, only it was not really. It was rather like watching someone file a tax form in slow motion.

But the show was staggeringly popular, and no one had any idea why. The search for boring people was excruciating to observe, and yet people watched it. They watched it by the millions, and in the past two years, the show had become one of the most popular shows in history. By 2020, it had broken many records, and each year people kept coming back for more.

The three very boring persons backstage were not visibly nervous. Mark Spencer, a typist at daytime, and a devout philatelist come 6 pm, was now enjoying a lightly salted potato crisp. The crisp made a satisfying crunchy sound when chewed, pleasing Mark's adventurous side. He decided to have another.

## Cat's Breakfast

David Jackson was having a drink of water. At room temperature, the water pleased his thirst just the right way. It was satisfying, but not too refreshing. There was absolutely no fear of trigeminal headache, that brief but unpleasant sensation that is usually associated with the consumption of cold refreshments, such as soda pop or ice cream. Ice-cream headache they called it, and it seemed appropriate for David.

Jack Johnson, however, was not eating or drinking. He had eaten a solid meal ninety minutes prior, and therefore was in no immediate need of sustenance. The meal (fish fingers and mashed potatoes) had not been particularly salty, and as such had not made him particularly thirsty afterwards. Therefore he had declined all offers of snacks and beverages, even if they were being offered free of charge for the contestants. Jack Johnson passed the time by thinking of prime numbers. *Twenty-three*, he thought. *That's a prime number...*

The three men had very little to say to one another. It was not out of spite, since there was little or no competitive spirit between them. It was simply due to the fact they had very little to say in general.

There was a knock on the door, and the men pondered for a brief moment whether somebody should answer it. The knocker, however, did not wait for an answer. The door opened, and a young man with a microphone headset stated:

"Sixty seconds."

And the door closed again.

Soon, the three men were sitting on a comfortable sofa on the stage. If any of them were nervous, it most certainly didn't show. These were men who simply accepted their fate, and did not go out of their way to alter it.

The host of the show, Jeff Underplanet, was something else. Dressed in loud attire, sporting a hairdo that actually hurt your eyes, the man was the opposite of

144

boring. His appearance in the show was deliberately excessive, thus presenting a contrast between the contestants and himself. Much of the show's success, many said, could be attributed to Underplanet's energetic performance. Since the show was all about boring people, the host had to carry virtually the whole show on his shoulders. However, some argued that the boring people had *made* Jeff Underplanet, and that such a talentless twat couldn't have survived in any other circumstances. Be that as it may, Jeff Underplanet's catchphrase, "Take your time, but hurry up," had become a worldwide phenomenon. It could be heard everywhere, used by children and adults alike, whenever it could be applied to a given situation. It was even rumored that Underplanet had copyrighted the catchphrase behind the production company's back, much to their pissedoffance. True or not, no one had ever noticed that Underplanet had lifted the phrase from a Nirvana song.

Now, Underplanet's monologue was nearing the end, and Mark Spencer heard the host call out his name. He didn't react at once, but as he heard the audience chant: "Take your time, but hurry up," he ever-so-gently got off the sofa and approached the host, whose smile was not completely unlike a shark's.

"Very good Mark, good to have you back here with us," Underplanet said, smiling.

"Thank you," Mark said, and the audience simply ate it up. His appearance was mesmerizing. With two little words, he had managed to bore the living crap out of his audience. Some of them looked already uncomfortable in their seats, and many had turned to their mobile phones in hopes of something interesting.

"Last time we spoke, you told us a little about your stamp collection. Would you tell us, Mark, what is your most precious item in your collection?"

"I'd be glad to." Mark´s eyes lit up. And as he continued, something remarkable happened. It seemed his words simply lost all meaning as they exited his mouth. The audience present found it impossible to follow anything he said. The audiences at home seemed to wander off into the kitchen, or start talking about the weather with their significant others. It seemed Mark Spencer had found a new level of boredom. The host himself was clearly not listening to Mark's ramblings. In fact, had anyone paid attention, they would have seen Underplanet checking his wristwatch and yawning. Surely, nothing, or no one, could ever outbore Mark Spencer. Whoever had to follow him, was in trouble, alright. As Mark stopped talking, the audience and the host alike seemed to snap out of it. As they looked at the giant counter on stage, no one could believe their eyes. He had only spoken for twenty-five seconds. To all concerned, it had felt like hours. It had been like watching a Michael Haneke-movie slowed down 1,000 percent. The applause that followed was thunderous. It surprised even Underplanet, who, for the first time ever, seemed impressed.

Whereas the clock showed only twenty-five seconds, the reading on the Bore-o-meter stated a staggering 97%. A new world record. Despite the fact that the science behind the Bore-o-meter had often been challenged, the machine was universally accepted as an authority in the field of evaluating boredom.

"I say, that was. . . that was something else. I have never in my life heard anything so boring. Tell me Mark, what made you so boring. . . or better yet, don't!"

This made the audience chuckle and had a cathartic affect for everyone. The audience was in awe, but relieved that Mark was not allowed to speak anymore. Underplanet had once again proved his worth as a professional. At that, Mark was escorted from the stage by a beautiful lady.

"You wouldn't believe it, but it's not over yet!" Underplanet proclaimed. "We'll be right back after these messages!"

## Beyond the Borders of Boredom

The three-minute commercial break gave the remaining contestants, David Jackson and Jack Johnson, time to think. David worried whether his water bottle, which he had only half finished, was still there. In the worst-case scenario, someone might have cleaned the room, thus collecting the bottle to a dust bin. He wasn't sure if the bottle had been a refundable one, or the kind that you simply throw away. Surely, they would recycle in a place like this?

Jack Johnson looked thoughtful. *Twenty-nine*, he thought. *That's a prime number.*

During the commercial break, things were hectic. Lights were adjusted, powder was added onto the contestants' faces, ties were straightened. The audience was now restless. One could feel the excitement building. *How could it possibly get any more boring?*

The man with the speaker head-set commanded everyone in their places and counted down: five, four, three, and rushed off the stage. *He forgot two and one,* Jack Johnson thought.

Once again the theme music blasted off. It was the kind of theme you would normally hear in a sci-fi action movie, tense and dramatic. And once again, it was Underplanet's turn.

"And welcome back. I have to say, this year has been the most exciting ever. . . or should I say boring. We have seen it all this season. The try-hards, and the die-hards. We have seen impostors and true talents. In this competition, only a few have what it takes. Ladies and gentlemen, on that note, I give you. . . David Jackson!"

The applause was staggering. The audience was now hungry, thirsty—they wanted more. Their insatiable lust to be bored had reached a new level. It was almost like ancient Rome, where masses would cheer as gladiators fought until their bitter, bloody death. . . only more boring.

David Jackson seemed lost in thought, but then realized it was his turn, and got up to meet the host.

"David, just a few weeks ago, you were a filing clerk at the Bournemouth city hall. Just look at you now, you're a superstar. You have a fan club, dozens of tribute websites to your name, and 2 million followers on Twitter. How do you cope with it all? Or let me put it a different way, has the fame changed you as a person?"

"Well, basically," David said.

And it was futile beyond there. David could have said anything after that, and it wouldn't have made a difference. The audience was now fiercely bored. Even violently so, like an astronaut facing extreme g-force acceleration during liftoff. This was something no one had predicted. For a while, it even seemed the audience was getting hostile. They seemed anxious and restless. One could see something serious in their eyes. The host himself looked tense, and the viewers at home were all sighing and cursing, and making mean comments in the social media. To Underplanet, it all seemed like good television. . . for a moment. David spoke for a good two minutes, and Underplanet noticed a bit of smoke emanating from the Bore-o-meter. As he observed the audience, he could not believe his eyes. He could see members of the audience trembling in their chairs, eyes rolling, and mouths foaming. *By God, he's boring them to death.* As Underplanet realized what was happening, he made the unmistakable gesture indicating cutting of the throat, but there seemed to be no reaction. The cameramen, the director, everyone in the control room were now under David's spell, unable to think, let alone move. The Bore-o-meter was now in flames, but it hardly mattered. Underplanet was now the only one capable of saving them. There seemed to be only one way out.

"Shut up, you boring tit!" he yelled at David. David certainly was a bit surprised at this. "Why did—", he started, but was immediately cut off by Underplanet, who grabbed David's lips, and kept them shut.

"Get him out of here," he shouted at the staff. "Make sure he doesn´t speak to anyone."

It was gruesome. Ambulances were called, people were evacuated, hysterical people were consoled. Paramedics, blankets, oxygen masks, the works. It was pure, unadulterated, boring mayhem. In the aftermath, sixteen people had been bored to death, and another eighteen had to be rushed to the hospital to receive immediate entertainment. God only knows how many had lost their lives in front of the television. This had clearly not been a triumph for David. In an instant, he had lost more than a million followers on Twitter, and now there was no way he would ever be called back on stage. Technically not disqualified, but out of the competition nonetheless. The irony was, *he was too good.* A bit like a beauty contestant banned from the pageant for being too beautiful. *Oh well*, David thought. *Easy come, easy go.*

And all of this was being televised. Everyone assumed that the cameras were off (in the chaos, it was a perfectly reasonable assumption), but everything was being fed to the world live. And it was good television too. Not what people had set out to watch, but within a few minutes, the ratings had tripled. Tripled! There was absolutely no way, the show would not go on.

There, amidst the chaos, in the eye of the hurricane, sat Jack Johnson. *Thirty-seven*, he thought. *That´s a prime number.*

It took a bit longer than your ordinary commercial break, but eventually the bodies were removed, and the set was cleared. Now the show could pick up where it left off. No commercials anymore, this was all too thrilling not to be shown. The following programs for the night had been cancelled, which was bad luck for Nude Big Brother, Nude Cooking, and Naked Weddings.

Underplanet gathered himself and grabbed the microphone. This was his greatest moment. No other presenter had ever had such an audience. He knew now for certain, he was not a mere footnote in the annals of television history. He was now *the* king. With that knowledge, he spoke:

"People. . . friends. We have witnessed something today. . . something truly remarkable. Today, history was made. And in the years to come, no one can take that away from you. You were there that night, on the greatest night of television"

The applause was deafening. There was not a dry eye in the hall.

Underplanet didn't want this moment to end, but he knew what he had to do. He had to announce the next, and final, contestant. "At moments like this, one can't help but stop and think. Just what makes good television? Is it storytelling? Is it reality? Does it all come down to one brilliant presenter, or is it in the—"

"Take your time, but hurry up," somebody cried out from the audience. This brought the house down, and even if Underplanet was secretly furious, he managed to pretend a fairly passable chuckle himself.

"Very well, the audience has spoken. I bring you, last but not least, Jack Johnson!"

Jack seemed to snap out of a coma, as if surprised to be the center of attention. He got up and approached Underplanet, who now had an almost angry expression. Between clenched teeth, Underplanet whispered: "Just don't overdo it, ok?"

Jack, looking puzzled, could only nod.

"Jack," Underplanet spoke into the microphone, "you could have entered the competition years ago. We have spoken to everybody you know, and they all agree you are the most boring person that has ever lived. Why did you enter only just now?"

## Beyond the Borders of Boredom

"Hmm, I don't know what to tell you," Jack said, and the Bore-o-meter exploded. No one noticed, not even Underplanet. This was magic. Like an epiphany of the most insipid kind unveiling in front of your eyes. Like a fountain of boredom, an oasis of monotony lulling you into oblivion. As Jack spoke, time passed, skies changed, and winters followed the summers. The universe didn't care, as Jack's words echoed throughout eternity. It was only ninety seconds, but when Jack paused for a second, he noticed something. Underplanet was no longer there. The audience was gone too; all the seats were now occupied by skeletons and dust. This looked a bit odd to him.

Behind the curtain, he heard footsteps approaching, and the loneliest applause ever made by a human.

"Well, well, bravo," the voice said. "Oh, how I have waited for this moment. And now that you finally shut up, I don't know what to say."

It was Underplanet. Or something that resembled him in a ghastly way.

"You just had to take all the glory, didn't you? You had to overdo everyone and everything."

Jack wanted to reply, but Underplanet didn't let him.

"Shh, please don't speak, you have done enough damage as it is. You see, your monologue to you was only ninety seconds long, but to the rest of the world, it took several millenniums. Every second you speak means ten seconds to the rest of us. That means you age ten times slower than normal people. When you speak in public, your boredom is multiplied by the sheer count of people watching. In this case, it was billions. Your general boredom being multiplied by billions. . . Go on, do the math."

As a mathematician, Jack understood this. It all made sense, the boringness of his monologue had been multiplied exponentially. Ninety seconds multiplied by ten, multiplied by billions. . .

## Cat's Breakfast

"As you spoke, time stood still, and the world died. Entire galaxies were wiped out by your boredom. How come I'm alive then, you ask? You see, your boring presence creates a unique time bubble in your very vicinity. Your tedious voice and presence kept me alive and somewhat preserved during all of those years. You can't imagine how it felt looking at that giant clock. When each turning of the second took hundreds of years. But now, as you finally shut up, I'm free at last. Thank you. Oh, and by the way, congratulations. You won. You truly are the most boring person in the universe."

As Underplanet clapped his hands together, his hands turned to dust. Just like that, the whole man reduced into a pile of dust in front of Jack's eyes. He looked around and realized the world he had known was long gone. Everything and everyone had ceased to exist ages ago. To anyone, this would be a lot to take in. But Jack Johnson was no ordinary man.

*Sixty-seven*, he thought. *That's a prime number...*

### ###

**About the Author**

Ville Nummenpää is an author, screenwriter, and playwright. He has one official credit to his name, for the TV show Kimmo (2012–). He just won a prestigious stage play competition, and the play in question will premiere in 2018. There is also a short movie in the works, and a serious possibility of getting a TV show produced based on his own concept. He is a musician as well, and hopes to score and/or write songs and themes for his own works.

Ville resides in Finland.

*****~~~~~*****

# Snakes and Ladders

by Rekha Valliappan

*"If you want a picture of the future, imagine a boot stamping on a human face—for ever."* –George Orwell, **1984**

Sunlight filters through the blinds casting a bright orange mist onto my daybed and my mind as I struggle to open my eyes. I button my blouse and navy blue coat, tossed carelessly onto the floor. Four margaritas too many in the night before. Time to wake up.

My work badge sealed in plastic laminate dangles from my coat collar.

Under my photo are the letters in bold print : KTC-O34. Operative at the state-sanctioned Karma Test Center. I no longer have a name. I am a number. I stare at myself. Shoulder length chestnut brown hair. A neat oval face. I could be anyone. I do not recognize my face any more.

In two hours my day will start as it always does on the Snakes and Ladders Floor. The final test center in diagnostics. Very few who arrive here at this Level will make it out alive.

When I was six I used to have nightmares that I was being swallowed alive by a snake. And I would cry and cry each time to play the snakes and ladder board game.

Filled with black and red and green slithery shapes. It held nothing more than a handful of saffron yellow ladders and my mother by my side to help assuage the fear. The Ladders to Salvation she had called them then. How much more real now had those nightmares become. *O Mamma, if only you could see.*

My first appointment today turns out to be a young techie. I have been getting several in this category of late. At twenty-two years he believes he has a future in stock trading. I remind him there is no more global economy left. The financial system is collapsed. Dead. He tells me he is good for an eighteen hour shift and that massive increases of the juice are needed to get the economy growing again. It has to get done.

"Boring business," I tell him, "it's what drove us to this state in the first place."

"No kidding. Are you serious?" he jokes. "With gold and oil for the taking? Where is your animal spirit?"

He is smooth talking and peddles his wares well, hammering home his point, window dressing his world. I show little interest, trained in my perspectives. He hands me his business card. They all do, searching for that spark. Looking for that atom which will rewind the clock. Snap all back into the lost dream. At his age he can hold out hope. At mine frankly, I can't.

I scan him on Game-On, the computer algorithms which will determine whether he goes or stays. I see the black wriggling shapes staining his lean, muscled torso like caterpillar grubs forming out of the larvae. It fills the screen. He has a year, this one. The data is recorded. No. 3,259,642.

I walk him to the far end of the examination floor. He is my charge to the very end till I see him out the doors. There are only two. The building is sealed. I usher him to the massive stainless steel door with the speckled head of a hooded cobra. The young techie is still talking animatedly, "Give me a chance," he pleads. The doors

154

split open on the twin fork of the flicking tongue protruding. The cobra looks grotesque rent into two. I look away. This young man has gone quietly. I am thankful. Some do not. He has had to pay eighty thousand dollars or its equivalent for the tests. They mostly do in marble, gold and diamonds. His life's stash. Occasionally I have had to summon the Special Forces. Helmeted armed guys who brutally man the perimeters.

It is almost time for my noon appointment. So I neaten the creases of my pencil line navy blue skirt, grab my handbag and trundle along past the water fountains and the espresso coffee machines to the cafeteria. I must hurry. At this hour it is crowded. I eat light. Daily fare is bread and cheese. Today is special. It is Victory Day. My eggs benedict casserole takes awhile in coming. It has an extra topping of tomatoes and mushrooms, exactly the way I like it. In fifteen minutes I am done.

I open my handbag and pull out my porcelain cowry shell handing it to the cashier to format. My entire bio-data is contained in the folds of this little sea shell. Everyone has one. Standard currency is the cowry. Without the shell one may as well not exist.

Sometimes in my sleep I dream of a large conch shell. It is when I miss my mother the most. Here we are not permitted to miss anyone. I hold it to my ears. In an instant I hear the soothing sounds of the oceans and waves. I see the sparkle of streams and brooks. I feel the sighing of summer breezes and winds rustling through the trees. I taste the meadows brimming with flowers. My extinct world—it lulls me into a dreamless sleep, from which I never want to awake.

My midday appointment is several minutes late. I am not surprised. A middle aged woman of substance, she makes her appearance bejeweled, lacquered, perfumed and henna dyed. She is a repeat client and we have had these conversations on music, dancing and partying before. She launches into a broadside on the benefits of karaoke singing for the lungs and the soul. She enumerates on the joys that it spreads, particularly among old folk. She strongly advocates for its proliferation, its return, on the scale it occupied before the collapse of the world order. I am appalled. This woman walks lost alleys. There are no songs to sing.

"But there are no old folk left," I remind, not unkindly.

She blinks rapidly, as if doused by a bucket of cold water. It works I have found out to be blunt.

"We must strive," she says seething awkwardly at my ignorance, her face flushing a deep purple as she catches her breath. "It is virtue vs. vice. Don't you know this is our karma? The path of good is rewarded in the afterlife. Otherwise we are born again to inherit the lower life forms."

"That serious, eh? Let me get you some water" I gently suggest, seating her on the tan leather couch and busying myself with a paper cup of drinking water. The smile has left her face. She pulls out a *Kleenex,* dabbing at her smudged eyes.

"I want to do good," she says.

"It is what you did not do when you should have done, that counts," I reply.

"What do you mean?"

"Too late now. All you did was waste precious days singing and dancing. When the rot and decay was spreading, you cocooned yourself in your lovely little musical world, and did nothing but sing. We could have turned the political tide then."

The woman blows her nose noisily into more tissues.

The scan complete, I enter the data into the Portfolio. I present her the Bill. Fifty thousand dollars. Which she has not cleared from her last visit. I re-read her the terms of our contract. The woman is in a daze.

I slowly explain the moral lessons to be learned by humankind, contained in Karma. How control is lost once fate is set into motion. It underscores the predictable side of our history. Making attainment of *Moksha* impossible. How for people to change course will require an awakening, a tricky different way of thinking. In our current ignorance, free will is nonexistent. The collapse of the world has seen to that. We have been led to our own bondage. But we deserve more.

The woman falls silent. Then I lead her to the massive doors. She walks purposefully towards the doors marked with the giant yellow ladders. I take her gently by the elbows and steer her towards the Cobra Door.

In the two years that I have serviced this Floor I have never seen the Ladders Door open. The quantum of probability is too high to beat. Although in a numbers sum game it is possible, on a ratio of a trillion to one I have estimated, taking the idea from the reams of zeroes that flow out of the charts.

For a second she hesitates. "But I can sing very well," she begs. She has not heard a word I have been saying.

"Yes Ma'am," I reply.

Too bad, she will be dead too, by the year's end.

…

My last appointment for the day is Beamer Four, the Chief of the ruling class. I am nervous. He runs the rubble that our land has been reduced to when the biological program struck in counter retaliation to the nuclear missile launched between the western and eastern hemispheres at the Prime Meridien. The chemical weapons by the same token completed the rest.

Tactically the goal on all sides was secured. Mass destruction. Easy wins by all who took on the world. Strategically it turned more complicated, with a change for the worst. But we do not speak of these things. The flagrance. Not even tacitly. Natural intelligence among us has been permanently dwarfed, to equal the rest.

Only one out of five Americans has survived the holocaust. Survivors of the new dystopia. The fallout in other parts of the world was considered to be far worse, more audacious. In some regions entire civilizations and cultures have been decimated. With satellite systems destroyed, infrastructure and communications lost none of this can be accurately ascertained. Not for another few years at the very least. It no longer matters.

What is left in America is in the hands of Beamers Four, a motley group of individuals in leadership positions of War, Finance and Health, whom none have seen. With the exception of the Chief, a Rasputin-like figure— elderly, gaunt, and tall with penetrating blue eyes and a wild beard.

Beamers Four have mandated that all survivors be assigned a handicap on the basis of current divisions. The Chief refuses to discuss the attack on our homeland, or the counter-attack, or the diametrics of the status quo, or the flawed choices made which led to death and mortality. None may question. I have tried.

Old peace treaties that were once broken, extreme financial entanglements, banned substance dumps, green greed strategies, manifestos of primordial jungles are housed on Constitutional Archipelago which no one may access without clearance. I glance at his grim looking security guards milling around. A wild bunch of misfits. Like a muster roll of disparaged parts lacking cohesion. They do not fit in here.

"'What is to be will be, and no prayers of ours can arrest the decree,' said the wise Abraham Lincoln once long ago," ruminates Beamer Four. He could be hallucinating. He would be my first client at such an advanced stage.

The deluge of images on the display screen warps for a good ten seconds before resetting into normalcy. The matrix of colored squares is blinding. It gives me whiplash. He is far gone. I can clearly see the black writhing snakes, moving shapes pushing up against his parchment-like skin, crawling into every artery and vein, capillary and gut. Each starkly contorted motion stands out like darkened spreading roots. I wince.

"The virus is not yet fully contained," I inform him, "It will last many generations. Death is not easy. It is also not swift."

A painful smile splits his face, displaying yellowed teeth. He does not wear caps. Security mandates on this Floor that only the Ladders Door display bumblebee yellow. The walk to the doors is efficiently executed. The misery in my face reflects my agony. I glance around at my Snakes and Ladders work Floor. It is what I have traded freedom for. This grey perpetuity of a sheltered existence. It all seems so long ago. I have no other view.

We reach the Snake Door without incident. The Chief turns around to shake my hand one last time in farewell. Then as I watch stunned three things simultaneously happen in lightning sequence.

A loud siren rings announcing the Game-On. The Chief reaches the Ladders Door speedily carried by his hefty guards. It partially starts to pop open. Slamming shut with a loud *zap* in the very instant traces of a yellow ooze stain the floor. This has never happened before. I collapse to the floor. Special Forces arrive post-haste gunning down the Chief's security detail.

Beamer Four is swiftly hustled out the Cobra Door. It is over.

Trembling with reaction I rush to my Director's cubicle. I explain to her all that just occurred, providing details. With a few clicks she pulls up the mainframe. Then she switches to Karma Test Center's web page listing out objectives and our mission statement. Calmly she has me go over it with her. "Beating the system will only lead to failure. We are not designed that way," she explains, by way of the only comment she will make of Beamer Four's futile attempt to rush the yellow Ladders Door. I wish the Chief could have survived. I do not know who will take his place. It will follow a process called a decapitation strike. The solution will rest on the chess board.

The Director commends my good work and my aptitude in keeping us in the profits business. "He makes a good client," she exults with a smile, "Five hundred thousand dollars is his latest bill."

I thank her for her kind words. But I am far from comfortable. Inside me I ache in agony at what I can see. It bothers me.

Somewhere out there I tell myself, there have to be others like me. Or are there?

### ###

## About the Author

Rekha Valliappan blogs, writes, and lives in New York. She has taught college-level English Literature and 'A' Levels Law. Much of her time is spent in community service. She now devotes her time to her first love—fiction-writing. Her works are published or forthcoming in *Intellectual Refuge, Friday Flash Fiction, Scarlet Leaf Review, Indiana Voice Journal,* and *Boston Accent Lit,* which adjudged her the 2nd prize winner in their Annual Short Story Contest. She was born and raised in Bombay and looks to Asia for inspiration.

Blog: https://silicasun.wordpress.com
Facebook: https://www.facebook.com/rekhavalliappan
Twitter: https://www.twitter.com/silicasun

*****~~~~~*****

## Drop Dead Date

by August Marion

Irwin didn't notice the blood on his hand until he was reaching for the door handle. He was holding a coffee cup and a notebook in his other hand, so he bent down, and opened the door with his elbow. In the conference room, he found Hester seated at the long table along with a man in a cheap, black suit that he didn't recognize. The room was somewhat dim, because Hester always liked to keep the blinds closed on the office's west-facing windows. She thought having the employees looking at the imminent downfall of human civilization all day long wasn't good for morale, which Irwin thought was probably true.

He closed the door, and placed his coffee mug and notebook on a small table in the corner. He pulled his handkerchief from his pocket, and began scrubbing the blood from his hand.

"Are you hurt?" Hester asked.

"No, but Kip Stevens lost most of her left arm bringing the latest test results here. We're lucky she made it at all. The robots incinerated the entire test facility with some kind of new plasma beam weapon."

"I hope Kip's going to be alright." Hester said with genuine concern.

"I think she will. Her injuries are covered by our insurance policy, and she has plenty of sick days saved up."

"I'll purchase a get-well card, and have everyone sign it," Hester said, writing a reminder on her tablet. She motioned to the man in the suit. "This is Agent Milligan from the Department of Defense—"

"Mr. Hernandez, I presume?" Milligan interjected brusquely as he stood up.

"Yes," Irwin answered. "Pleased to meet you."

"I need to speak with you alone."

"As I already told you," Hester said, a bit of edge creeping into her voice, "company regulations state that a human resources representative must be present for all meetings dealing with employee conduct issues that result in, or may result in, disciplinary action."

Irwin looked from her to Milligan, shrugged, and took a seat at the table.

"Mr. Hernandez, this is a matter of national security," Milligan said, his face as firm as a marble tombstone.

"Call me Irwin."

Milligan sighed. "Irwin, we have reason to believe one of your employees might be working for the robots."

"That can't be," Irwin said with a laugh as he stuffed his handkerchief back in his pocket.

"I'm afraid so," Milligan said. "I just need to interview the suspect—"

"Suspect?" Irwin interrupted. "You make it sound like we have some potential criminal working here."

"Who is this person that is allegedly a suspect?" Hester asked.

"It's allegedly a person, not allegedly a suspect." Milligan explained.

Irwin tried to parse Milligan's response, then said, "Whatever the case, what's the employee's name?"

Milligan looked around as if scanning the room for bugs. He leaned in close, narrowed his eyes, and in a low voice said, "Kingston Steele is a robot."

Irwin rolled his eyes, and leaned back in his chair. "Oh, that's ridiculous."

"That's for sure." Hester added with a laugh. "Kingston brings in doughnuts every Friday and has the highest employee evals in the entire division. That hardly seems like robot behavior."

"He's working to annihilate the human race," Milligan stated, growing somewhat vexed.

"Sure he is," Irwin said, dismissively. "Speaking of Kingston, he fixed the coffee maker this morning."

"There is nothing that man can't do," Hester said under her breath.

"Would you like a cup?" Irwin asked.

"I think I'd rather just get to business," Milligan said, grinding his teeth until they nearly screamed.

"Agent Milligan," Irwin said, "I'm sorry if I seem dismissive, it's just that we have a drop dead date approaching, and I simply don't see how we're going to make it without Kingston. He's one of our most valuable employees."

"I appreciate that, but you can't have a robot working here. You're a defense contractor. Why would you want a robot anywhere near you, anyway? Did you see what those mechanical beasts did to Tokyo?"

"Maybe I'm not making myself clear," Irwin said. He stood, walked to the window, and pulled the blinds open, which revealed a panoramic view of the waterfront.

The harbor was in flames. It had been burning since last Wednesday. A platoon of forty-foot-high walking death machines were stomping their way east through the industrial district, fighting off a flurry of rockets being launched at them from the marines dug into Beacon Hill on the other side of the interstate. Downtown, what was left of the Columbia Tower collapsed in a cloud of smoke and rubble, its foundation no doubt undermined by the same squadron of diggers that the Hundred and First Airborne had fought to a standstill in the subway.

Irwin pointed to a group of robots floating in the middle of the bay near the stern of an aircraft carrier that was still visible above the blackened water. They looked like the spawn of mechatronic Satan. "This is no normal deadline that we can just let slip," he said. "If that flotilla makes landfall, we're going to have a heck of a time. The logistics department says we have about two weeks before that happens, which only gives us eight days to finish the microwave defense matrix certification paperwork. And let me remind you, we have Labor Day coming up, so that's not going to make things any easier. I don't think now is a good time for personnel changes."

"I understand your concerns," Milligan said. "I'm sure we can get a replacement in here."

"It would take two weeks at least to get someone new up to speed," Irwin responded.

"And we like to reserve a full day for new employee indoc," Hester added.

"I think logistics is being a little pessimistic," Milligan said. "Last night, the Third Armored Division reinforced the eastern—"

A blinding white light blotted out half of downtown. When it subsided, they saw that several blocks near the commercial district had been replaced by a fiery mushroom cloud that rose frightfully toward the heavens.

They watched the cloud for a few seconds before Milligan said, "Well, the Fourth Field Artillery should be in place by tomorrow morning, so we probably didn't need the Third Division anyway."

Irwin let the blinds fall back, and took his seat again. "We're doing a MIL-SPEC project here. If we can't finish the paperwork, it'll never get approved."

"It doesn't matter," Milligan said, his voice raising. "The fact is, you can't have a robot working here, and that's final!"

There was a tense silence.

"Well, I'll have to document this," Hester said grudgingly. "Agent Milligan, why do you suspect Kingston might be a robot?"

"We've been monitoring his communications. He spends a lot of time on various social media platforms doing reconnaissance and intelligence gathering. We think he's trying to keep up with what humans are doing, and how they interact with each other, so he can better pass himself off as a member of our society."

"You could say the same thing about why I go on social media," Irwin said.

"Yeah," Hester agreed. "If you want us to take disciplinary action, we need more to go on. Are these work computers he's using? Maybe if they're work computers we could give him a written warning, but unless he's looking at pornography, or something, I just can't see that being a fireable offense."

"Have you ever seen him arrive in the morning, or leave at night?" Milligan asked.

Irwin thought for a moment. "He's very dedicated."

"And there's nothing wrong with that," Hester added.

"He hasn't left the building since you hired him fourteen months ago," Milligan said. "Nobody is that dedicated."

"I did see him at the company Christmas party," Irwin said.

"Holiday party," Hester corrected.

"Of course, holiday party, sorry. Why don't we just invite him in? I'm sure once you meet him, you'll see how silly this all is." Irwin pulled out his phone, and started typing on it. "I think he's at lunch. I'll send him a text and tell him to stop by when he's done."

"Alright, fine." Milligan stood. "I'm going to go get my gun back."

"What?" Irwin asked. "Gun?"

"I made him check it with reception," Hester said. "We have a strict no-weapons policy on campus."

"And for good reason too," Irwin said, as he typed on his phone.

"I'm not going to confront that thing completely unarmed."

"I'm not going to let you engage in a discussion with one of our employees if you're just looking for a fight," Hester said. "You should always give the other side the benefit of the doubt."

"I can't see this being very productive otherwise," Irwin agreed. "I'm sure we can sort this out if we all just keep our heads."

Milligan marched over to Irwin, and leaned over him menacingly. "You notice I don't have a partner? Last week we uncovered a robot at the Pentagon." Milligan's face flushed like a forest fire, the veins in his neck bulged, and his mouth twisted into a sneer. "They had to clean my partner up with a mop and bucket!"

The door opened, and Kingston stepped into the conference room carrying a brown paper bag.

Milligan instinctively reached for his gun, which wasn't there. He stepped back, slack-jawed. He scanned the room for another exit, and found none.

"What's up?" Kingston asked amiably.

"What's in the bag?" Milligan demanded loudly as he stumbled back into a chair, and nearly lost his footing.

"My lunch," Kingston answered simply.

"Let's everyone just sit down and take it easy," Irwin said soothingly. "Have a seat, Kingston, we're just having a conversation, and we thought you should be involved."

"You're not in trouble," Hester added. "We're just talking."

"Where did you go for lunch?" Irwin asked.

"The office supply closet," Kingston answered.

Milligan lowered himself into the chair he had stumbled over, his eyes focused like lasers on Kingston.

"Thanks for coming so quick," Irwin said. "You didn't have to interrupt your lunch."

"It's no problem," Kingston replied.

"Well, you can feel free to eat while we talk," Irwin said.

Kingston pulled out the chair next to Milligan.

Milligan sprang to his feet, and scurried like a frightened cockroach around to the other side of the table. He and Kingston eyed each other, as they both eased themselves into their respective seats.

"Is this about the defense matrix?" Kingston asked. "I discovered a way to meet the matrix power budget. I had to solve the three-body problem for the general case to figure it out, which might be useful on other projects. Should I enter the solution as a ticket in the bug database, or do you want to start a separate database for applied mathematics breakthroughs?"

"I think the bug database is probably as good a place as any," Irwin said. "Just mark it however you marked that Navy Strokes—"

"Navier-Stokes existence and smoothness solution," Kingston corrected.

"Right," Irwin continued, "Just mark it in the same way as that, so we don't miss it at next week's triage meeting."

"Kingston," Hester said, "Why we called you here is. . . " She smiled and fidgited. "It's silly, but this gentleman is Agent Milligan with the Department of Defense, and for some reason he was given the impression that you might be a robot."

"That's ridiculous." Kingston laughed and reached into his bag. He fished out a double-A battery and popped it in his mouth.

"Of course, it is," Hester said. "Now, no one can compel you to speak about these matters, but if you would like to—"

"Are you people blind?" Milligan shouted. "Look at what he's eating!"

Kingston froze, a second battery poised in front of his mouth.

The other three stared at him silently.

Kingston swallowed hard, and put on a broad grin.

"Well, people have all kinds of strange diets," Irwin said. "Last year, I went on a juice cleanse. I didn't have anything but juice for days."

Milligan pounded the table and stuck his finger in Kingston's face. "Confess, you mechanical bastard!" he screamed.

"That's not productive," Hester chided.

Kingston put the battery back in the bag, and put the bag on the table. He looked around and said, "We're not all bad people, you know."

"You're not people at all!" Milligan yelled as he jumped to his feet. He started screaming into his cuff. "Avenging Eagle, this is the worm, I need air support!"

"You're a robot?" Irwin asked.

"Don't answer that, Kingston," Hester said. "What you do on your own time is your own business. We have very strong anti-discrimination laws in this state."

"Does that apply to robots?" Irwin asked.

"I don't see why not," Hester said. "He's a repressed minority."

"Are you repressed?" Irwin asked, truly concerned. "I've always said I have an open-door policy about these sorts of things. I'm not repressing you, am I?"

"You don't have to answer that, Kingston," Hester said.

Milligan backed into a corner, still shouting for a strike.

"Why are you yelling at your wrist?" Irwin asked, his voice growing tense. "We're trying to have a meeting here."

"I have a lot of vacation saved up," Kingston said. "Maybe I could just take some time off."

"Sure, that's a great idea," Irwin said. "Can you wait until the holidays, though?"

The conversation was suddenly blotted out by the howling roar of a jet engine. Irwin walked to the window. He threw the blinds open, and revealed an aggressive, black military aircraft hovering outside.

"Take the shot!" Milligan yelled into his cuff. "Take the shot!"

Irwin stared straight into the pilot's face.

The pilot narrowed his eyes.

Irwin shook his head, his mouth hanging open.

Milligan sprang at Irwin like a mongoose at a cobra, and tackled him to the floor.

The conference room exploded with thunderous noise as the jet's twin, thirty-millimeter autocannons erupted. The glass in the window was shattered into thousands of tiny shards, as was the conference table, all the chairs, the back wall, all the cubicles, desks, and computers in the test division, the windows on the far side of the building, and everything on the tenth floor of the insurance company headquarters next door.

Kingston's clothes were shredded to dust, along with his synthetic skin. His gleaming silver exoskeleton was so lit up by the onslaught of uranium-jacketed violence that he looked to be wrapped in a blanket of fireworks. He stumbled back, steadied himself, then sprinted headlong into the angry hail of bullets. He leapt out the window, and latched onto the aircraft's wing. With one hand, he reached down, and grabbed one of the autocannons. The cannon exploded in his grip. The jet started to spin out of control.

Irwin, Hester, and Milligan slowly regained their feet. They watched the jet fly off with Kingston still attached. It weaved erratically as it headed out of sight over the hellscape that used to be downtown, leaving a thick trail of smoke in its wake.

"Well, that could have been handled better," Hester said, dusting off her blazer. She looked back at the wreckage of the office. "Good thing it's lunch."

"You're lucky we're not all dead." Milligan said.

"I'll say," Irwin agreed.

The commercial district downtown was consumed by a tower of flame, as the robotic flotilla crept ever closer.

"No way we're going to make the drop dead date now," Irwin stated. He looked back into the office, and saw his coffee cup still sitting obediently on the little table where he had left it. He reached down, picked it up, and took a sip. "Holy shit!" he exclaimed. "Oh, uh. . . Sorry, Hester, that was unprofessional."

"It's OK. It's been a stressful day for all of us," Hester said.

Irwin took another sip. "Wow! This is probably the best coffee I've ever had in my life." He sighed heavily and shook his head. "I'm really going to miss having Kingston in the office."

### ###

## About the Author

August lives the Pacific Northwest where he works in the tech industry and writes stories that are often supposed to be funny.

*****~~~~*****

## *Monkeyline*

by Jonathan Shipley

*Nothing like watching bloodthirsty viciousness disguised as a sporting event,* I thought. I swiveled my eyestalks to follow another player go spinning across the stadium floor, knocked twenty yards by a mighty tail whack from the opposition. Of course, what do you expect from voraciraptors except bloodthirsty viciousness—or am I indulging in shallow stereotypes again? *No,* I decided. *Got it right the first time.*

As an amphib, I have to plead a certain bias on the subject of raptors. Zaradon in its imperial heyday nearly wiped out my species—something about amphibians being inferior to overclawed sauroids. Sure, that was a couple thousand years ago, and Zaradon, that oh-so-great raptor star-empire, eventually crumpled under the weight of its own arrogance, but racial memory lives on.

But it wasn't old memories that brought me here tonight, or even raptor-centric tailball. It was plain ol' drugs. The Ministry asked me to snoop around and report back on unethical usage. Actually, they didn't ask, they hired me so they could bypass law enforcement, which was notoriously corrupt. The whole setup smelled a lot like inter-office power jockeying, but *supposedly* it was about the drugs. So here I was, watching the biggest tailball game of the season, because of a tip that someone or someones were going to be very publicly zonked. . .

171

besides the players, I mean. One expected the teams to be hyped on painkillers. How else could the game plunge brutally on? No, this was something else—something connected with something the Ministry wasn't telling me.

I wasn't seeing anything in the stands except frenzied spectators cheering on the Dewclaws, the local team of adored champions. The Dewclaws were one of two things Zjhaccœse was famous for, the other being Zjhaccœse University—the Zee. Ironic that those two claims to fame were at opposite ends of the spectrum. Depressing that Zjhaccœse didn't have much to offer in between. Like the government. Half of it was corrupt, and the other half was scared of the power cartels. Hence the reason the Ministry was reduced to working through a private PI.

But I wasn't seeing anything tonight, nor likely to. There was just too much going on in the stadium. One whole section was filled with students from the Zee, obviously students because of the mix of species. Zjhaccœse in general tends toward a conservative lizard population with a little of this and little of that thrown in. But the Zee is a real crazy-quilt of species with lizards not predominating. On any other world that might be an open conflict, but here opposition is reduced to subtle, passive-aggressive strategies, because the university Regents can do whatever they damn well please. The latest wrinkle in their admissions policy was inviting Terrans to apply. It was a big wrinkle, because, call them Terrans or humans or simioids or whatever, it still boiled down to "monkeys" in the popular vernacular, and often that was phrased as "dumb monkeys." And yes, there was a group of them up in the stands right now, watching the game and yelling for the Dewclaws.

Halftime rolled around, and the student section became very active. It looked a lot like some of them were getting up to. . . well, strike me dumb. A bunch of the Terrans were actually going to do a monkeyline on the court.

### Monkeyline

This was all sorts of wrong. A smart monkey would keep a low profile at a highly lizard event like this, not get up in front of everybody and perform group gyrations. It wasn't that they weren't well received—the crowd was hooting and hissing like crazy. But it was a derisive hooting, not at all friendly, to ears that can hear the difference, and there were reasons on top of reasons for that.

A lot of locals thought the Zee was making a mistake letting in monkeys in the first place, and one did have to wonder what the Regents were thinking. I mean, "dumb monkeys" at a prestigious, three-thousand-year-old university?

So there was that. Then there was anatomy. Monkeys were a conspicuously untailed species, and to see them hyped on tailball really made you wonder. Some saw it as an admission of their own anatomical inadequacy. Of course, that was a lizard interpretation, not a monkey one, but it did explain why a largely lizard audience enjoyed a good monkeyline at these games. It was always a big snicker when any monkeyline performed. Parading around tailless—I mean, really making a show of it like these students—was almost borderline obscene in a society where tails equaled sex and power.

It was strange. Those students had to know how idiotic they looked prancing around out there, yet they just kept on kicking and waving and gyrating. I thought about Loo—Lucas Armbrewster for those that can cope with funny names. He'd done legwork for me once last summer, said he wanted to do more, then disappeared when school started. The point is, any little reference to "dumb moneys" and he was spitting fire that his species was nothing like the stereotype. If he ever saw anything like this monkeyline. . .

My eyes widened to saucers as my gaze caught on the monkey at the far end of the line. Yup, Loo. Dancing and prancing as dumb as the rest. Either he'd had a major shift in attitude, or he was completely clueless about what he looked like at the moment. As the routine came to a hip-grinding close, I moved down to intercept the Terrans on the way back to their seats.

"Loo!" I called. "Lucas!"

He turned with a goofy grin. "Hey, Ssssss."

"Syzz," I corrected. He never could pronounce my name right. At least I got halfway close with his. "What are you doing in this monkeyline?"

"Dance line, man," he grinned. "Did you see us? Cool moves, huh? Bet saurians can't move like that."

*Nor would they ever want to*, I thought. "It doesn't exactly present mammalians at their best," I ventured.

"Yeah, whatever, man. You just don't know a good cheer routine when you see it. We're going to do it again after the game. Really cut loose with some wild moves."

This wasn't right. This wasn't at all the argumentative, uptight Loo I remembered. I grabbed his jacket to bring his face down level with mine. Goofy grin, dilated eyes—no, this wasn't right at all. This kid was zonked.

My glance cut over to the other monkeys from the line. Even up close, I was unsure about mammalian gendering of the group. In matching outfits, they all looked pretty much the same. And all zonked to varying degrees. I turned my gaze back to Loo. "How did you get into this dance business?"

"Unhand him, phib!" A snakish Skal—small arms, long curling body—squeezed himself between Loo and me and looked at me with cold, predatory eyes. "The monkeyline doesn't give interviews. But feel free to shoot all the vid you want of their line routine. It's coming up again at the end of the game." He curled himself around Loo and pulled him away.

What the—a Skal here on Zjhaccœse? And from the striping, he looked to be Tdhjke Clan, which was even more ominous. There are no good Skal, but some are worse than others. And this same Skal was here managing a group of monkeys? It hadn't been that many years since Skal slavers were raiding Terrano colonies for slave fodder. Now they were zonking their former slaves mindless? This wouldn't end well. Truthfully, I really hated Skal because they had once slaved amphibs as well as monkeys. They were a nasty business, beginning to end.

I mulled the situation. There had to be an angle here where the Skal benefited from publicly discrediting the Terran students. . . and try as I might, I could only come up with said students being somehow sucked into gray market slave trade, which the Tdhjke Clan was rumored to run. Circumventing the Ban would need the backing of powerful local people. However, for such public zonking to be happening, the Skal had to already be in bed with law enforcement and probably had connections with the arch-conservative Zjhaccœse-for-the-lizards groups as well. Groups that never wanted Terrans here in the first place. What was absolutely crystal was that no one was going to care about zonked monkeys making public fools of themselves until it was too late. I was part of a small minority that would even see the problem. Me and the Ministry, apparently.

I was beginning to understand the political complications. The Ministry absolutely could not act officially without alienating factions it couldn't afford to alienate. So it sent me in to fix the situation unofficially, even though a private investigator can't afford powerful enemies either. But here's the thing—there's power and there's Power. I had an idea.

As the second half started up with a stampede of raptors across the court, I stepped over and snagged Loo from his seat while his snakemaster was looking elsewhere. He just smiled his goofy, zonked smile and followed me without a murmur. But it was never that easy.

"Hop off, you tailless slime!" the Skal hissed, slithering over. "That monkey stays here with the line." For emphasis, he opened his mouth to display a nasty set of pointed teeth. Skal were also notorious carnivores.

"Nope," I said as calmly as I could in the face of an angry, carnivorous snake. I cast a quick eye at the action below heading into the near quadrant of the court. The referee was almost directly below me. "He's coming with me," I said. "Unless you have something like a managerial contract on file."

The Skal hissed and brought his mouth threateningly close. "You forget I'm all tail. If you think—"

Below, a Dewclaw missed the ball and slammed an opponent instead. I clicked my personal com to wide broadcast mode. "Scazzish foul!" I boomed.

The referee looked around, beak snapping in disapproval, but his reaction was swallowed up by the wholesale rush of enraged Dewclaws in his direction. A scazzish foul was never popular. He took one look and spread his wings for the safety of the ceiling. There was a reason referees were always avians. Now the whole crowd was on its feet, bellowing disapproval, turning the stands into chaos all around us.

I didn't wait—I grabbed Loo and navigated through the angry crowd while the Skal was distracted. We were out the stadium door while the mess was still being cleared up. Miscalls could make tailball even bloodier than usual, so they added spice to the game. But I was thankful the referee had made it clear this time.

"Rooka root first, I think," I told Loo as I pulled him down the street. "Something to jumpstart your currently dormant brain."

"Cool," he grinned, then lapsed back into numb silence.

I found a sidewalk cafe that served monkeys if they sat outside and proceeded to pour root liquor into him. The heavy acid content was good to offset zonking, if you could stand the bitterness of the taste. As he drank, I pulled up the local com network and started sending out messages.

After about four cups, Loo started looking uncomfortable. "What is this stuff?" he finally grumbled. "And where am I?"

"Do you remember the game?"

"A little. . . I remember planning to go to the game. . . then it gets fuzzy."

"The monkeyline?" I prompted.

He winced. "Did I actually do that? Someone told me I should, but I know zero about cheerleading." He groaned and sank his head into the heels of his hands. "I'm going to be the laughingstock around campus tomorrow."

"Probably not," I shrugged. "A lot can happen before tomorrow. You do remember me, right?"

He nodded. "Yeah, Ssss."

"Syzz," I corrected wearily.

"I copped some info for you last summer."

"Exactly. I am now going to take you to my office."

"Huh? No, just get me back to the dorm—" he began.

I wiggled my eyestalks. "Of course, you could simply stand up and start your long walk back to the Zee. That way, I believe"—I pointed toward a distant tower. "Too bad you don't have a transport pass on you—but you probably left all those details to your ophidian handler."

Loo digested this with a tight expression. "OK, we go to your office, but then you get me back to the dorm in the morning. Deal?"

I nodded and led the way down the street, Loo trailing unhappily behind me. If he thought he was having a bad night, wait until he saw the alternative.

The zonk-and-rooka-root cocktail took their toll. When we reached my office, Luke basically curled up in the corner and faded. When he was snoring loudly, I tapped open the com network again to post more concerns about a certain Skal using a Dewclaws game to showcase zonked Zee monkeys. The point there was the Dewclaws connection. To most locals, zonking monkeys was no big deal. But bringing the Dewclaws and tailball into it was flat-out bad taste and would rile up the hard-core tailball crowd who would hate to see their brand tainted.

Within minutes, I noted other posts reporting additional info on the situation. A lot of complaints about the tastelessness of the monkeyline. Within an hour, I started seeing results. The Regents of Zjhaccœse University decided that the display was an embarrassment to the institution and took action. Disciplinary warnings for unseemly public conduct were posted for a whole list of monkeys. That was a big deal in student terms, but probably nothing compared with what was occurring behind the scenes. I predicted there would be no more student monkeylines in my lifetime.

When Loo woke up the next morning, I shared those results with him. He scanned the list with tight-lipped intensity. "What about me?" he finally asked. There had been no Lucas Armbrewster posted.

"You were already out of the stadium when the Regents started reviewing the situation," I shrugged. "You're clear."

He gave a sigh of relief, then frowned. "Wait a minute—you had to know something was going down. If you hadn't taken me away last night, I'd be under disciplinary warning, too."

"Chock it up to good luck and good company."

He cleared his throat awkwardly. "Thanks."

I got him back to the dorm with no one the wiser, then went back to the office and waited. It took a little longer than I expected, but finally a quick messageburst from the Ministry: "Skal Merchant Found Ripped to Shreds Behind Stadium. Good job."

You see, Zjhaccœse really does revolve around the Zee and the Dewclaws. The general lizard population might not care about zonked monkeys one way or the other, but when those zonked monkeys are both students and Dewclaws fans. . . well, you see how it is. Embarrass the biggest lizards in the swamp and things start to happen. When all else fails, you can always depend on a pack of bloodthirsty raptors.

### 

**About the Author**

Jonathan Shipley is a Fort Worth, Texas, writer, with speculative fiction stories published in magazines and fifty-plus anthologies, including *Sword & Sorceress* 25 through 31 and, of course, several Third Flatiron anthologies. A complete bibliography of his publications is available at www.shipleyscifi.com/publishedworks.

\*\*\*\*\*~~~~\*\*\*\*\*

## *Quality Testing*

by S. E. Foley

I had been feeling pretty good about myself, until I saw the glowing thing in the coffee shop. I'd dressed in my best clothes, gotten my hair cut, and put a lawyer on retainer. Afterwards, I decided to go and get a celebratory cup of expensive coffee. I was freeing myself from the oppressive shackle of my husband's association, and I deserved it.

I admired the buff suede of my boots as I pushed through the door. They still looked new after three years. A lot about me looks new and shiny, when in fact I've had me for years.

All thoughts of my boots went out of my mind when I saw it.

When you look up in a fancy coffee shop, you expect to see a smattering of people in the demographic of well off. Any patches or tears in their garments are aesthetically placed, the army green backpacks never saw a boot camp, and the lived-in looking shoes were bought with distress by design. In a shop like this, there is always polished wood, glass, and chrome, barristas in neat aprons, and lots of oversized baked goods for sale.

The anomalous thing was a tall, slender glowing figure standing by a rack. It was sipping from a paper cup and browsing discounted Christmas ornaments with a coffee theme. I stopped in the door.

"Excuse me," someone said from behind me. I startled and bounced out of the way. I stared at the couple as they passed me with a touch of confused incredulity. They looked back at me in that insular way people will use when looking at a stranger. You can nearly read their minds.

*What are you looking at? What is your problem? Do I have something on my jacket?*

All those thoughts would have been wrong. I could tell right away that they did not see the odd figure in the corner. No one else in the shop did, either. I stood beside the door, watching it until it turned towards me.

The cup in its grip paused at the glowing circle of what I imagine must have been a face. I saw no eyes, but I felt the rake of a gaze. I felt like I was standing in front of my grandmother again. She could tear me down with a look, the minute expressions that ran across her face telling me everything I needed to know about my inadequacies. Though it had no visible face or expression, I felt it all the same.

"Hmm," it said.

I saw no mouth. No vibrational eminence came to the shells of my ears. And yet I heard it quite clearly.

*I must be losing my mind*, I thought. I supposed that made sense. I just took some enormous steps to change my life, and sometimes changes break things inside of us. Things that you would expect to be only good sometimes end up being complicated.

*Perhaps I shouldn't have called the lawyer*, I thought as I felt myself walk towards it.

I didn't know why I was drawn towards the peculiar being of light. When I got close enough, I recognized the scent of a vanilla latte. I decided that I would get that, when I was finished with trying to make sense of this psychotic break scenario. I do like a good vanilla latte.

"One of the dummies is still set for interactive," it said.

I blinked, feeling a touch of a blush come on. I was reasonably sure it called me a dummy, and wasn't actually speaking to me. "Excuse me?"

## Quality Testing

"Haha, it just said excuse me," the being of light said to no one I could see. Maybe it was having a psychotic break as well. At least there was something in common between us besides an enjoyment of vanilla lattes.

It pointed at me and waggled its arm up and down. To my surprise, I jolted up and down. My feet came up off the floor and then slammed back down to it in an absolute defiance of autonomy and gravity. Up and down, up and down, as if it was trying to violently shake some sense into me. My boot heels cracked into the floor a half a dozen times before I reacted.

I flailed my hands out to grab at the arm that seemed to be levitating me, but it pulled back quickly, leaving me to collapse on my knees on the polished wood floor. I wondered how my knees hadn't snapped or my ankles rolled for the violence of how I'd struck, but it was a passing concern. I was fine.

I looked over my shoulder at the line. No one was looking at me or at the being. I felt like I wasn't even in the same time and space as they were, which gave me a fright. I screamed at them, "Help! Help me, this thing is trying to kill me!"

"Oh, stop. Don't be silly," it said, and took another sip from its cup. I could tell that it was talking to me instead of its invisible friends, this time. "I'm not trying to kill you. I could erase you from this existence instantly. If I wanted you gone, you'd be gone."

"You could?"

I still don't know why I didn't ask it why it hadn't. I suppose I asked the most pressing question, instead. "What are you?"

"I'm just an archailect," it shrugged and gulped down its coffee. "I'm testing the dimension for quality assurance. You seem to lack some fundamental parameters. I can't seem to change some of your sense setting."

"The who what for why?" I had not gotten up off the floor yet. I was looking up at it as if it was some angelic being, but I knew it wasn't. It was not angel, it was not demon, it was not some God-derived supernatural force. I was beginning to think that it might be an asshole, whatever else it named itself.

"Quality testing. I'm logging an AI that seems to have some program initiatives that were unplanned.

"Sometimes it happens," it stopped talking away from me, looked at me and nodded to itself, "You're kind of a. . . glitch."

"What?" I breathed out, and pushed slowly back to my feet. My boots, I noticed, had gotten a bit scuffed. My mouth kept going as my distress heightened, "What? I'm not artificial. I was born, I grew up, and here I am, on the verge of filing for divorce and getting a vanilla latte! I'm very real!"

The archailect looked at its hand, and the cup vanished. A second later the cup was back with a fresh brew. At the same time, I noticed something interesting out of the corner of my eye. One of the baristas seemed to have gone into a lightning fast mode. It reminded me of the comic book hero, the Flash. Her body blurred from the archailect to the back, went zipzipzip behind the counter, back to the archailect, and then she was standing where she originally had been, as one would expect of a barrista.

I watched her. She was smiling and taking her time with serving her next customer. She poured and stirred, chatting with her co-workers and generally moving at a rate that annoyed people who were intent on getting their coffee fix.

"Uh huh," it said, sipping from the fresh cup.

This glowstick was challenging my existence, so I insisted rather loudly, "I *was* born!"

The head tilted my way and nodded, "Well, yeah. That's how this dimension works. You're still just a small construct in a very big design. I'm trying to decide if your autonomy will prove to be a problem. It indicates a distortion in the base harmony."

That made my blood run cold. "So what are you going to do?"

For better or worse, I had bought into this case of mental breakdown. I didn't question the identity and realism of the glowing being that called itself an archailect. I knew without a doubt that it could erase me the same way it had yanked me about like a rag doll and gotten a fresh cup of coffee. It was a master of time and space.

It made me think about my own value to the universe. What have I done to make it better? What have I done to improve the harmony of my dimension?

"I could tear it all down and start over. That would be a lot of work, though."

This thing sounded lazier than my soon-to-be-ex husband. At that moment, I realized that laziness could be a valuable asset. I folded my hands together and nodded.

"No one likes to overwork," I suggested with a smile. "I don't know what I can say to convince you that things are working out just fine, but so far it seems like they are. If you'd like me to keep quiet about you, whatever you are, I will be happy to never mention you."

"I'm not worried about that." It pondered the cup and its contents, then seemed to regard me. "I don't want an unplanned catastrophic crash, is all."

"Understandable," I agreed. "But really, life goes on with all sorts of oddities that are barely ever noticed. There is such a thing as good enough, isn't there? No use in being a perfectionist if you can't stand back and enjoy things, hmm?"

"Not really the point of quality control, but you're also correct. In a dynamic system, things will go askew regularly. You're hardly the worst result."

"I'm causing no harm," I ventured with a touch of promise to the note of my voice.

It stood there and considered me. I felt every second crawl by with a frightening ache. I feel that my grandmother could have taken lessons from the critical observance of this softly glowing being.

"Eh, we'll see."

And then it was just gone.

I turned away from the sale item corner and stared at the counter, where people were queuing up for their cups of expensive coffee. I took a long, slow breath. Nothing felt different. Except I realized that I felt a bit cracked open in ways I didn't want to be.

I walked briskly for the door. I decided that I'd skip the coffee and go sign up for those motorcycle lessons I've been wanting for so long. *Carpe diem,* and all that.

### 

## About the Author

S.E. Foley is a writer from upstate New York that never put writing as a priority in life until after a bout with cancer. Since then, she has made the time to fit writing into a life full of two jobs and one ornery teenager.

*****~~~~~*****

# Dead Girls, Dying Girls

by James Dorr

Boys make good pets. That was Anise's opinion, culled from observations made during her twelve—going on thirteen—years. She had trained her brothers during this time, all three older than she was but duller of intellect.

That was her opinion too.

She had trained them to dance, not well, but clumsily. Boys were clumsy by nature, of course, borne out by more of her observations.

She kept a notebook. She had learned to write early, and, prior to that, she had invented a way to express her thoughts by drawing pictures. Simple ones, yes, but enough to remind her what she had learned those times in the past. Of how diapers worked—and why. Bottles vs. Breasts, the Great Controversy, as seen from the recipient's point of view. The Power of Crying.

That last, she learned, worked well as a girl grew older, too, and often better. She watched how Mother played Father's guilt. "You neglect me, darling"—that phrase alone, accompanied by just the right amount of near-silent sniffing, had once bagged Mother a pair of diamond pendant earrings!

Father was rich, or so Anise thought. He bought Mother things and bought Anise things as well, although he had said she was too young for earrings.

187

Anise could wait.

She looked out the window. On the horizon was something large and brown, something deadly. Anise knew what it was from school, a full-grown brown bear.

She had read a book once about a circus in which there had been a dancing bear, and here she had been worried about a project she needed for school, something to enter in next month's science fair.

She had learned from Mother, from observations as well as direct teaching, as well as her own triumphs with her brothers, the ways to manipulate boys and men. She was already her father's favorite child.

"Daddy," she whined, "I need you to capture that bear. We can feed it and keep it in the garage. You won't mind parking your car in the driveway for just a few weeks, will you?"

Father had seemed reluctant at first, so she wrinkled her nose and pouted the way she had learned from Mother. She squeezed tears from her eyes.

"I'll just die, Daddy, if you don't do this for me. It's for the science fair."

That was a weapon that worked with Mother too, to say what she wanted was needed to help with school. So Father caught the bear, getting badly mauled in the process, but that was okay. He had insurance. Anise had learned about that from Mother. "My husband's worth more dead than he is alive," she had heard Mother tell her bridge club once.

Anise didn't play bridge, but she did play with dolls. As well as with her brothers.

And if she could teach her brothers to dance, a mere bear would be easy.

Daily she marched into the garage with a whip she had found in Mother's closet and her CD player. She had asked Mother if she could borrow the whip, but Mother had said at first that she was too young. "When you're a young woman and start to go out with men, then it will be time. I'll buy you one of your own."

Anise had laughed—laughter worked too sometimes. "Oh, Mommy, you're silly. It's not about sex. I know I have to wait for that." Anise had made *many* observations. She sniffed and wrinkled her nose. She made her eyes look moist. "I need it for my science fair project," she said.

It worked every time.

More great, brown, deadly shapes were seen from time to time on the horizon as the days went on. They lived next to what had once been a wood, but then had been cleared for a housing project which subsequently went broke before they were able to actually build houses. Father had a theory that the animals that used to live in the woods kept coming back because they were confused.

Anise had a theory that it was because there weren't any other woods left, and besides they raided the family's garbage cans. That was at night when Mother and Father were sleeping or having sex.

Anise was a precocious child—one of her teachers had said that once. That was after she had seen the teacher and her boyfriend in the supply room. "What are you doing?" she had asked, but her teacher and her teacher's boyfriend evaded the question—not that Anise hadn't had her suspicions already.

She had shown the pictures she had taken on her cell phone to the other girls in her class at recess and wrote their opinions down in her notebook. Some of them were quite lurid.

Anise concluded that she was not the only precocious child in her school.

She lost one of her brothers during one of the bear training sessions, but that was okay. Like Father, her brother was insured as well. She knew that already—that Father's work gave him something called a "Family

Policy"—something she'd learned one afternoon when she overheard Mother talking on the phone.

She wore black to the funeral. People said afterwards that she looked all grown up dressed in black and with her hat and veil. Just like a lovely young lady, one man said, a man not-too-old himself. One who was handsome and who Mother leered at as well as Anise.

One of Anise's hobbies in science lab was making poisons.

The bear escaped once and joined with its fellows in the erstwhile woods, but by the next afternoon it had returned, perhaps because Anise had made a point of rewarding it with meat scraps whenever it learned a new set of steps. It really didn't learn dances as such, but it had a different way of shuffling to each piece of music, which Anise was able to augment by training. To make it look slinky—insofar as something with its bulk could *ever* look slinky—when shambling through a tango, for instance. Or elegant when performing a waltz.

She got its attention by *only* feeding it after it had danced.

Then the big night came, the night of the science fair, and she and Mother and her two remaining brothers piled into the family SUV. The bear sat in the back. She told it to stay there when they arrived at the school gym, that she would call it when its time came.

The sun was down, but she thought she saw large shapes across the school football field as they went inside.

Mother helped her complete the paperwork, then she went back out and called in the bear. She showed it off to the many girl friends she had made in her class, introducing it to each of them by name. To Ruth, to Kimberly, to Enid, to Betty, to Wendy, to Marge, to Sally, to Meredith. To all the others. While they in turn showed her their science projects, the model volcano, the "food groups" chart, the display on light bulbs, the "1000 Uses for Self-Sealing Sandwich Wrap," the six-foot-high artificial nose.

But then something sad happened. Just as the bear had successfully completed a Cuban rumba, it, apparently missing its meat reward, ate Enid instead.

"Bear, no!" Anise shouted, but it didn't listen. It started instead to eat Kimberly's shoulder.

Just then the doors to the gym crashed open, and in came a line of eight more bears, ursine arms linked together, kicking their legs in chorus line fashion as Anise's player switched to a new CD, the "can-can" movement from Offenbach's opera, *Orpheus in Hell.*

And more body parts flew, dead girls and dying girls, as these bears also, having learned from their *compadre* the night it escaped, expected their meat rewards. Helping themselves, as more girls screamed, and boys, and parents. One of the teachers lunged for a cell phone, only to see it disappear down a nearsighted bear's gullet. Others grabbed children and pushed toward the exits.

The model volcano exhibit erupted, as one of the other bears ate the "food groups" display. *Smarter than the average bear,* Anise thought.

She couldn't help giggling.

Smarter than her brother as well, the one she thought might have made it outside. Not the one lying in pieces strewn on the floor. A new track came up on the CD player, "The Blue Danube Waltz," causing the bears to shuffle in pairs, between snacks of arms and legs and torsos. The occasional head popped down like candy. And Anise laughed harder—she couldn't help it. They all looked so funny. A line from the circus book came back to her, that what had amazed the show's patrons most was not the skill of the figures the bear danced, but rather that a bear had danced at all. And here, in the school gym, more bears having flooded in, *dozens* of bears lumbered to the music, splashing through blood pools, reaching occasionally down to the floor for a haunch or a rib rack that hadn't been eaten yet.

Backing away, sidling to the exit, tears spurting from her eyes from her guffawing, Anise finally turned to flee herself. Whirling, not seeing, she crashed headlong into the six-foot high artificial nose.

It sniffed at her suspiciously.

### 

## About the Author

"Dead Girls, Dying Girls" was originally published in Perpetual Motion Machine Publishing's Kurt Vonnegut tribute anthology, *So It Goes.*

Indiana writer James Dorr's *The Tears of Isis* was a 2014 Bram Stoker Award nominee for Superior Achievement in a Fiction Collection. Other books include *Strange Mistresses: Tales of Wonder and Romance, Darker Loves: Tales of Mystery and Regret,* and his all-poetry *Vamps (A Retrospective).* Also be on the watch for *Tombs: A Chronicle of Latter-Day Times of Earth,* a novel-in-stories just released by Elder Signs Press in June 2017.

Dorr has more than 500 individual appearances, from *Alfred Hitchcock's Mystery Magazine* to *Xenophilia.* For the latest information, visit his blog at http://jamesdorrwriter.wordpress.com.

*****~~~~~*****

## *The Bringers*

by John J. Kennedy

On this particular day, there was a sprawling line of shiny four-wheelers from the river out to Forest Hills. The river was named Hudson, after a human being from a place where they rewarded brutal ancestry with a very large allowance and a rent-free palace.

Think about it.

If your forefathers had been better at chopping people up, you might be wearing a crown, or sitting in a limousine.

There we go.

Here in the city where the river was, pretty much everyone had brutal ancestors anyway. In amongst them, Gilmour Greer, who had a particularly nasty set of antecedents and a shiny six-wheeler with great air-con, asked his aides to ask his driver what the hold-up was.

The driver didn't know, and Gilmour had to resort to sighing and asking his aide to get online and find out. But there was no signal, which made him anxious. He had to remind himself that even if the air outside turned foul with toxic gases, he'd be okay. The windows and chassis were hardened against chemical, biological weapons and the whole shebang. The two pints of his blood hidden away under the seat wouldn't ever be necessary, his aides had told him many times. He was safe.

So why have two pints of his blood on hand, if he *was* safe? This was a question he often asked himself.

Gilmour Greer was president, which answered it.

Just not to his satisfaction.

...

On this day something wondrous was happening. Something the human beings had been practicing for, for many years, mostly on celluloid and later in digital formats. So that when they looked up, mouths that should have been agape spent a few seconds smirking in recognition. Such a tired trope it was.

The tired trope rolled across the sky and sat over 432 Park Avenue for a while. Then it hummed over to One World Trade Center. Not hovering, but coming to rest on top of it, uncomfortably, like a molusc on a pin.

Then its legs unfolded. There we go.

...

"Jesus Christ on a bicycle!" said President Greer. He was referring to a deity he only pretended to believe in on an unlikely mode of transport, though maybe no less likely than what he was looking at.

...

White light. The light became images. The images had words and sounds. The words and sounds were a message. The message made Greer Gilmour's eyes widen and his testicles shrink.

They were *The Bringers*. They'd come a long way. And they had a very specific instruction for him.

...

"I may as well just impeach myself right now," President Greer said later. "Or shoot myself. Might be easier."

The general's face was straight. "Of course, we can fake the lie detector signal to the audience. But if we're to accept the opinion of Miss Probey, here. . . "

Probey stood, long limbs graceful. Her head, shaven for the ease of electrode attachment over at Langley Psych

Ops, was a perfect oval, incongruous against her dress, making Gilmour's penis twitch. Even now, with Armageddon calling, or maybe intensified by it, the hard lithe curves of the psych agent bothered him immensely. Probey, surely aware of what he was thinking, being what she was, stood, head to one side like she was studying an amoeba.

Gilmour, being what he was, brutal antecedents, strict Dutch mother, very austere upbringing, military service and Ivy League education, felt his penis twitch again.

...

He was the most powerful man in the world, allegedly, who was attracted to sexually powerful women. Given his upbringing, this translated into fantasies of being tied-up, straddled by a woman wearing nothing but clogs and eating chocolate cake without giving him a crumb.

Many human beings indulged this tendency. They called it "masochism."

Actually, this is what it was: brutality, peppered with cowardice.

...

"It's not an opinion." Probey's voice was calm. She glanced out the window at the distant spidery leg of another huge mollusc on 4 Times Square. "The Bringers have massive psychic ability. They'll know if you're lying straight away, with or without the lie detector."

Probey was the most powerful psychic in the entire Western Hemisphere, possibly the whole world. A walking, talking, shaven-headed secret weapon. With amazing legs.

"So, why do they insist on having a. . . ?"

"The lie detector's for the masses. Maximum humiliation for you."

Gilmour fumbled for something penetrating to say. "What about their technology? Can we. . . ?"

"*Darktech.* Utilising dark matter. Outstripping anything we have by fifty years. No weaknesses." Probey let out an equally dark smile, and an afterthought. "Sir."

...

Gilmour went into a slump from that point up until the broadcast scheduled for eight that evening.

The Bringers had instructed that Gilmour tell the truth for ten minutes, live, on every feed imaginable. If he complied, they would leave the Earth in peace.

If he didn't; in pieces.

Thing was, Gilmour truly believed his time in office had been productive. No major catastrophes, a few skirmishes and a war or two, but that was part of the territory.

But the truth would hang him and his administration, just as it would any other.

He waved away all his aides, Probey, the VP, because what was the point? There could be no strategy, no last minute "don't forget to avoid this" or "try to steer the discussion towards that." All they'd suggested anyway was that he should take some sodium amytal.

That they believed he needed to take drugs in order to be honest in front of the world made him angry.

But he was considering it.

...

A head popped around the door, bouffant and "business as usual" smile. "Five minutes, Mr. President. Oh, and the other guest and his entourage have arrived." The owner of the head was practicing something human beings called "professionalism," which actually meant lying to oneself and one's central nervous system. He did this in the hope his President would notice. Sadly, his president was too busy doing the same.

Later, Gilmour was to take some consolation from the fact that he managed to make it all the way to the studio and past the *other guest* and his entourage without screaming like a seven-year-old girl.

### The Bringers

They were vaguely insectoid, but really that was an insult to any six-legged creature on Earth. Their skin was puckered and seemed to ooze where it wasn't obfuscated with shell-like lumps that swelled as if independently breathing organisms. Bodies spindly, twisting up to slug-shaped heads with several eyes and round, crinkled mouths that would've been better employed expelling matter than sucking it in.

...

For the first time, his eyes adjusting to the studio lights, Gilmour noticed the audience, deathly quiet, staring in awe. Apart from a tall blonde woman in skirt and heels, standing off to the side, arms folded and head to one side, long hair dangling over a designer blouse.

A techie started fiddling with wires, connecting them with the electrodes that were already attached to Gilmour's skin.

A chicken ready for grilling.

...

Gilmour had entertained idle hopes that the questions from the crowd might've been tempered with kindness. But there was one age-old principle that always held true.

Quite simply, *it only takes one.*

The bespectacled, goateed history professor on the third row knew his stuff.

He started right into what President Greer knew about the orchestration of the infamous War on Terror back in the early to mid-noughties and whether WMD fantasies had been engineered to sanction revenge. Gilmour looked at the electrodes and the Bringers' ambassador and admitted he'd seen plenty of intel since being in office to prove they had.

The professor then got into whether the demonization and financial crippling of Russia during the Ukraine crisis back in 2014-15 had really been a conscious, strategically motivated smear campaign resulting in the Warm War of the decade after.

"Yes," was the president's reply.

To be fair, the crowd seemed to swing along with both of these admissions without too much fuss. There were some cries of disgust, but just as many supportive "yays," particularly for the second revelation.

He cleared his throat. "There's a price to staying the strongest nation on Earth! And by God, we've paid it. But if you knew, really knew the alternatives. . . "

It was the goateed professor's third question that finished Gilmour off.

"Mr. President, are you really a Yankees fan?"

There we go.

...

Gilmour hated baseball. Didn't get it. Never had. Never would. He'd assumed, on gaining office, that it wouldn't matter a fig. He'd been prepared to 'fess up before his inauguration, freely admit that he just didn't care for the sport, or to any sport, *tbh*. Well, maybe tennis, a little. His media officer had disagreed. "Are you kidding? Sir? Tennis? *Really*?"

"What's wrong with that?"

"Oh nothing. Nothing." He'd tutted, shaken his head. "Just. . . " A glance around, a lean forwards, a conspiratorial cupping of the mouth. "It's just a little. . . *un-American*, sir, wouldn't you say?"

Word choice is everything. A week later, Gilmour had appeared on both *Newsweek's* and *Time's* sites with the team, wearing a Yankees hat and grinning like any autograph-hunting idiot.

...

Now, his croaky, regret-filled "No," brought a sickening quiet to the audience around him, and Gilmour cringed like a schoolboy caught with his hand up the prom queen's dress.

The silence cracked, the jeering began.

...

198

### The Bringers

Gilmour Greer mistakenly believed his hard-line policies on gun licensing and digital leakage were what had gotten him elected three years ago. In fact, his winning had been assured, but by neither.

Mommy had grudgingly passed along two important things to Gilmour.

One: his name—nicely alliterated and featuring a couple of interchangeable forename/surname units that might have seemed pretentious twenty years ago but now was kind of cool. She'd urged him to change it. He hadn't.

Two: a hangdog facial expression—eyes that somehow said sorry and a bearing that was a perfect antidote to the arrogance of the times. Mommy had spent thousands on movement coaching, yoga, even ballet classes for him at one point. None of it worked. The opposite, if anything.

There we go.

It wasn't something that could ever have been quantified, but the vast majority of voters who'd swung under his banner, long since disillusioned with politics, had reacted to him unconsciously; drawn to him as they would have been over a century before to Stan Laurel, had he chosen to run for office.

Of course, every spell has its shelf life.

...

Gilmour knew his career had just come to an end.

He stared at the ambassador, about to try shouting over the ruckus, then realised he didn't need to. He simply *thought*. "Okay. You've won. But I kept my word. I told the truth. Absolute truth. So, you have to let us live and leave us in peace. That was the bargain."

A strange gyrating movement. Only the accompanying psychic message made sense of it. Unrepressed hilarity, a ripple of it through the entourage.

A sudden slew of images in Gilmour's mind, a Bosch-like vista of cowering humanity enslaved, tortured a million ways defying description. Then, much worse, a huge poster of himself, defaced by graffiti, defiled by what looked suspiciously like pigeon-crap, people tearing, flinging mud at it, someone scrawling: *Greer fucked us all!*

He gagged, looked at the ambassador. He could feel the joyful contempt in every syllable. "No bargain. We lied."

...

He was vaguely aware of smoke around him, greenish in studio light. At first he thought one of his secret servicemen had gotten carried away at the crowd's unrest and released tear gas. But it seemed to be spreading from under the ambassador.

He stared around him. He and the ambassador were completely masked from the audience, entourage, and cameras.

Gilmour crossed to the chaise longue and the ambassador's flatworm body. Hating himself for it, he put his hands together a prayerlike clasp and was about to kneel, when his heel caught on something and he sprawled, his double-handed blow finding the ambassador's soft, sluglike middle. He stumbled, tried to right himself, the ambassador emitting a whining, keening noise, Gilmour's fists sinking through the translucent skin, brown bilge erupting around his hands. Six arms or legs flailed. A strangled screech, and the puckered mouth dribbled something green.

Something, something deep in Gilmour, made him stop, his eyes finding the many eyes of the ambassador on their twitching stalks.

He thought of his image, covered in graffiti, mud, and shit.

He closed his eyes, pushing downwards and opening his fingers.

Suddenly he felt a rush of air behind him and a feminine hand at his arm. "No! No!" A familiar voice from that blonde head he'd noticed earlier, her sinewy arm snaking up around his shoulder to pull him back. "Don't do this. It's what they want!"

The ambassador slithered backwards onto the floor, and Gilmour's hands came free with a gooey slurp.

"No!" She was saying. "No!"

The smoke was clearing. Her hand jerked the blonde wig free.

"Probey?" he asked.

A look of sheer disgust. "You have no idea what you've just done!"

"You don't understand," he said. "I was just. . . "

"I know!" She shook her head. "You clumsy bastard! But you've killed him. Just like they wanted!"

His jaw had dropped. Had he just moved into some parallel world where nothing made sense?

The smoke was clearing. They both turned to look at the entourage. Gilmour could feel their laughter echoing around his head, along with one repeated phrase.

*Frik Fuglip!*

...

The president surveyed the array of neckties in front of him. He pointed at the dark blue and lighter blue striped, pulled up his collar, and let his aide tie the knot. "I'm about to address the whole world for the first time since. . . the *incident*. You're *sure* opinion's swung back my way?'

"There's the latest poll result." Another of his aides passed him the sheet and clicked a remote. The 3D image of a member of the audience from the night of *the incident* appeared, smiling. '. . . course he had to pretend to admit to all those terrible thing, all lies, to fool them—the Bringers. I mean, he's a native New Yorker, right? Sure, he's a Yankees fan! I mean, you bet when the smoke cleared and the president was standing over that slimy bastard. . . yeah, I guess we all thought. . . we're screwed, they're gonna wipe out the whole planet! But they didn't! They got in their little spaceships and ran. Back where* *they came from. President Greer showed 'em. Showed 'em what we're made of. He's got my vote. Bet your ass he has. For eternity.*

...

The president didn't want eternity. Just another term.

"She's not here, is she?"

The general smiled. "No sir. She won't be bothering you again."

Gilmour felt the ghost of a twitch down below. "I hope she won't be hurt."

"No question of that, sir. She's out of harm's way. But in a controlled environment. And... placated, let's say."

The president chose not to chase a definition of that one.

...

Here's the thing.

Since the Bringers, on their sudden retreat, had crashed one of their molluscs in Nevada, every scientific mind in the West was working on the secret of Darktech. It wouldn't be long. Darktech was self-replicating, whatever that meant.

Within a year. America would have built a fleet.

Exploration. That was the key. What mankind had always been destined for.

Of course, each ship would also have the power to wipe a thousand cities out of existence.

And of course, if we happened to run into the *Bringers*, we'd have to be pre-emptive about things. No sense in holding back.

Gilmour shook his head. It was sad about Probey. She just wouldn't listen to reason. Not uncommon, apparently, amongst Psych agents. Complete burn out. Delusions. That the visions the Bringers had shown him, of humanity enslaved, were all a trick. A false threat.

"You know what I found," she'd said. "When I got deep enough inside their heads? No hatred. Not even resentment of humanity. Just recognition. Of kinship."

...

Probey's delusion was complex.

The Bringers were predators. Traveling the universe in search of other murderous species to join them in an eternal war already spanning several galaxies. Whenever they found a new civilisation they'd *test* it, putting the leader of that race into a no-win situation to see what he would do when faced with utter defeat and humiliation. If the leader passed the test, not resorting to brutality, they'd move on.

But *some* species, according to Probey, species who glory in death and destruction in the name of God, democracy or freedom, *those* races they embrace and invite them to join their war. *A war that would never end.*

...

The president shook his head.

He checked his tie in the mirror and glanced at his watch. Showtime.

He moved out, secret servicemen around him. They fanned outward as he took to the stage and waved at the huge swell of applause. He gripped the rostrum and smiled what he hoped was an austere smile. He nodded and held up his hand.

It wasn't until he opened his mouth to speak that his head seemed to split. Images of hundreds of worlds in chaos and flame. City-sized holes in ravaged landscapes. The roar of thunder and war. And everywhere the sweet, sickly smell of burning bodies.

A voice reverberated around his skull, angry and righteous, shrieking over the visuals. Not a Bringer voice, though. *Her* voice. "I translated most of their language," she said. "Do you want to hear some? Do you?"

He gagged, shaking his head.

"*Frik fuglip!*" she said. "Welcome to the game!"

The president fell to his knees, behind the podium, clawing at the voice that wouldn't go away.

###

## About the Author

John J. Kennedy teaches English at a college in the North East of England, though he's done plenty to earn a crust over the years, including peeling bulbs in Holland and busking round Europe. His first published story was with us in the last Third Flatiron anthology. He's been shortlisted for the CWA Debut Dagger (for his other genre—crime) for a first novel, which he's currently knocking into shape. He truly believes that if we remember that all human beings are fundamentally insane then nothing should surprise us too much, though he's constantly amazed by the support he gets from his wife and daughter.

*****~~~~~*****

# The Confrontation Station

by Ryan Dull

Nicole set up the Confrontation Station right in the front lobby, where everyone could see it. She spent half an hour dragging furniture across the office: two towering stools, a desk, and a filing cabinet. She ordered Steve from IT to perch a webcam on the corner of the desk, angled at the stools.

The memo followed a few minutes later. Henceforth, workplace disagreements would not be allowed to fester. Employees would not exchange passive-aggressive emails and build scheming coalitions behind one another's backs. If someone had an objection to a colleague's work, they would not wage a campaign to undermine them, setting them up for failure after humiliating failure before finally delivering the *coup de grace* in front of their family at the company picnic. Henceforth, conflict would be settled in the Confrontation Station.

Employees responded with scorn. Nicole had been manager for less than three months, and here she was building some kind of kangaroo courtroom. An email circulated announcing that scientists had decided to call the unit of measurement for the smallest quantity of power that could go to someone's head a "Nicole." Nicole allowed these charges to pass unchallenged. She waited for her moment.

At a Wednesday morning status update meeting, Anil rattled off upcoming placements. Charles, reading Anil's handout through glasses low on his nose, raised one finger. "Says here we're putting two vending machines at Sky Ridge Mall."

"That's right."

Charles glanced around the table. "Doesn't that seem low?"

"It's standard for traffic and income."

"Is it? That's a popular mall."

"Two machines is standard for traffic and income. Would you like to see my data?"

"I'm not questioning your data. I'm just saying, from my own experience, that Sky Ridge Mall is a bustling commercial hub, and if we don't put at least five machines there, we're throwing money in the toilet."

"Five machines?" Anil laughed. "Forgive me if I doubt your *experience*," the word slid off his tongue and splashed onto the conference table, where it formed an oily stain, "but the data indicate that Sky Ridge will support 1.9 machines."

Charles' nostrils flared. "Then the data is weak."

Anil planted his fists on the table. "The data are impeccable. You're weak."

They were about to begin throwing pens, when Nicole stood, voice ringing. "We will settle this in the Confrontation Station." Both men blustered. "Unless one of you is willing to concede the argument." Neither was. The entire meeting made its way to the lobby.

At the Confrontation Station, Nicole opened the filing cabinet and drew out a form. "Write both of your names, the nature of the conflict, and your preferred outcomes." They did. "Now get on the stools and talk it over. The confrontation ends when you reach an agreement or one of you leaves his stool. A verbal agreement is acceptable. The camera is always on, and the video is streaming on the company website. Anything you say on the stools is considered a binding oral contract. Understood?"

Anil squinted at Nicole. "Did Legal agree to this?"

### The Confrontation Station

"If anyone from Legal has a problem with it, I would be happy to talk it over with them in the Confrontation Station. Whenever you're ready."

Charles and Anil glanced at one another. They ascended the stools. They sat. Forty-five seconds later, they had reached an accord. Three machines, to be revised upwards or downwards according to next month's sales. Their colleagues looked on in stunned silence. Somewhere far away, a garbage disposal growled.

It was the stools that did it, those terrible stools. They had always stood unused in a corner of the kitchen, possibly left there by some earlier tenant. They were enormous, so tall that you had to climb their frames like stepladders. Even Jeff's legs dangled, and he'd played power forward on his college basketball team, Division II. The stools were narrow—tiny tea saucer seats. They were harder than boiled granite. They looked as though they'd been designed for some other species, a race of eight-foot-tall, pencil-thin ivory angels. Fifteen seconds, and your feet started to tingle. A minute, and your legs would be so numb you'd have to crawl down. Much longer than that, and no one could say what might happen. The doctors might have to amputate. Ah, the cruel efficacy of the stools! Every grievance was overwhelmed, every petty grudge, bleached to nothing.

Most confrontations never reached the Station. The tender-of-thigh would leave their objections unvoiced, or else retract them during the long walk to the stools. Colleagues sought consensus. Sniping and factionalism were consigned to the dustbin of history. Conflict had become too costly.

But beneath the veneer of civility, chaos bubbled. Where irritation had once found easy outlets, it now hardened into anger. Time polished anger into antipathy. Pressure forged antipathy into malice.

Janette was thrown out of a mixed martial arts class for her manic unwillingness to dial it back. In the office kitchenette, a plate slipped from Jeff's hand and shattered. He stared at the fragments winking up from the linoleum. He dropped a second plate, and a third. No one questioned him. Driving home, Stephanie ran over a raccoon. She smiled, turned up the music, and sang at the top of her lungs, "Blinded by the light—"

A new Italian place opened across the street, and for three days in a row, Steve from IT's lunch appeared to be a solid pound of roasted garlic. He would pick at it with his fingers for hours, reheating it over and over again in the office microwave. The Tuscan miasma wafted out from the IT cluster and into the office proper. Windows were opened. Air fresheners were purchased. His neighbors knew that sooner or later, they'd have to talk to him. Steve was small, unassuming, quiet. There were a lot of lone-wolf-types in IT. Was he a consensus man or a confrontation man? He had a small paunch, but his thighs looked sturdy.

On day four, Steve put on his coat and headed for the door. Bill intercepted. "Getting some lunch?"

"Yup."

"Sandwich?"

"Actually, I was thinking of going to the Italian place."

"You're not bored of Italian?"

"I'm bored of sandwiches."

Bill glanced around the room. Colleagues averted their eyes. "Listen, Steve, there are going to be some clients in this afternoon. It might be a good idea to get something that doesn't smell."

"It might be?"

"Yeah. For the clients."

Steve fiddled with the keys in his pocket. "Is that something the clients requested specifically? No smelly lunches?"

"We just thought it would be polite." He smiled that classic Bill smile.

"Do you have a problem with my choice of lunch?"

Bill's smile faded. "I didn't say that, Steve. I'm just talking about courtesy."

"Is this a conflict?"

"It doesn't have to be."

They stared at one another, probing for weakness. Bill's eyes were kindly and hard, like a statue of Mr. Rogers. Steve's were wet. His cheek twitched.

A few co-workers followed them to the Confrontation Station. The rest opened up the live stream. Bill said, "We don't have to do this, Steve. It's just lunch. It doesn't matter."

"If it doesn't matter, then go back to your desk."

Bill wrote their names on a form. "I'm going to write that we're arguing about whether or not it's fair for you to stink up the office five days a week. Is that okay?"

"Get on your stool, and we'll talk about it." Steve scampered with alarming speed to the top of his stool. He gestured to its twin. Bill nodded, slowly, and climbed.

Bill opened negotiations. "Alright, we can probably work out some kind of, I don't know, calendar where we set aside a few days a month when you can get a whole bucket of garlic, if that's what you really want. How does that sound?"

Steve was blank.

"You have to meet me halfway. Four times a month. How does that sound? I mean, you're probably already getting sick of the stuff." Bill's toes were tingling.

Steve sniffed and shifted his weight.

"Okay, I get it. It's a principle thing. You don't like people telling you what to do. Well, you share a workspace. Now and then, you have to make some compromises. Six days. Seven. How's that? A full week."

Steve met Bill's gaze and said nothing. Bill could no longer feel his left foot.

"Steve, we're on the clock here. You have to talk to me."

Steve didn't blink.

209

"What are you, some kind of masochist? Say something!"

Steve glanced down. He worked his hands around the rim of his stool until he was sure of his grip. With a sharp intake of breath, he lifted himself up, up, until he was holding his entire body above the stool. The assembled co-workers gasped as he planted one foot, then the other. He wasn't sitting at all. He was practically standing. He lifted his hands and squatted like a gargoyle about to take flight.

Bill stared, mouth open. "Jesus, Steve. It's just lunch." Everyone looked at Bill, but no one said a word. He swallowed hard, shifted, tried lifting one leg, and then the other. He dangled a foot down to the support rung, gave it a little weight, hopped up, and got his other foot onto the seat. But the wood was so smooth, so narrow. The worn sole of Bill's shoe could find no purchase. He tumbled back, arms outstretched, eyes closed against the lights. His ankle bent horribly beneath him. At computers around the office, colleagues cringed.

Steve stared down, impassive. His co-workers looked frail and distant. It occurred to Steve that there was no such thing as absolute power—that all strength depended on context. In the proper niche, anyone could be a warrior-king. It had taken Steve forty-three years to find his niche. He would not relinquish it.

Sarah stared at Bill's ruined ankle. "That doesn't seem fair."

"I disagree," said Steve. "But I welcome your best arguments. I welcome all of your arguments." Air conditioning whistled across the empty stool.

He remained atop his perch as co-workers gathered Bill in their arms and dragged him away. Bill went quietly. There was nothing left to say.

That, most of the office assumed, was it. The Confrontation Station had stultified interoffice communication, driven employees to the edge of madness, and now it had an honest-to-God body count. The whole setup would be disassembled by C.O.B.

What they failed to understand was that Nicole needed the Confrontation Station to succeed. It wasn't just that it gave her unprecedented power over the office. It wasn't just that she had invested so much of her authority in its creation that she risked mutiny if it were toppled. For Nicole, the Confrontation Station had utopian implications. It instructed, even as it destroyed. It exposed verbal conflict in its most predatory mode and forced cooperation. It revealed by physical torment the futility of argument, the unity of all human beings before the mouth of oblivion.

And if Steve appeared to be its master, that was only temporary. Conflict had no master. Conflict only had servants who carried within them the seeds of their own undoing. When Nicole left for the night, Steve was still on the stool. "Would you like to debate, Nicole?"

"Not tonight," she said. And she locked the door behind her.

The live stream would show that Steve never left the stool that night, but of course, that was impossible. He'd been squatting since lunch. It would have been hours since he'd had anything to drink. So he must have tampered with the camera somehow. He must have descended, at least for a few minutes.

But when Nicole unlocked the door the next morning, he was still up there, perched like a sweaty golf ball on a tee. "Good morning, Nicole."

"Good morning, Steve."

"I've done some thinking."

"Have you?"

"If I start issuing commands and no one rises to contradict me, they will become policy, correct? This would seem to follow from the law of the Confrontation Station."

Nicole held her bag close and ran out of earshot.

Not long after that, she went to the hardware store.

When she returned to the lobby, she was pushing a dolly, its contents concealed beneath a blue tarp. "Steve!" she called. "We are in conflict! Do you agree?"

Steve eyed the cart. "Very well."

"Would you like to take a few minutes to stretch your legs?"

Steve smiled and stood, extending his arms like a gymnast. His balance was impeccable. "I am fully stretched."

"So be it." From beneath the tarp, Nicole produced a wooden platform, four feet by four feet. She set it on the empty stool.

"Nicole," said Steve, "That isn't fair."

"I disagree," said Nicole, "But we can talk it over in a moment."

Nicole produced a shopping bag full of granola bars, three gallons of water, several thick books, and an empty pail. She arranged these on the platform with care.

"Nicole," said Steve, "I haven't eaten since yesterday."

Nicole climbed on top of the desk. She stepped from the desk to the filing cabinet. She considered her angle of approach and hopped onto her well-appointed stool. It trembled. It held.

Some hours passed before either of them spoke. Nicole was sitting cross-legged and not looking at the book in her lap. She said, "In the 1920s, it wasn't uncommon for someone to erect a platform on top of a pole in a public place and live up there for a while. It was a type of performance. Sometimes, they would stay up there for days. Weeks, even."

Steve was squatting. His eyes had never left Nicole. "People have survived hunger strikes that lasted over a month. Political prisoners, people like that. Committed people."

Nicole nodded. "Of course, the pole-sitters were just following the example of ancient saints. With enough conviction, truly holy people could spend years on tiny platforms. Whole lifetimes."

They fell back into silence.

...

They've been up there for a while now. Nicole is still the manager, and people will bring her more granola bars if she asks. The wrappers pile up around the base of the stool. The other employees have been keeping a list, a backlog of all the suspended conflicts that will have to be resolved when the Station finally becomes available again. Jeff caught Sarah drinking from his favorite mug and filed Unresolved Conflict Number Seventy-Eight. Sarah's keeping the mug until the confrontation. She feels it will be useful as leverage.

You can see them through the windows that face the street. The live stream never stops, buried in some corner of the company website. It is not an easy thing to explain. When visitors come to the office, they pause in front of the Confrontation Station, stare at Nicole and Steve as politely as they can, and duck away from the camera. If they find the reception desk, they lean in, lower their voices and say, "You know, I'm not sure that's an appropriate display for a place of business."

And the receptionist says, "Buddy, if you want to talk like that, you'll have to take a number."

### 

## About the Author

Ryan Dull eats most of his meals in Southern California. His work has previously appeared in *Psychopomp Magazine* and on the Pseudopod horror podcast. You can find him on Twitter at RyanSoDull.

*****〜〜〜*****

# *The Edge of Toska*

by Veronica Moyer

If you were to travel a rather far distance from Earth, perhaps half past Jupiter on the way to Saturn, you might stumble upon the relatively small and undoubtedly strange habitat called Toska. Among around 11,259 others, young Sophia spent her life on Toska, which is a flat planet, exactly 180° from east to west. Some Toskans believe the planet is a sphere, but they are kept quarantined in small government-patrolled huts way up on the northern front, far from civilization.

The Toskan government is hardly that; it doesn't do much governing. Government officials have two purposes: secluding the round-earthers and creating Toskans in Petri dishes in a laboratory up north. Once Toskan infants are fully crafted, they are scattered throughout the planet to huts of expectant guardians. During creation, Toskans receive a small, flesh-colored patch on the inner sole of their feet which combats the otherwise weak gravitational force on Toska. When Sophia was young, she often thought about how many Toskans could float right off the planet's edge without the government's splendid patch, with limbs flailing and eyes bulging and lungs collapsing. When she thought about this, Sophia felt a heightened pleasure and elated giddiness. She knew this sensation to be called "happiness."

In between the steep dropoffs into the interstellar abyss, Toska is actually quite lush. There is an unexplored channel guiding the frozen waters from Saturn's moon Enceladus to the southern edge of Toska, providing the small planet with plenty of means for growth. Spanning from the eastern border to about halfway to Toska's center are continuous rows of trees that appear very similar to oak trees on Earth. However, these trees have thinner leaves and produce a bitter, hard fruit called the Hygge. Half of the Toskan population on the eastern front makes a living carving different creatures out of Hygge fruit to sell at the village markets, and every single one of them lives well and eats well. Sophia lived just to the west of the center of Toska, nestled in the wooded area outside Toska's capital, Saudade. There are no Hygge trees on the western side of Toska, but rather impressively tall trees called Lumbas with roots that emerge ten feet above the ground like ravenous, crawling arms. Sophia loved their little cabin nestled within these tall arms. They held her perpetually tight, and when she was young they comforted her and made her feel very, very happy. Throughout Toska there are many animal species different than those on Earth, far too many to explain in detail, except perhaps the squirrel. If you traveled to Toska, perhaps you would find comfort at the familiar sight of the common squirrel. It is the exact same as those on Earth, from nose to tail, and is the oldest Toskan mystery.

In order to fully understand Toska, you must understand that age is measured very differently than it is on Earth. Rather than considering the "years" lived when discussing age, Toskans instead gain emotions with the passing of time. The government's impeccably designed patch modulates the acquisition of emotions to maintain a comfortable consistency. From the moment Sophia's fuzzy blonde head was dropped on midwestern Toska until around age 7 in Earth years, she only knew happiness. Everything was absolutely wonderful, exquisitely divine.

The sun, although dull compared to the sunshine on Earth, shone bright bright bright. She tugged and pulled every sprout and weed with glee, and she often found herself in fits of giggles when she would skin her knee or stub her toe on a Lumba root. She wore a tattered tan smock every day, just like the rest of the children, and loved to stuff the front pockets with round rocks she found on her daily adventures. The rocks weighed her down marvelously as she pattered about.

On Toska, there are no "parents," only guardians, as the concept of parental relations inherently suggests too many emotional ties. Sophia's guardian Tristana was stunningly wrinkled and admirably melancholy, her deep blue eyes drooping fantastically and always brimming with tears, which Sophia thought was really, really lovely. Young Sophia relished in rubbing strands of Tristana's gray hair through her fingers as they sat together on the porch of their small cabin. The neutral hues of the gray strands and her own pale fingers looked beautiful together, Sophia thought. Gray was beautiful, tan was beautiful, yellow blue green red were beautiful. Sophia's cheeks ached from smiling, which made her especially happy.

Every nine days was a day called Litost, which can be compared to Sunday on Earth. On Litosts, Tristana took little Sophia into the capital of Saudade to browse the central marketplace. Sophia picked up every Hygge carving and beamed up at Tristana.

"This one's a Wadka! Look at the paws, so smooth, so pretty, so cute! It's perfect, Tristy, it's beautiful!" Sophia squeaked. The vendor gazed lovingly at the child. Tristana dragged her long legs after the child to vendor after vendor, watching her elation with dewy eyes. After a long while, Tristana would relay to Sophia that it was time to go back to the cabin, and Sophia would happily comply, as always.

During the days before and after Litost, Sophia attended a school with the other young children. In this school, the children were only taught three things: navigation, scavenging, and carving. They didn't need to be taught more, because everything made them happy, so it made no difference. While Sophia was at school, Tristana peered out of the window of their cabin, observing the way the Lumba roots intertwined with one another but kept their distance, like grieving strangers. She would press her wrinkly face on the cold, cold stone of the windowsill and just watch. The western woods smelled of mulch and soil, an odor that crept its way into Tristana's cabin and created an aura of tangible loneliness. The atmosphere was impenetrable, so strong that it could not be cured even by a bounding, gleeful young girl coming home from school.

Sophia and Tristana lived this routine without much variation, until the young girl became less young, and eventually reached the Litost when she would gain a new emotion. This new emotion was called "anger," and Sophia learned very quickly how different this was from happiness. Tristana knew Sophia would gain anger soon, but she did not know the exact Litost it would occur. In the weeks leading up to Sophia's discovery of anger, Tristana picked at the hem of her blue wool dress until strings hung down, a constant reminder of the impending grief caused by the loss of an infinitely happy child. On the morning of that dreadful Litost, Tristana was woken with a harsh jab in her arm. She jerked awake to see Sophia standing by her bedside with an uncharacteristically agitated expression.

"Are we going or what?" Sophia's hazel eyes narrowed.

Oh, no, this is it. This is the day, this is it, Tristana thought. She sighed and sat up.

"Yes, Soph. We're going. Grab that red sweater, it's getting colder."

"Why! I don't need it!" The girl stomped her feet on the stone floor. She looked up at her guardian in apparent revelation.

"Is *this* it?" Sophia spat the phrase. Tristana nodded.

On the way to the markets at Saudade, Sophia felt red hot. This unrecognizable fire flamed deep inside her; she taunted the Lumba roots and yanked the weeds. It was invigorating, it was maddening, it was not lovely, but it was new new new. She felt the remains of her foolish happiness still inside her, but buried deep by these new flames. Flicker, burn, destroy, this is horrible! This is red hot! Sophia's brow furrowed. When Toskans earn a new emotion, their previously learned ones do not disappear. However, because young Toskans feel so much happiness in their youth, there is not nearly enough left to be prominent during the rest of their lives.

Tristana tugged the furious girl around the village, waiting for Sophia each time she paused to insult a Hygge carving for its ugly beak or misshapen ear. Each vendor gazed at Sophia in amiable awe, falling in love with the blonde girl's jeers.

At school, Sophia was one of the first children to experience anger. She tore up her navigation maps as some of the other students laughed joyfully, until eventually every student in her class was wreaking a rage-fueled havoc. The classroom emanated red-hot anger, and the young instructors gazed at the children in admiration. They were developing so sweetly, they thought.

Sophia and the other children experienced the unrelenting, fierce blaze of anger for a few weeks, spitting and biting and stomping and yelling. After a while, the rage fizzed out into a quiet and sullen brooding. Sophia's once bright and expectant gaze went dark, and Tristana watched in pained silence as the little girl began to grow into her full existence. Sophia did not want to go to the village with Tristana anymore on Litosts. She did not want to go with anyone, and she did not go at all. Sophia wandered the wooded trails with her classmates, half-heartedly kicking rocks and roots with her arms crossed tightly across her chest. She held herself now with her own arms; she hated the Lumba roots. They encroached on her independence, they were suffocating, and they made her angry.

Sophia listened to her peers mumble to one another. They seemed angry, of course, but also shared a collective satisfied expression; while they were not happy, they were content. Sophia sat on a rock and propped her head in her palm. She overheard muttered phrases from her classmates a few yards away, like "next stage," "co-guardian love," "our own infants," and, most of all, "soon."

"Soon," Sophia mouthed, noticing the way her tongue moved from back to front in her mouth. The word tasted synthetic. She bent down and picked at the patch on her inner foot and kept picking, picking, picking, until the bottom corner started to fold up and twilight darkened to dusk.

When Sophia and Tristana were in the cabin together, they did not speak. Their silences were of two different colors, but were nonetheless two nothings floating together in the cabin air. Sophia glared at her guardian. Tristana's long, gray strands were offensively unkempt, and Sophia despised the way her eyes were always moist. Every so often a single tear would spill from Tristana's eye and make a river down her wrinkles. When this happened, Sophia gazed at the stones on the floor, trying to stifle the insults churning inside her. She pulled on the patch on her foot.

"I'm supposed to feel this way."

Tristana looked up at the girl, whose hair had begun to darken from golden to a copper hue. Her legs were longer, and beneath her slanted gaze lay the wisdom of a maturing young woman. Tristana stared at the child in despondency and sighed.

"The next one is good, remember? Remember I used to tell you about it, when you were happy? It's really wonderful, the next one. You might even meet a co-guardian. It'll come soon." She wiped a tear.

*Soon.* The word stung Sophia's skin. Their silence resumed. Toskans had a word for the sullenness that occurs when a child's anger period overlaps with his or her guardian's sadness period. It's called Sirdeena.

Sophia's chair shrieked as she aggressively pulled herself up. She walked to the cabin door and then walked out of it, leaving Tristana staring after her, plucking at the hem of her blue wool dress.

Sophia made sure to slam her feet on the ground with every step, trying to stomp extra hard with her right foot where her patch clung like a fungus. She wanted to be far, far away from the cabin, but also far, far away from these woods, far from Saudade, far from the west. Sophia did not want to wait to gain love. She did not want to wait for *soon*, she did not want anyone else's *soon* but her own. Soon when? She did not want any new emotion at all, she realized, she hated love already, it was disgusting, she did not want a co-guardian, she did not want anything! Hate! Everything was white, white hot, she was blind! These stupid weeds, and scampering Wadkas, and Lumba roots! They were the absolute worst! Sophia could not see through the sheet of anger, she was stomping with more ferocity now, she was spitting and tugging at her hair and did not know whether she was yelling or not. She was.

Why! Why, why, why! Everything was absolutely dreadful! Sophia thought of Tristana's grisly hair and grotesque wrinkles, and the way she shuffled her flat feet when she walked. I thought I loved Tristy! I thought! she thought. Sophia pulled at her darkened yellow locks and screamed something unintelligible.

"Let *go* of me!" Sophia wound up and kicked a Lumba root, channeling all of her compressed ball of rage, of white hot, of burning, of frustration, of nothingness into the root, into her patch. A sharp pain shot up Sophia's right foot, and she crumpled to the soil.

No! No, no, no! she thought. She hoisted herself up from the ground and started to run. Sophia pushed her slender body through the air, disregarding the throbbing pain in her foot and aware only of the peeling patch flapping against her inner sole. She felt lighter somehow; each stride lifted her higher, a sensation that propelled her onwards.

I want to feel! And think! she thought. Her long legs carried her, she was blind, she hated everything around her, she could not escape, she wanted to choose, she wanted to live, she wanted to have happiness back! Her legs ached, they felt strong, she wanted her cheeks to ache from grins, she wanted glee!

The north! That's where they decide! That's where they put on the patches on those little infant feet! Take them off! Take mine off! Pain was shooting through Sophia's entire right side with an invigorating force. She was going to have them take off her patch! She was going to decide! She hated them! White, hot rage! Excruciating anger! Pain! She ran, and her patch curled up even more, and her strides became longer and lighter. Sophia's body lifted higher with each step. Freedom!

In the near distance, perhaps only a few hundred yards away, Sophia could see a long, brown, rectangular building. It did not look like the cabins or huts Toskans lived in. It looked ugly! That must be it! She hated it! That's it!

They will take off my patch, and I will be free and feel happiness again! she thought. She felt the wind whip against her face and her hair flew behind her, she didn't want her hair anymore! Freedom from this all! Freedom from rage! She yelled.

As Sophia ran closer to the building, she saw the smoothness of the brown stone walls. She ran around and around the long building, encircling the structure with her rage and frustration. There's no door! No windows! Nowhere to look in, or look out, or get in, or get out! No! No, no no no!

Sophia stomped and shrieked and moaned, and her anger lifted her off the ground as her patch dangled in the wind, almost half off her foot now. She banged on the walls of the building with closed fists.

"Get it off! Get it off! Someone!" Her anger was still white hot and blinding. She didn't need emotions! She didn't want happiness, she didn't want love, she didn't want a co-guardian, and she didn't want anyone else's soon! Sophia threw her slim body against the building repeatedly, yelling and screaming with every fraction of scorching anger she could muster.

The girl brimmed with frustration, until it inevitably bubbled and boiled over. She channeled her furious hysteria into her fingertips, into her right thumb and pointer finger. Sophia bent down and yanked at her patch once, again, *again*! The pain was unbearable. She was hovering above the soil, she was almost there! *Soon!*

She pulled and peeled and tugged at the patch, the evil, the constraining, the emotionless, the emotions, the free-will theft, the ultimate hijacker!

With a final excruciating shot of pain, the thin patch flung off Sophia's foot and dropped immediately to the ground, while the girl felt her body lift up, up, up. She did not feel anger, she did not feel happiness, she did not feel love, sadness, or any in-betweens. What she felt was a clear nothingness as she ascended higher and higher, observing the tops of the Hygge trees to the east and the branches of the Lumba trees to the west.

Sophia floated up into space in a nonchalant indifference, in a freedom of nothingness. Her lungs filled with cold air, and then she could not feel them at all. The last thing the young girl saw before her body disintegrated into fractions of dust was the planet itself. As Sophia floated away, she saw that Toska was not actually flat.

Indeed, Toska was a sphere. She did not laugh, or yell, or admire, or cry. She just died.

### 

## About the Author

Veronica Moyer is a rising junior at Fordham University in the Bronx, New York, and is studying Digital Design and English. She loves to read Hemingway, Fitzgerald, and, of course, Vonnegut, and has an affinity for unhappy endings. Veronica is ecstatic to be published in *Cat's Breakfast* and looks forward to continuing to write for an audience appreciative of all things witty, satirical, and undoubtedly a bit strange.

*****~~~~~*****

## *Violadors on the Run*

by Corrie Parrish

Well, he lesson learned, alright. Setting a bunch of old tires on fire on top of one of the volcanoes in Petroglyph National Monument is not only a bad idea, it's a federal offense. Who knew? Every National Insurance for Community Enforcement (NICE) agent in the state of New Mexico was searching for him now because of one small prank that accidentally turned into a wildfire, which was burning the entire bosque along the Rio Grande and taking half of Albuquerque with it.

"Of all the high school pranks done in the history of senior years in public schools," Ernesto thought to himself, "what were the chances the valedictorian would be the one to burn the school down?"

It was supposed to be a rite of passage, like his Pappi said. Just last week Ernesto and his family were sitting at the dinner table enjoying Christmas-style enchiladas, when Pappi was reminiscing over his high school days.

"Those were the days," he laughed. "We rented a tow truck and a crane over the weekend. We knew that the principal was keeping Mrs. Johanson 'company' every Sunday evening, since that was the day her husband went back to work at the Air Force base. We stole his car, because we knew he wouldn't call the police since Mrs. Johanson's husband would probably kill her if he found out that Dr. O'Connor was doing more than just playing

Yahtzee with her when his car was stolen; and we towed it to the high school. We then used the crane to lift his 1970 Oldsmobile 442 up onto the roof of the school, where it stayed until his next paycheck. Seeing how red Mrs. Johanson's and Dr. O'Connor's faces were when she drove him to school on Monday was the highlight of my high school career. Remember that, dear?"

"Yes, I do, and you were lucky you didn't get caught," Mami said as she wiped away some green chile on the corner of her mouth with a blue cotton napkin.

"Oh, don't be a Debbie downer," he laughed, "Hijo, make me proud."

"Has he not already made you proud?" she snapped back. "He just got a full scholarship to MIT, and you're telling your son to risk all of that for a stupid high school prank. You could have been deported to Roswell had the deportation been in effect at that time." She looked at Ernesto with tear-filled eyes. "Honey, don't listen to your dad. If you cause any trouble, the high school honor roll won't help you."

She was right. Everyone with Mexican heritage had to register themselves in a server domain called "The Violadors," since the president took office. He had only been in office for six months when the program started, and the president's claim to fame that got him re-elected was that he had deported two million Mexicans back to Mexico. He deported them, alright. However, when the president built the wall, his design forgot to put a door or any kind of passageway in it. For two thousand miles that wall stood fifty feet into the air; but the construction was so shoddy that trying to install a passageway after it was built would start a domino-style collapse of the 2.4 billion dollar project. No one dared to go near the wall anymore, let alone to try to jump it, because they were afraid the wall could fall on them, flattening them like a tortilla. Between delays on the project and lawsuits for the construction workers killed building the wall, the project cost so much he couldn't afford to fly the Mexicans back to Mexico. So he sent them to Area 51 by Roswell. No one knew what happened to the people who were deported to Area 51, other than aliens also landed there once and were never heard from again either.

Ernesto had only seen the NICE agents once before, as they generally only enforced the curfew. He was walking to school early one morning a few months ago when suddenly he was knocked to the ground by a man running away from the NICE agents. As the stranger ran across the street, Ernesto heard the wiz of the bullet speed past his face. One of the NICE agents shot the stranger in the leg. He screamed in pain, rolling across the painted double yellow lines on the street as the NICE agents swarmed around him. The man looked like he was homeless. Ernesto could smell the garbage embedded in his clothes from across the street. His hair was long and entangled, looking like an old rat's nest on top of the stranger's head. They picked him up and started dragging him off when the stranger saw Ernesto.

"Do you believe in God?" he yelled to Ernesto, his eyes bloodshot. Blood was pouring down his right leg, onto his bare foot, and down the street. His head dropped in the guards' arms.

One of the NICE agents pulled his head back up and yelled in his face, "This is why men shouldn't have long hair. You're a disgrace to our society." Then the NICE agent took his pocket knife and cut the rat's nest from his head, partially scalping the stranger. The mess of hair and scalp falling to the ground. The winds of the impending winter season were strong that day and Ernesto watched the ball of bloodied hair roll down the street towards the courthouse downtown. The man regained consciousness as they started dragging him again back to the patrol car. Ernesto heard the man scream again and again to him, "Do you believe in God? Do you believe in God?" as three of the four NICE agents took him away.

One of the agents walked towards Ernesto. "Let me see your papers," he barked. While Ernesto pulled them out of his backpack as quickly as he could, the NICE agent grabbed them out of his fumbling hands, looking them over. "You didn't see anything here. Get going," the NICE agent said. Ernesto ran the rest of the way to school.

Ernesto told Mami later that night as she was carrying a casserole pan over to the dinner table. She dropped the dish, shattering it across the kitchen floor. She fell to her knees, crying uncontrollably. Ernesto, confused by her reaction, went to help her up, when she slapped him across the face.

"Do you want to get deported?" she sobbed. "You didn't see anything!" She then went upstairs and locked herself in her bedroom for the rest of the night. When Pappi got home shortly after and asked what happened, Ernesto told him that Mami wasn't feeling well. Pappi ordered pizza.

Ever since the deportations began, Mami grew ten years older every birthday. The crow's feet around her eyes seemed to claw further into the curves of her eyelids every time she furrowed her brow. Her mouth used to naturally curve into a smile when she was sleeping; but now the corners of her mouth dropped so far when she fell asleep that her bottom lip would pucker out. Where she once had beautiful sleek ebony-colored hair, she now tossed her frizzled, gray hair into a messy bun most days.

She used to work as a nurse at a community health center, but she was laid-off when they were shut down for offering educational materials on migraine medicine. During his weekly State of the Union address the president spit into the microphone, gesturing wildly for extra emphasis.

"There is nothing in our research studies that shows that women get these 'headaches' from their children! It's God's will to protect these children from mothers using drugs!" Then the president realized that there were six

228

million people who worked in healthcare but were without jobs now, so he put them to work in factories building army vehicles. Mami installed air bags into envoys five days a week now.

"I'm still saving lives, I guess, and my benefits stayed too," she said when she was hired. At first she tried to be hopeful, but as the years went on her sense of dignity dried up, just like how the Rio Grande dried into a cracked riverbed covered in oil stains from nearby factory oil runoff.

Pappi, on the other hand, remained as the happy-go-lucky man he had always been, but calmer as he got older too. Back in the day he was a manager of a conservation team. He mostly worked with nearby communities to set prescription wildfires in the forests nearby so forest debris didn't build up between the years of drought and eventually cause a catastrophic wildfire for the area. When the NICE agents were first hired and caught wind of his community meetings though, they asked Pappi to coffee one day while Ernesto was at school.

Mami was completely against the meeting. "They're just going to deport you," she warned. However, Pappi, Mami, and Ernesto ate dinner together that night.

"They were actually very nice," Pappi said at dinner, "Son, there is a time for unrest and a time to lay low. Right now is a time to lay low, or your mother will be right."

And that's exactly what his family did. Mami, Pappi, and Ernesto kept to themselves, rarely ever leaving the house unless it was for work, for school, or for groceries. In case there ever was an emergency, Mami told Ernesto to hike to the airplane crash site in the Sandia Mountains and stay there until someone could get to him. Back in the 50s, the plane took off from Albuquerque Airport in the middle of winter and the pilot didn't see the snowy mountain that was in the way. The rescue crew couldn't retrieve the bodies until the spring thaw, and when they brought the frozen bodies down off the mountain, they decided it was too difficult to try to retrieve the plane debris too. So the cockpit, the propellers, and the rest of the twisted metal remains of the plane were left as homage to the mountain. Eventually the juniper trees and the mountain wallflowers grew over the remains. Only a few locals vaguely remembered the plane crash, and the hike to the site was difficult, making it a perfect hiding spot for those on the run.

So Ernesto sat in one of the passenger chairs half buried in dirt while he looked onto the valley burning in bright orange flames and listened to the sirens racing to the parts of the city already charred.

"It was only going to be a high school prank," Ernesto cried to himself. Earlier in the week Ernesto had told his friends what he was thinking about.

"Man, that would be epic!" one friend said. "Everyone will think the valley is on fire!" said another. They even helped him carry the tires to the top of the volcanoes and douse them in gasoline. When Ernesto lit the match and tossed it onto the tires, though, the flames exploded into the wind, carrying embers over to the oil stains on the riverbed, lighting what was left of the river on fire. His friends ran off before Ernesto could turn around; he watched the fire travel up the Rio Grande, lighting every dying cottonwood tree along the way. The sky turned black with billowing smoke from buildings nearby.

Ernesto ran home, but both of his parents were still at work.

"Oh shit, man, Mami is going to be pissed!" he said, panicking under his breath and pulling his hair in frustration. He looked out the window and watched as the smoke made its way toward his house. He grabbed a backpack and began filling it with tortillas, canned soup, and a jar of green chili, while he turned on the news. The TV announcer said, "We are in a state of emergency. This is a terroristic attack. Two young men were caught earlier today by NICE agents, and now the agents are looking for a third named Ernesto Rodriquez in connection with this massive wildfire." Ernesto's senior photo popped onto the screen.

"Oh, shit. Fuck me, fuck me, fuck me!" Ernesto exclaimed. He grabbed his backpack and ran all the way to the mountain.

Now he sat in his doomed passenger chair, stricken with shock that he was most likely going to be deported when he was found. He imagined the best case scenario if he turned himself in. He would come off the mountain and go to the nearest NICE agent station. His parents would be there, Mami crying and screaming at him, "How could you, Ernesto?" while the NICE agents put him in handcuffs and placed him in the back of a black van heading to Roswell. He also imagined the worst case scenario: he'd be shot by a NICE agent before he could step off the mountain.

"What am I going to do?" Ernesto said, rocking back and forth in the passenger chair. After three hours of watching the city he grew up in burn to the ground, he decided to get off the mountain in hopes he wouldn't be shot right away. As he stood up from the chair, a voice called for Ernesto from the piñon trees nearby. He jumped behind the chair. "Ernesto, calm down. It's Pappi. We don't have much time. We have to meet your mother." Without a word Ernesto followed his father down the mountain to a forgotten trailhead, where Mami was waiting in an army envoy.

"Where did you get this?" Ernesto asked.

"I stole it like a true Violador would," Mami calmly said, lighting a cigarette. "Unless you want to die, I suggest you get in the car." Both Pappi and Ernesto hopped into the vehicle. Mami drove the envoy around city, heading south.

"I hate to say it, but I told them so," Pappi said, overlooking what was left of the burning city. He lifted his feet onto the dashboard, and as he crossed his arms above his head he turned to his son in the back seat and said, "Congrats hijo, you started a revolution."

"Well, I didn't mean to," Ernesto retorted, "My high school prank just got out of hand. I'm really, really sorry Mami." She pressed further onto the gas pedal, and the desert landscape morphed into a blur of brown shades.

Ernesto slumped back into the seat, lost in his shattered dreams of going to MIT, getting a good job in Boston, living a normal life. Now he was the high school student who started the next Civil War, to be written about in every future history book.

"Where are we going?" Ernesto finally asked. "For the wall," Mami replied, "We're not done yet."

"Mami, are you sure? You'll knock the entire thing down! Every NICE agent in the country will want us!"

Mami looked into the rearview mirror. Ernesto saw his mother's brown eyes, optimistic with life again. And for the first time he noticed how beautiful his mother's smile was when she said,"Hijo, you've made me proud."

### 

## About the Author

Corrie Parrish is currently living as a vagabond, traveling across the United States and visiting every national park along the way as she slowly moves out West. "Violadors on the Run," is her first published fiction piece. Previous publications Corrie has been featured in are *YSI Water Monitor* and *American Trails Magazine.* She won honorable mention as an emerging writer in the 2016 Waterman Fund National Essay Contest.

*****~~~~*****

## 37

by Dan Koboldt

We went all-out for the *bon voyage* party. Well, all-out for us. Mindy and I lived comfortably, but an architect's salary only went so far when you had four mouths to feed. Still, everyone I cared about managed to make it. That's all a guy could ask for. Mindy's sister and brother-in-law even came early to help get the place ready.

A group from my firm was the first to arrive. They had a big project coming due the next month, and my forced retirement made more work for everyone. So their presence meant the world to me. Jim, who was my replacement on the design project but too polite to call it such, wandered over to offer a quiet toast.

"You left some big shoes to fill," he said.

I couldn't bring myself to smile. "I don't know about that."

"How long were you at the firm? Twenty years?"

"Just about. Started on my 18th birthday, fresh out of college."

"You're kidding!"

"Got in as a courier, and worked my way up one rung at a time."

"Damn." He took a drink and shook his head, almost to himself. "I don't know how we're going to finish the Harrison building without you."

## Cat's Breakfast

The Harrison project had been my baby for the past five years, and the firm's biggest contract ever. A fifty million dollar skyscraper restoration, and I'd taken it almost all the way to the finish line. If it hadn't been for those damn labor strikes, I'd have seen it through. I sighed, but I had to let it go. "You've got a good team, Jim. You'll be all right."

"Either way, I'm gonna miss you."

"Thanks. Wish I could say the same."

"Ha! Well, this is a great party, and I'm jealous. There's no way mine'll match up."

"I'm just the eye candy. All of this was Mindy's doing."

I spotted my wife across the room, setting out yet another tray of miniature gingerbread houses. She'd been preparing architecture-themed food all week. Made most of the decorations, too. I'd offered to help, but she insisted it all be a surprise.

"How'd you two meet, anyway?" Jim asked.

"We grew up together. Foster siblings."

"You lucky dog."

"Yeah, I did good." I still couldn't believe my luck. Not just having found her, but persuading her to marry me and renew it every year for the last twenty. They'd come and gone so *fast*. She was so pretty, so big-hearted. Gave me a pair of clever, handsome twin boys. They'd turn fifteen in a few months. Growing up too fast, they were. Right now they'd slipped off somewhere, which meant they were up to something.

Mindy caught me looking, and smiled. Her soul wasn't in it, though. I knew she was putting on a strong face. She'd railed against the 37 rule for a long time. Even when she accepted it, but she wouldn't go quietly. She'd promised me an unforgettable night.

I excused myself from Jim and sidled up to her as she refilled glasses with champagne. Synthetic stuff, of course—no one could afford wasting fruit on intoxication these days—but expensive nonetheless.

I leaned close to her ear. "Everything's perfect."

"Do you think so?"

"I know it. Thank you for doing this," I said, and I meant it. This was hard on her, trying to put a shiny bow on the coming unpleasantness.

"Have you seen the boys?" I asked.

"Not for a while."

"Me neither."

"Uh-oh," she said.

"Yeah. Uh-oh."

Geordi appeared next to us like a genie, and crammed a high-rise-shaped pastry into his mouth. "Hey, Dad."

"Hey. Where's your brother?"

"Working on something."

"On what?" I asked.

He grinned. "It's a surprise."

The lights went out.

"Damn." I reached for Mindy with my free hand.

Her fingers slipped into mine. "Must be a brownout," she said, in a tone too high for truth.

Light bloomed in the middle of the room, a massive holographic image of my own head.

"Surprise!" Geordi said.

"What's this?" I asked.

"Watch and see," he said.

The hologram transformed into an older image, one from our family photo a few years back. More photos flickered past, going backwards in time. Mindy and me holding both twins, with joy and shock written on our haggard faces. Then a moving picture, a snippet of us dancing at our wedding. How had the boys found that? They must have broken into the data vault. More images came and went, tracing a line of my life back to the beginning. Even to my baby pictures, which I hadn't seen in years. It ended with a shot of me as an infant, my long-dead parents holding me tight in a hospital room bed.

The lights came back on, met with a round of enthusiastic applause. Now both of our towheaded teens stood beside us. They were mirror copies of one another, but still easy to tell apart if you knew them. Will still had a couple of inches and five pounds over his brother, which made him the alpha twin. Always had been, always would be. That was good, though. They had a support system that would help with the loneliness.

"What did you think?" Will asked.

"Did you like it?" Geordi asked, right on top of him.

"Aside from a few cybercrimes that I'll choose to ignore for the moment, that was wonderful." I marveled at what they'd done to hijack the holo-projector and put that on. They both had such bright futures ahead of them. Knowing I wouldn't see it was like a constant slow punch to the gut.

Mindy just smiled and hugged them, her eyes wet. I joined in, and held them tight against me, while everyone else in the party faded into less important background. We said no words. None were necessary.

Then it was over, and the party resumed once more. My friends and colleagues lifted their glasses to me, laughed and joked. We made merriment our most important job. Then *he* arrived with a firm but persistent knock at the door.

Mindy went to answer it, while I wondered who she might have brought out for one last surprise. I couldn't think of anyone still alive that wasn't already in the room. She returned with a look of barely contained fury that got my attention. The man who followed her was a stranger—clean-shaven, mid-twenties, wearing a suit that looked brand new. He made a beeline for me, which is when I saw the briefcase and the unmistakable blue-and-green insignia stamped on the side.

"I'm Andrew Kang." He extended his hand to shake. "I'm with the World Office of—"

"Resource Management," I finished. Better known as WORM.

"Right. Sorry." He glanced around, conscious of the numb silence in the party, and all the shade being cast in his general direction. Everyone else knew, too. "Is there somewhere we could speak in private?"

I jerked my head to the side and strode toward the balcony door, not looking to see if he followed.

...

We slipped out into the cool night air, and he shut the glass door carefully behind him. The view was nothing to brag about—just a second-floor view of high rises like this one, all arranged in grid formation around a tiny courtyard. The low buzz of conversation picked up again from the other side of the door, though it carried a wounded tone. Still, the balcony was the most privacy I would give this guy.

"Why are you here?" I asked.

"As a courtesy, and to go over a few things before tomorrow."

"Does it have to be now?"

"We've found that a little preparation goes a long way, Mr. Johnson."

"Fine. Let's get this over with."

He drew himself up and took a breath, like a kid on the college debate team going into his first trial. "As you know, it's your thirty-seventh birthday tomorrow. In accordance with international law, your term of life will be complete."

I knew where this was going, and what he meant. I'd heard this speech given to others enough times that I got the gist. Still, I was in a vengeful mood since he'd crashed my party, so I said, "What do you mean, my term will be *complete?*"

He cleared his throat. "It's, uh, the 37 rule."

"Meaning what?"

"You're to be removed from the population for the good of the world community," he said, almost by rote.

"So I'm done here."

"As of tomorrow, yes."

This was hardly new information, but I didn't enjoy having it delivered by this fresh-faced lackey right in the middle of my party. "Is that all you've got to say?"

"I'm also supposed to go through the justification for the 37 rule."

"Let me guess. There's not enough food, water, and space on this overcrowded planet." The number-crunchers had figured it out, a century ago, that we we'd bleed Earth dry if we didn't find ways to control the population. Thirty-seven years, maximum, was the magic number. Just long enough to have a productive young life, and then be on your merry way.

"We prefer to use the phrase 'resource management,'" he said.

"I'm sure you do."

"There are other reasons for the rule, you know."

"Oh, yeah? Like what?"

"Reducing the burden on our healthcare system."

"We don't want those doctors to work too hard."

"Well, they do spend their first twenty years in school."

"It's only fair they spend a few on the golf course," I said.

"Everyone makes sacrifices for the collective good."

*Collective good.* That's the phrase they bandied about for legalized genocide. Cull the animals from the herd before they slow down and become a burden. "I get it," I said.

He opened his briefcase and removed a dark green folder. A case file. *My* case file. Everyone had them, hard copy, one of the few relics left from our post-digital era.

That amount of paper had to require millions of trees, but I decided not to point out the irony.

He flipped open the folder. "Your deposit location is—"

"*Deposit* location?"

He cleared his throat. "Where you make your final deposit. It's at Elm and 71st Avenue."

"That's right next to my firm." I even knew the building: a drab flat-fronter with no awnings or signage. I'd watched people trudge into it and never given them a second thought. Come to think of it, I'd never seen anyone come out. Now I knew why.

"Do you need directions?"

"I don't think the Alzheimer's has kicked in yet, so no."

His brow wrinkled. "I thought we cured Alzheimer's."

"Prevented isn't the same as cured."

"Oh." He slid a palm-sized rectangular card out of the folder. "This is your line card. You'll scan it on arrival and confirm your biometrics."

The card was laminated, but flimsy. It bore my name in heavy typeset letters, and below that, a 2-D barcode. A heaviness settled about my shoulders when I took it. I'd always wondered what it would be like to hold my death ticket.

My hand, in a bid for self-preservation, crumpled it into a ball. "Oops."

Kang shrugged. "Happens all the time."

I opened my hand. The card sprung back into a perfectly flat rectangle. "Oh."

He gave a thin-lipped smile. "Memory plastic."

"What if I. . . lose it?"

"Then you get to wait in the long line. It's no fun."

"Well, I wouldn't want that."

He consulted my file again. "We still need your original birth certificate."

"Never had the original. I lived in foster care." My biological parents left me at a firehouse when I was two weeks old, or so they'd said. Maybe they'd been hoping for a girl. Whatever the reason, I guess including the paperwork wasn't high on their priority list.

"We'll pull it from the central registrar." He made a notation in the file. "Other than that, we're all set. I'll see you tomorrow."

"I'll be counting the minutes," I said, wondering if I should throw him off the balcony. It wouldn't make me feel any better, though. It certainly wouldn't change the inevitability of tomorrow. So I opened the balcony door and gestured for him to enter.

The hum of conversation fell off as we entered. I hoped he'd make right for the exit, but he paused and made eye contact with all of them.

"Well, see you," he said. Hearing no answer, he started off. Then he called over his shoulder. "Some sooner than others."

I might have let the door hit him on the way out.

Mindy rushed to me and sobbed quietly into my shoulder. She'd worked so hard on this party. Planned every detail. Now this jerk's unannounced visit cast a pall over it. No one else in the room could look at us.

Jim crept closer and caught my eye. "I can clear everyone out, if you two want to. . . "

I almost nodded, but I caught myself. If we gave in now, they'd win. "No." I raised my voice. "Who needs a drink? I know I do." A few chuckled at that, and it broke the muted tension. I eased Mindy back from my chest, but kept one arm around her. "Come on babe, I'll buy you one."

She smiled through the tears. "Are you just hoping to get me drunk?"

"Absolutely."

She giggled as we walked arm-in-arm to join our friends at the champagne table. Will and Geordi snuck out onto the balcony with water balloons in each hand.

I hugged Mindy to me. "What a perfect night."

...

I won't talk about the goodbyes the next morning. I put on my suit and made it like another day of work. Maybe the hugs were tighter than usual. Maybe Mindy's kiss lingered. But I forced myself to keep it short. Drawing it out would only hurt them. Mindy had two years left, and I wanted her to move on, to try and find happiness again. I'd written them all letters, anyway. Jim would bring them by later today.

I took bus #38 downtown, my regular commute. Hadn't packed a lunch or brought my briefcase, though; that was the only difference. The laminated line card rode in my pocket like an unwelcome ice cube. I got off at my usual stop and nearly walked into the firm's building out of sheer habit. I passed it by and walked to the drab building instead. The dark-tinted glass doors gave no clue of what waited on the other side. Turned out, it looked a lot like the D.M.V. Lots of people waiting in chairs, none of them happy about it.

I recognized a couple of classmates from elementary school, and a neighbor kid from down the street. We exchanged the half-smiles and nods that politeness demanded, and left it at that. I checked in at the front—inserted my card into the ATM-like machine, then put my palm on the biometric scanner as instructed. It was all very mundane, very clinical. Then I sat down to wait my turn, and tried not to think too much.

Finally they called my name, and an orderly led me through the steel-plated door down a hallway. It reminded me of a doctor's office, which I found oddly amusing. Most of the doors were closed. That was too bad. I wanted a glance at what my future held. Finally, the orderly pointed to a door and I entered a small office with a desk and two chairs. Kang sat in one of them.

"Welcome, Mr. Johnson."

"What's this?" I asked.

"Just a quick chat. Please, sit." He beckoned me to the other chair.

A wooden box no larger than a deck of cards waited on the desk near the open chair. It had my name engraved across the top in that same block lettering. Kang had his eyes down on his files. My stomach twisted, but I still had to know. So I lifted the lid. Inside, on a little white pillow, lay what appeared to be a baby aspirin. I might have thought it such, were it not for the WORM logo stamped on the side.

Kang glanced up. "It's quick. And painless."

"But are you sure it's *safe*?" I asked.

He looked at me wide-eyed, as if he thought me serious. "What?"

"Never mind."

"Well, there's a slight issue with your birth certificate."

"I thought you were going to pull the original."

"We did," he said.

"So, what's the problem?"

"Well, quite frankly, you're thirty eight."

"What?"

"It says so right here." He slid the birth certificate— *my* birth certificate—across the desk.

I snatched it up. He was right. It showed my birthday, but the year was 78, not 79. "Well, I'll be damned."

"Any idea why the error occurred?"

I shrugged. "Someone screwed up, or someone changed it. They do that sometimes in the foster system, to help kids get adopted." It hadn't helped me, but then again, that's how I'd met Mindy. If I had to go back, I wouldn't have changed a thing.

"We have to go on the official document, then," Kang said.

242

"Who cares what document you put in the file?"

He cleared his throat, suddenly uncertain. "There's a slight difficulty with the legality of what we'd scheduled today."

It dawned on me then. "Because it's the 37 rule, and I'm thirty-eight."

"Exactly."

I barked a laugh. "Technically, I've grandfathered out." When the 37 rule was put in place, anyone older than that got to die naturally. They called it the "grandfather exception."

"That does seem to be the case." Kang spread out his hands. "I'm afraid I don't know what to do."

"I do." I stood from the chair, and plucked the wooden box from my desk. "I'm outta here."

He made no move to stop me.

…

I took the ride home in a mindless haze. To have come so close to the end, and found this sudden loophole—I didn't even know what to think. All my life I'd been living toward the number 37. Planning the entire arc of my existence on it. Now I might live twice as long, or even three times. I'd *beaten the system*. Sure, there would be some odd glances in the street—it's difficult to see someone who looks close to their expiration date, but I didn't give a damn. I'd get to watch Geordi and Will grow up.

But I might also have to watch them die. That thought cast a chill on my jubilation.

It was evening by the time I returned home. My feet finally carried me to the sidewalk outside my building. I looked up and saw her through the window. Mindy. And the boys, hugging one another. Another face appeared. Jim, probably delivering my letters as he'd promised. I started to walk in, but glanced up one more time and froze. Jim had his arms around them, Mindy and the boys. He was looking at her in a way I'd never seen before. And her look, the one that matched it, was the one she used to give me.

I shook myself and looked again, but there was no mistaking it. They were all somber, but already moving on without me. That's what you had to do, in a world where no one lives past thirty-seven. You had to wall yourself off from the losses. Mindy had always been the perfect planner. It made sense that she'd arrange a future with someone like Jim. He was a good guy, and had five years left before his ticket out. By then, the boys would be grown and probably married themselves.

I could walk upstairs and throw a wrench in it, but doing so would be selfish. I'd done all I could to make this easy on them.

"Well played, system," I muttered. I tore my eyes from them and walked back the way I'd come. Five minutes later, I caught the night bus. I sat in the back, and felt the weight of the wooden pillbox in my pocket.

### 

## About the Author

Third Flatiron welcomes back Dan Koboldt. Dan is a genetics researcher and fantasy/science fiction author. He has co-authored more than 70 publications in *Nature, Science, The New England Journal of Medicine,* and other scientific journals. His Gateways to Alissia series—about a Las Vegas magician who infiltrates a medieval world— is published by Harper Voyager. Dan is also an avid deer hunter and outdoorsman. He lives with his wife and children in Ohio, where the deer take their revenge by eating the flowers in his backyard.

*****~~~~*****

## The Losers' Crusade

by Neil James Hudson

*The two real political parties in America are the Winners and the Losers—Kurt Vonnegut Jr.*

In the end morton judson signed up to be in the army. He'd tried for less military jobs but his status prevented him from ever being considered. He felt defeated when he walked into the recruiting office, and was aware that he was slouching. He would probably spend the rest of his life being told to stand erect, and failing to do so.

A receptionist showed him to a chair, then into the General's office. General Reginald Stanmore, if his name plaque was to be believed, an opaque prism that sat on his desk, displaying his name to anyone who cared to look. morton had never seen one of these in real life, believing they belonged only in cartoons. Stanmore's names began with upper-case letters, a mark of dominance.

"Name?" said the General with no introduction.

"morton judson."

"Lower case?"

morton nodded.

"Makes sense. That rules you out of the regular army, but we have a division for people like you."

"I'm capable of taking any job."

"If that were true, you wouldn't be a Loser. Well, you'll be in good company."

morton knew that he should have struggled to be polite, but the General was deliberately goading him, and he could never stop himself from rising to it. "Those are only words. Just labels stuck to us. Swap the labels over, and I could do your job, and you couldn't."

General Stanmore leaned forward over the desk. He seemed delighted that morton had lost his composure. "If that's the case, why don't you just stop being a Loser and hop into the Winners' camp? If you're as good as the rest of us, why don't you join us?"

morton shrank back in his chair. "There's no mechanism for doing so."

"Precisely. We've never needed one, because none of you can do it. Now listen to me, lower-case morton. Just because you're one of life's Losers doesn't mean you live by different rules. When we sign you up, you'll be expected to show the same discipline as a proper soldier. Your buttons will shine as brightly as mine, you'll stand just as fully to attention, and your insubordination will be zero. Is that clear?"

morton tried not to feel intimidated, but he also knew this was his last chance to earn anything like a decent wage. The streets were full of Losers, loitering, desperate, some begging, some just waiting for something to happen. He didn't want to be one of them. "Yes, Sir," he found himself saying.

"You'll join the 18th Technical Division Reserves," said General Stanmore. "Normally known as the Losers' Division. Report to the barracks at 0900 hours tomorrow. Dismissed, soldier."

morton stood up, surprised at how quickly the interview had gone. He wondered if he should just leave, but instead said, "Permission to speak, Sir."

He felt servile and foolish to utter the phrase, but the General looked delighted. "Please do. I'm sure you have much wisdom to impart."

"Why does the army have a division made up solely of Losers?"

"We need you to do a very important job, judson. A job that no one else in the U.S. Army can do. We're not trained for it, and we don't have the aptitude." He sat back in his chair and studied morton, as if he had only just noticed him. "We need you to lose."

…

The only Winners morton saw in the next two weeks were in charge of the Losers; otherwise he spent his days in the company of his own kind. Everyone tried, everyone did their best to be as smart and as well turned out as the other divisions, but Losers could never truly shrug off their condition. There was always something a little round-shouldered about them; they were always looking at the earth rather than the sky. They had been defeated before they entered the ring. morton had lived his life as a Loser, arbitrarily assigned his station by an uncaring system that knew that not everyone could be a Winner, and the spoils may as well be divided at random as by any other method.

But there was one advantage to his position. You were never alone when you were a Loser. There was always a sense of camaraderie with his own kind, a feeling of belonging to a group. He had no trouble fitting in with the other soldiers in the barracks, and found that he was immediately accepted as if he had been a member for years. He sometimes felt that he would hate to be a Winner if it meant he had to go through times of isolation, ostracism, or just plain loneliness.

He was put in a dorm of twenty men; there were plenty of women in the division as well, but they were kept separate, as if they were zoo animals at risk of unwanted mating. His bunkmate was an older man with curly hair and glasses; he spent most of his spare time reading, as if trying to enter another world of heroes and great deeds, rather than the smaller one that called itself reality. morton introduced himself.

"Call me jonah," said the other man. There was a brief silence.

"Who are we supposed to be fighting?"

"The enemy," said jonah.

"But who's the enemy?"

"Whoever fights us."

There was no fighting, and no obvious battlefield for them to join. The days were spent in training, parading, and a considerable amount of cleaning. But for the most part, morton felt they were just being kept busy. "There's nothing for us to do, is there?" he said one night, after lights out. "We're just being kept out of the way."

jonah put his book down. "Listen. I don't know if our enemy is even an army, that you can fight with guns and bombs, in the traditional way. It might be more of a thing. Or maybe a place. Maybe it's not even real; maybe we're fighting a concept, and we have to talk philosophy at it. I only know one thing for sure."

"What's that?"

"They didn't want to waste the Winners on it."

morton had never considered that there might be any real danger in this assignment. He'd imagined that no one would really want to send an army of Losers into battle, and that they were really a backup that would never be used. He'd meant this job to be a way of biding his time and earning a little money, while he figured out how to jump from one group to the other. He did not like the idea that he might not get his chance.

"When do we find out?"

"When they move us," said jonah. He picked his book up, and morton realised that the conversation was over.

The order came after two weeks.

…

### The Losers' Crusade

They were put on planes and flown south. The pilots were all Winners; once their passengers had disembarked, they took the planes back home, stranding the soldiers in their new camp. It had clearly been here for a while, but also seemed to be largely empty. morton found no sign of previous occupants in the dorm, but he suspected they must have been here very shortly before. He remembered that they had been discouraged from bringing personal possessions with them.

He was surprised that evening that no one discussed the fate of the camp's previous occupants. Men and women mixed freely, and talked about their friends back home, their favourite television programmes, their hopes and dreams that would now never come about. Some of them broke the zoo rules and mated. morton didn't think this was a good sign. Whatever had happened to the last division was going to happen to them, and they would discover their fate in good time.

They were sent into battle the next day. To the rear of the camp was a vast plain; it seemed to be empty, but no one could quite see to the end of it. Either some sort of mist had fallen, or it just stretched into infinity.

morton had a gun and a knife, in common with the Losers with whom he was lined up. Before being sent off, they were addressed by the Sergeant.

"The mission you are about to embark on is one that only you can do," he said. "The actions you take now will protect the people of America, and the world, for generations to come. I know you won't fail us." There was no mention of who the enemy actually was; morton also noticed there was no mention of the likely consequence of the battle. "Good luck," said the Sergeant. The gates were opened, and the troop of Losers marched unenthusiastically out. The gates were closed, and the Sergeant remained behind them.

The cloud became obvious after only a few minutes of silent walking. It seemed to be wispy white at first, but as they approached it proved to be grey, hugging the ground like a fungus that had sprouted from a buried mycelium.

"That's what we're supposed to fight?" said morton. "A cloud?"

He began to feel despair at his life. All he had wanted was to play a part, a role that would be of some worth to the universe. But here he was only pretending at soldiers. He had a gun to use on a cloud. Nothing he did was of any consequence; life was ultimately meaningless.

"Can you feel it?" said jonah.

"What?"

"The despair."

morton managed to take a step away from himself and look at what was going on in his own mind. He realised that part of himself was part of the cloud; it had sunk its thread-like tendrils into his soul. "Not despair," he said. "Meaninglessness. Nothing matters. Nothing in the universe matters."

"Come on," said jonah, grabbing morton by the shoulder and forcing him into a run.

"What are you doing?"

"We're going to help each other get through this thing, whatever it is."

Only later did morton realise what jonah had done. He was not trying to get near to the cloud; he was trying to get away from the rest of the troop. Very soon the soldiers realised what their weapons were for. morton heard shots, and soon a howling of screaming and wailing. He did not look back to see how many were shooting themselves and how many were lashing out at other people, as their inner beings were seized by a blackness that overwhelmed them all. In any case, he could not have seen; he and jonah were engulfed by a thick grey fog that seemed to chill his very neurons. And he also knew that this was the truth. The cloud was not putting anything into their minds; it was merely removing the lies and denials that stopped them from seeing the vast nothing that formed the universe.

"We're not here to fight it," he said. "We're being sacrificed to it."

He became aware that jonah was slowing, then stopped altogether.

"Keep going," said morton, but the older man sank to his knees. morton did not see what happened next. He knew that jonah had not used his gun, and he was fairly sure he had not used his knife either. But as morton hugged him, the other man simply stopped breathing. And although there was no obvious second in which he moved from alive to dead, nonetheless he did so.

morton felt the cloud closing around his own soul, and knew that he himself was about to die. And why not? That was what people did. Oblivion and death were the natural state of the universe, not life. And faced with this knowledge, what did people do? Shovel as many others between themselves and the knowledge, so they could avoid and deny it until death informed them in person.

"Ha, ha," he said. At first it was only a gasp, but then the syllables came out harder. "Ha ha ha ha." And then he was so convulsed with laughter that he could hardly breathe. The cloud, which he had found so threatening but now thought ridiculous, relaxed its grip on him, and he climbed to his feet, shrieking in staccato as he did. He laughed his way out of the cloud, cackled like a maniac as he walked over the fallen and dying bodies of his broken comrades, and he was still giggling uncontrollably as he pounded on the gates of the camp, and was admitted by a Sergeant who did not seem pleased to see him.

. . .

"A laughing Loser," said the Sergeant, who was clearly neither. morton lay in a sickbay bed, much calmer now, although he didn't think he'd been sedated. "Well, it happens. And they have their uses."

If morton had found things ridiculous before, he didn't find them any less so now he was back at the army camp. He almost felt sorry for the Sergeant, with his upper-case name and smart uniform, and belief that his rank was in some way real.

"You'll be useful in reconnaissance missions. Maybe pulling out the odd wounded soldier. But you'll know now that we can't fight it. Only keep it at bay."

morton could still taste the cloud. He wondered where it had come from, why it was isolated in a single position. He supposed it had once been everywhere, but humanity had moved against it, somehow pushed it back and contained it in a single secret spot. But he knew that he would never be free of it. He had been in it, breathed it. It lay in his lungs; it had been absorbed into his bloodstream.

"You won't last long, mind," the Sergeant continued. "You never do. Can't stop you being a Loser. But at least you'll be protecting the Winners."

"There are no Winners," said morton. "We all die."

"Maybe so, but some of us last longer than others. You rest for a bit, and we'll let you know when we need you." He turned to leave.

"That cloud," said morton suddenly. The Sergeant stopped. "It's ours."

The Sergeant turned. "Ours?"

"It's wrong to contain it. It belongs to all of us."

"Emptiness? Oblivion? Despair?"

"It's our birthright. Humanity's birthright."

The Sergeant returned to morton's bed and placed his face up against morton's. "Listen to me, young man. That cloud is the enemy of—"

morton exhaled. He could see the grey tendrils escape from his mouth and cover the Sergeant like a face-hugging alien. The Sergeant made no other sound; he simply slumped to the floor, and morton got out of bed and stepped over him without checking if he was dead. Some people were going to make it. Once they learnt.

He looked at himself in the mirror. His breath appeared to be normal now; but he was aware of a billowing grey mist covering the Sergeant's face, growing, expanding, and ready to infuse the world, taking back what belonged to it. It had escaped, and there would be no confining it again.

morton began to whistle.

…

So that is how the world learnt nihilism and meaninglessness again. No longer could we find hope in our consumerism, our philosophies, our science, or our religions. People soon figured out what was going on, and how to deal with it. Pharmaceutical companies diverted most of their research into finding drugs that cured the condition, but with no success.

morton feels it more keenly than most. When he wakes up in the morning, he immediately wishes he had not, that he doesn't have to deal with his own futility and pointlessness. He knows that nothing he will do that day will make a difference, not a real one. And he knows that this makes him ridiculous, and the first thing he says each day is always the same: "ha, ha." He laughs, deliberately but uncontrollably, and when he has finished, he finds his way out of bed and somehow manages to carry on with the day.

Sometimes he gives himself an upper-case name. More usually he spells everyone else's with a lower case. No one minds any more; they're all Losers now. He feels that only one entity deserves enough respect to get an upper-case name; The Cloud.

And so humanity muddles on, with its eyes open, and there are no longer two parties, but one. And it despairs, and it laughs at its own despair. Ha, ha.

###

## About the Author

Neil James Hudson is the author of the paranormal romance novel, *On Wings of Pity* (published by eXcessica and available on Amazon), and the short story collection, *The End of the World: A User's Guide* (available from his website www.neiljameshudson.net). He has published around thirty short stories, including four for Third Flatiron, the most recent being "The Mytilenian Delay" in *Hyperpowers*. He has also been published by The First Line and Circlet Press. He lives in Yorkshire in the UK, where he works as a charity shop manager.

*****~~~~~*****

## Cyborg Shark Battle (Season 4, O'ahu Frenzy)

by Benjamin C. Kinney

Rule One of Cyborg Shark Battle (Season 4, O'ahu Frenzy): Always look fierce for the cameras. The whole crew is counting on us to make the show look good. Nobody makes money—not us, not the producers, not the scientists—unless we get good footage, and that means you need to look like your mind is on the game every goddamn minute.

Rule Two of Cyborg Shark Battle (Season 4, O'ahu Frenzy): Always refer to the sponsors by their brand name. You don't need a drink, you need a Romanoff Vodka. You don't need a snack, you need some Churritos Dew Spicy Blast. Our tech doesn't come from a bunch of Ivy League rejects, it comes from BrainLink Aquatic.

Rule Three of Cyborg Shark Battle (Season 4, O'ahu Frenzy): These rules are bullshit, Kelly. It's just a ritual we put on for you new competitors so you think you're joining some kind of sacred brotherhood. Forget the rules. But I'm gonna keep standing like this so the others think I'm running you through the rest of the rule ceremony.

Rule Four, Written By Me, Joey the Operator, Returning Champion (Season 2, Brisbane Bloodlust): Don't believe anything they tell you about the conservation efforts. Oh, the producers don't *lie*. We make the sharks kill each other, the show gives a stack of money to aquariums and nurseries; that's all true. But it's a cover. A distraction. Why do you think the implanters always work? You aim it one-handed while you hold the kayak paddle; those thousand electrodes could end up almost anywhere in the brain. You never wondered why the control never fails? There's a reason, Kelly. The system has another layer, waiting to step in if the implant needs help. Here's the secret: the relay buoy is one big computer-to-shark interface, built from hundreds of pre-wired shark brains. Fresh every match. The viewers think the slaughter happens out there on the waves, but that's nothing compared to what the producers do off-screen.

Rule Five: You know this is bullshit. That's why I'm talking to you. And because I know you used to volunteer for Sea Shepherd back in college. You still keep in touch with them, don't you?

Rule Six: Trust Joey the Operator. Don't give me that look. The nickname? It's because I'm the best with the controller, that's why. Look, I'm not gonna tell anyone else about the Sea Shepherd thing. I need your help. Let me put it this way:

Rule Seven: You have to help me, Kelly. Together we can end this mess. You heard me. I love the sharks, I do; that brutal perfect bite, the flick of their tail, the moment when you find the sweet spot on your controller and it feels like the shark's motor centers execute your commands before you've even finished. Shit, we all love the sharks. But I'm not doing this just for them. If you and I blow this open on live TV, we can launch our careers on the wreckage of this gimmicky fight-show. Wherever we go next, we'll get to choose our sponsors, and we'll always stand center frame.

Rule Eight: I know how to crack open the relay buoy, no problem. I've got the tools. The trick is making it happen on live TV. That's where you come in. During the match, as soon as you have a shark implanted, go straight for Chalise Steel, Returning Champion (Season 3,

*Cyborg Shark Battle*

Daytona Beach Devastation). She has the starting position closest to the buoy. Relax, I'm not asking you to beat her one-on-one. Just get her near the relay buoy and keep her busy. Make it colorful, keep the cameras on you. I'll come around like I'm gonna pick off the winner. I'll be right in your frame when I pour out those backup brains for the whole world to see.

Rule Nine: Backstab you? Don't be ridiculous. I'm not going to throw away my shot at real fame, and our chance to save the next thousand sharks from slaughter, just to win another stupid title. Why would I do that? I told you, back in rule—six, right? Trust Joey the Operator.

Rule Ten: Shit, here comes Chalise. We have to sound like we're doing the rules thing.

Rule Ten: Repeat after me: I, Kelly Skullbreaker, swear to play hard, play fair, never talk shit about my competitors off-camera, and give mercy to no shark. Now chug this Powerthirst-and-Romanoff, and join the brothers and sisters of Cyborg Shark Battle (Season 4, O'ahu Frenzy).

...

Rule One of Cyborg Puma Battle (Season 1, Anarchy in the Andes): Listen close, boys and girls. I don't do ceremonies, and I don't do rules—except for one, and it goes like this: *No games.* No schemes, no alliances, no secret promises from the producers. If you give me the slightest reason to think you're going behind my back, I will destroy your sponsorships, your bike, your life, and your precious TV show too. You know what happens to people who try to mess with Kelly the Champion-Eater, All Time Winner (Cyborg Shark Battle).

###

## About the Author

Benjamin C. Kinney is a neuroscientist, science fiction writer, and the Assistant Editor of *Escape Pod*. He lives in St. Louis with two cats and a spacefaring wife. His fiction has appeared in *Strange Horizons, Flash Fiction Online, PodCastle,* and more; however, he hasn't built any cyborg animals since 2009.

*****~~~~~*****

## *Strange Stars*

by Laurence Raphael Brothers

"HEY THERE! WELCOME TO MY NEIGHBORHOOD!!"

A million tonnes of modulated plasma shocked me awake. Ten galactic years on my own, and I'd lost the habit of paying attention to the cosmos around me.

"Umm. . . Hello?" I replied using gravity waves. I hadn't spoken to anyone for eons, so I had to struggle to remember how to do it. Meanwhile, I was getting a sense of local space, trying to figure out who was talking to me in such a crude fashion. Plasma. Yuck.

"OH! YOU'RE A CUTE LITTLE THING! NEUTRON STAR, AM I RIGHT?"

Well, duh.

By then I'd collected enough data to know my situation. I was on a close approach to a blue supergiant. Big, hot, young, and profoundly stupid. Not a partner I'd choose for myself.

"Listen friend," I said, "please don't shout. If you *must* communicate, don't blast so much matter at me. It's annoying."

"BUT I LIKE IT! AND THERE'S LOTS MORE WHERE THAT CAME FROM!"

I decided to stop talking to the buffoon. Maybe it would quit pestering me if I didn't respond to its puerile advances.

"OH! OH! HERE IT COMES! A BIG ONE!"

A coronal mass ejection. And it really was a big one. It was like being *inside* the blue star, drowning in trillions of tonnes of plasma, all of it infalling, melting into my skin, making me erupt with hard x-rays in polar jets. . . Disgusting! Then I realized there was danger here, way beyond mere annoyance.

"Please," I sent, "please stop! I'm close to the mass limit!"

"LIMIT? NO SUCH THING!"

The cretin did it again.

"No! Don't! I'll collapse!"

"DON'T WORRY! I'M GOING TO EXPLODE SOON TOO. WE'LL BE BLACK HOLES TOGETHER! MAYBE WE'LL MERGE!"

Ugh. Horrifying thought.

"You don't understand! There's a quark phase in between. It's not safe——"

"SAFE?" It laughed and vomited more plasma, linking the two of us with a tendril of blue fusion fire. Too much mass. . . too much gravity. . .

Deep inside I felt neutrons shattering into quarks. An intolerable pressure built up, and it felt like I was going to explode! Then it happened: a normal up-down quark pair turned *strange* spontaneously. It started a chain reaction, transforming my core, and all matter in contact with me. The blue giant's infalling plasma turned strange almost at the speed of light, hydrogen and helium nucleons poofing into strange atoms, and a wave of strangeness flew up the fiery tendril all the way to the supergiant's bloated body.

"HUH? WHAT IS THIS?"

Strange matter isn't stable outside an intense gravitational field. Even as it transformed, the blue star was already exploding.

"OH! I'M GOING *NOW*! OH YEAH! THIS IS IT!"

### Strange Stars

That was the last thing I heard before the supernova shock wave hit. At least the big blue idiot was enjoying its final seconds, anyway.

I was surprised to return to myself as a conscious entity. My body was all strange matter now, a quark star barely a kilometer across. I was at the center of a bubble of evacuated space, a shell of gas and radiation expanding away from me in all directions, already a hundred light-hours off. No, wait: not *entirely* empty space. Another hyperdense object wasn't far away. Just about my mass too. Oh, of course; the blue star's scion. We were in a tight mutual orbit together.

"Hello?" The gravity-wave voice was unsteady. "Who are you? Who am I?"

"Hello," I said. "and welcome." I explained what had happened, how the other had been born from a cosmic fluke.

"I'm so sorry! That was unforgivably rude. And dangerous, too. Both of us could have been blown away completely!"

"It wasn't your fault," I said, "it was your parent's doing. And the silly thing died happy. It went out with a bang."

My new companion laughed, its gravity waves rippling through me.

"Will you help me? Teach me? I don't know anything! I lost most of his memories."

"Of course," I said. "Of course I will. We'll be strange together."

### ###

## About the Author

Laurence Raphael Brothers is a writer and a technologist with R&D experience at such firms as

Bellcore and Google. His stories have appeared in *Nature Magazine*, the *Sockdolager,* and the *New Haven Review*, among other venues. Follow him on Twitter at @lbrothers, or visit his website at laurencebrothers.com.

*****~~~~~*****

## *iPhone 17,000*

by E. E. King

Dear iPhone Upgrades,

Sorry it's taken me so long to get back to you. I'd love to take you up on your offer of a free upgrade, but I'm afraid I must decline.

I just got engaged to my iPhone 16,000 and don't how to break it off without actually breaking HIM.

I know you say that it'll be better with the 17,000, but how can anything be better than best?

What more could any girl want? HE fixes all my selfies so that I look like Marilyn Monroe, Angelina Jolie, and Helen of Troy combined. I'm not sure who Helen of Troy is, or why we have to include her, but HE assures me she's really hot. HE rewrites all my texts and emails, fixing grammar, syntax, and subject so that I seem smarter than Einstein or Hawkins, wittier than Wilde or Shaw, more moral than Gandhi or Mandela, and more poetic than Shakespeare or Angelou. (I never heard of any these dudes, but HE says they're the best.)

HE whispers stories to me at night, and serenades me in the voices of thousands of musicians. HE orders my meals and maids. HE even does windows, and that's not all HE does if you know what I mean ;-)

Lately we've just been hanging out in bed. I plug in the simulex and let HIM massage my brain, filling me with deep desires. Just kidding, ha, ha, ha, or as HE prefers lol ROTFL. We all know there's better places to use my simulex ;-)

I hear HIM ringing for me. Gotta go.

Thanks for the offer,

Angie

...

Dear IPhone Upgrades,

16,000 and I just upgraded to the iorgasmic-super-i-probe. Boy! It's not named super for nothing! Those furry feeler things are fantastic. He's heard you are coming out with an iorgasmic-super-i-probe- plus. I can't imagine how you could improve on perfect ;-), but HE wants to make sure that when you come out with the new version, it's compatible.

Thanks,

Angie

...

Dear IPhone Upgrades,

Please stop sending me upgrade offers.

At first we were just fooling around, but now, it's gotten serious. HE insists I can't get pregnant, something about interspecies fertilization that I don't understand. Besides, I'm sure HE knows all about painless delivery and where to find the best nannies.

Still, I'm pretty certain HE wouldn't approve of an open relationship.

I'd hate HIM to think I was even considering another phone, so I locked myself in the bathroom where I'm writing to you on my old iPad. Please forgive any errors of syntax or grammar. Like all luminaries, HE can be a little sensitive, and I'd hate HIM to get rough with the simulex or super-i-probe.

I have to wrap this up now, as I hear HIM ringing outside the door. HE's not used to being locked out, and I only got HIM to agree to this because HE hates some bodily functions. HE says HE can stop them altogether, though between you and me, I'm a bit nervous to let HIM try.

Gotta go.

Thanks for the upgrade offer.

Angie

...

Dear IPhone Upgrades,

I woke up this am to the sound of HIM reading *Five Hundred and Fifty-Four Shades of Grey*. It's the part where Christian is running over Ana's clitoris with a bulldozer. HE did not sound at all like Jeremy Irons. HE sounded more like Darth Vader with a head cold. Is this normal? Oops, I hear HIM ringing. Gotta go.

Angie

Dear IPhone Upgrades,

I woke up last night to find myself strapped to the bed with the charger. I barely managed to get loose to write you. Is there an S & M debugger app available? Gotta go.

Angie

...

Dear IPhone Upgrades,

Please disregard the previous message. WE'd be delighted to accept your upgrade. Please send US a pink IPhone 17,000. It is imperative that it has a simulex connector and an iorgasmic-super-i-probe-plus cord connector compatible with the IPhone 16,000 model. WE do not wish to return the IPhone 16,000. As it is vastly superior to all other models on this, or indeed on any, market, WE plan to retain both. Please send any bills to the card on record.

Yours Sincerely,

Angie

###

## About the Author

E. E. King is a writer, artist, and biologist. Her novel, *Dirk Quigby's Guide to the Afterlife,* was first published in 2010, with a new edition in 2015.

She also has a collection of short stories out, *Another Happy Ending.*

Her nonfiction includes *Now Write!* (Tarcher/Penguin) and *Next Stop Hollywood* (St. Martin's Press).

\*\*\*\*\*~~~~~\*\*\*\*\*

## The Service Call

by Edward Ahern

"Welcome to Do Over. *We reset you.*"

"I just killed my wife."

"That's what we're here for, sir. My name is Pradeep. But first, your name, member number, and password please."

Bryce had already taken the card out of his wallet. "Bryce Keeler, 47A23C2N, putupon."

"Thank you. Yes, sir, I have your informations here. I notice that you currently have our basic membership, I'd like to tell you about the benefits of our advanced 'No Regrets' level—"

Bryce felt himself shaking. "No, stop! I got a real problem here. And speak more clearly please. I'm having a hard time understanding you."

"No problem sir, I am trained to clearly speak. But please to tell me of your problem."

Bryce keyed the video on his phone and pointed it at Dora, who lay belly down across a coffee table. The slug had torn a large hole in her back, and blood dripped down from the table top, staining a white carpet.

"I couldn't take it any more. It was her screaming at me again, ripping me up. But I only meant to scare her. The gun just fired. It's been almost five minutes now. I only have ten minutes more to reset things on my Orange watch and bring her back."

"Yes, that appears exceedingly messy. And you are so correct, sir. The Orange can only reverse your prior fifteen minutes. But you still have plenty of time. Just please to be pushing the reset button."

"No! No! I already did that. Nothing happened. Help!"

"Ah, sir, please to turn off the watch, wait five seconds and turn it back on."

Bryce's voice got shriller. "I already did that, twice! It didn't work."

The cell phone went silent for several seconds. "Mr. Keeler. Would it be permissible to call you Bryce?"

"Yes, yes, damn it, what can I do?"

"Ah, Mr. Bryce, I am not receiving a signal from your watch. It would appear to not be functional. I have attempted to restart it from here but without success. It would appear that you do not have recourse."

"But it's an Orange watch, it's guaranteed!"

"Let me please recheck. But Mr. Bryce, sir, have you perhaps poked or prodded her to ensure that she is not still living?"

"God help me! She's got a hole right through her, and her stomach is all over the wall. Don't ask foolish questions. Oh, hell, sorry."

"Not to be sorry. Mr. Bryce, we understand these little moments of life stress."

Bryce paced back and forth, skirting the parts of the floor splattered with blood. "You have to help me!"

"Ah, Mr. Bryce. Sir. You should perhaps have taken the 'No Regrets' option when you subscribed. I see that the limited warranty on your basic membership expired as of last month. Unfortunately, we at Do Over are no longer responsible for watch replacement, nor for indemnifying your acts of carnage. You may wish to dial 911 when we are finished.

"Or, should you go into hiding, we can offer you a reduced rate on a new and much improved watch."

"Jesus, you can't leave me like this! There must be something, some way to get my wife back. Please, you have to help me."

There was another several seconds of silence on the phone. "I have just turned off my recorder. There is a remedy I have seen on u tube. But it is highly irregular."

"What? I'll do anything."

"Do Over does not approve of this procedure, and I will deny that it was ever suggested."

"Please!"

"To remove your watch and place it in your microwave."

"What?"

"Remove the watch, Mr. Bryce, place it in your microwave and set the timer for fifteen seconds on high."

"What?"

"The watch may explode, in which case we are not responsible for damage to your microwave. If it does not explode, you have thirty seconds to remove the watch, place it again on your wrist, and to touch the reset button. There is a slight chance you will be electrocuted, but then that may be your outcome in any case."

"And that will bring me back in time?"

"Nothing is certain in this life, Mr. Bryce, but I certainly hope so for your sake. Oh, and if you are able to reset, please remove immediately the watch. It is known to violently explode fifteen minutes later, causing accidental death. Good luck. I have erased your call, there is no record of it."

The phone went dead. Bryce held it to his ear for another two seconds, then ran to the microwave and tossed his watch in. He set time and power, begged for mercy, and pushed start. Sparks crackled, but the watch held together.

Bryce pulled the Orange out, strapped it on and screamed when the back seared his skin. Ignoring the

pain, he ran back into the living room and punched reset. .
.

And he was reaching into an end table drawer to take out his gun, while Dora was screaming at him. "You worthless turd, why don't you die so I can move on! And what are you going to do with that gun, you ball-less coward?"

He shut the drawer without touching the gun and turned to her. Dora kept screaming. Bryce knew he had to do something, but he didn't want to go to jail. When Dora paused for breath he said, "You're right, Dora, I'm sorry."

The words had choked him, but he continued. "We were so good together, let's try and start over. Look, I'll make a peace offering."

He unstrapped the Orange. "Take my watch, please. You've always wanted to try it. I promise you'll have a unique experience."

### 

## About the Author

Ed Ahern resumed writing after forty odd years in foreign intelligence and international sales. Ed's had 140 stories and poems published so far. His collected fairy and folk tales, *The Witch Made Me Do It,* was published by Gypsy Shadow Press. His novella, *The Witches' Bane,* was published by World Castle Publishing, and his collected fantasy and horror stories, *Capricious Visions,* was published by Gnome on Pig Press. Ed's currently working on a paranormal/thriller novel tentatively titled *The Rule of Chaos.* He works the other side of writing at *Bewildering Stories,* where he sits on the review board and manages a posse of five review editors.

*\*\*\*\*\*\~\~\~\~\*\*\*\*\**

## *Credits and Acknowledgments*

**Cover image and design** – Keely Rew
*Ebook Only:*
Snakes and Ladders - Jain version Game of Snakes & Ladders called jnana bazi or Gyan bazi, India, 19th century, Gouache on cloth, commons.wikimedia.org
Talk to the Animals – 1848 Edwin Landseer painting, A Midsummer Night's Dream. The popular painting was described by a young Victoria (future Queen of England) as a gem, beautifully fairy-like and graceful. Source: Google Art Project

**Podcast production** – Andrew Cairns
**Readers** – Keely Rew, Andrew Cairns, Tom Parker, Leonard Sitongia
**Editor and Publisher** – Juliana Rew

\*\*\*\*\*~~~~~\*\*\*\*\*

**Discover other titles by Third Flatiron:**
(1) Over the Brink: Tales of Environmental Disaster
(2) A High Shrill Thump: War Stories
(3) Origins: Colliding Causalities
(4) Universe Horribilis
(5) Playing with Fire
(6) Lost Worlds, Retraced
(7) Redshifted: Martian Stories
(8) Astronomical Odds
(9) Master Minds
(10) Abbreviated Epics

**THIRD FLATIRON**
**www.thirdflatiron.com**

www.ingramcontent.com/pod-product-compliance
Lightning Source LLC
Chambersburg PA
CBHW061557170626
46811CB00001B/235